D0170244

Praise for *True Story*

"A spellbinding debut . . . Petty leaps from genre to genre with dizzying velocity . . . to show the way trauma works on us, how it shapes our lived experience. . . . Tantalizing us with the 'truth' about what really happened to Alice . . . even as the term itself feels increasingly useless, deceptive."

—Megan Abbott, *The New York Times Book Review*

"A gripping, ripped-from-headlines tale."　　　　　　*—People*

"Extraordinary . . . Fans of the formal inventiveness and twisty-turny narratives of *Trust Exercise* and *A Visit from the Goon Squad* will be immediately engrossed."　　　　　　—R. Eric Thomas, *Elle*

"Part thriller, part social commentary . . . A masterclass in creative form."　　　　　　*—Good Housekeeping*

"Among the best [books] I've read this year. It's an exhilarating read . . . and the twist at the end all but requires you to go back to page one."　　　　　　—Perrie Samotin, *Glamour*

"*True Story* [was] able to remind me of the pleasure of reading when I was certain I had lost it forever. . . . [It's] that surprisingly hard-to-find gem, [one of those] books I will stay up all night for, books that will make me forget where I am, and yet the sentences are also nice, and the mind behind them very sharp."

—Nadja Spiegelman, *The Paris Review*

"[I] found a lot of comfort in the recognition (and awe!) I felt while reading *True Story*."　　　　　　—Tavi Gevinson, *HuffPost*

"An impressive literary crime novel along the lines of Megan Abbott and Laura Lippman with great pacing and formal experimentation . . . A dazzling puzzle." —*CrimeReads*

"A powerful and thought-provoking examination of how the manipulation of stories can shape whole lives." —*The Guardian* (London)

"Unfolds like a mystery, flitting between genres to weave an inventive tale . . . that keeps you hooked until the very end." —*BuzzFeed*

"This novel fits into a mini-phenomenon I think of as 'the *Gone Girl*–ing of literary fiction,' which includes Taffy Brodesser-Akner's *Fleishman Is in Trouble*, Lisa Halliday's *Asymmetry*, and Susan Choi's *Trust Exercise.* . . . *True Story* is a delectable addition to the trendlet. [Petty writes] with great skill and intelligence." —Molly Young, *Vulture*

"With every page, *True Story* gets . . . more inventive, with slow and fast twists that challenge conventional notions of power, sexual assault, and our understanding of truth." —*Goop*

"Blurring genres and subverting structure, Petty examines the ways narratives are woven and take root while trying to untangle the truth." —*The Millions*

"Extend[s] the legacy of *Speak*." —*Bitch*

"I literally cannot believe this book exists. A mind-blowing, page-turning, un-put-downable, heartwarming, empathetic, formally inventive horror suspense thriller, with a life-affirming and timely feminist message? What? This would be an amazing fifteenth novel for a person to have written and it is Kate Reed Petty's first one. What an incredible talent!" —Elif Batuman, author of *The Idiot*

PENGUIN BOOKS

TRUE STORY

Kate Reed Petty has been recognized with a *Narrative* magazine
30 Below Award, as well as grants and scholarships from the Robert
Deutsch Foundation, The Mount, Bloedel Reserve, and the Sewanee
Writers' Conference. Her short fiction has been published in *Electric
Literature*, *American Short Fiction*, *Blackbird*, *Ambit*, *Nat. Brut*, and *Los
Angeles Review of Books*, and she has a master of letters from the University
of St. Andrews in Scotland. She lives in Baltimore.

To access Penguin Readers Guides online,
visit penguinrandomhouse.com.

TRUE STORY

a novel

. . .

Kate Reed Petty

PENGUIN BOOKS

PENGUIN BOOKS
An imprint of Penguin Random House LLC
penguinrandomhouse.com

First published in the United States of America by Viking,
an imprint of Penguin Random House LLC, 2020
Published in Penguin Books 2021

ISBN 9781984877703 (paperback)

THE LIBRARY OF CONGRESS HAS CATALOGED THE HARDCOVER EDITION AS FOLLOWS:
Names: Petty, Kate Reed, author.
Title: True story : a novel / Kate Reed Petty.
Description: [New York] : Viking, [2020]
Identifiers: LCCN 2020006573 (print) | LCCN 2020006574 (ebook) |
ISBN 9781984877680 (hardcover) | ISBN 9781984877697 (ebook) |
ISBN 9780593296417 (international edition)
Classification: LCC PS3616.E895 T78 2020 (print) | LCC PS3616.E895 (ebook) |
DDC 813/.6—dc23
LC record available at https://lccn.loc.gov/2020006573
LC ebook record available at https://lccn.loc.gov/2020006574

Printed in the United States of America
1st Printing

DESIGNED BY MEIGHAN CAVANAUGH

We are, I am, you are
by cowardice or courage
the one who find our way
back to this scene
carrying a knife, a camera
a book of myths
in which
our names do not appear.

— Adrienne Rich, "Diving into the Wreck"

BARCELONA

2015

When you last came to ask for this story, I'd already been hiding out in Barcelona for years. I live in an airy studio on the top floor of a five-story building, with tile floors and a big sliding glass door that opens onto a patio; the patio is lined with terra-cotta pots too heavy to move, left by the previous tenants and overflowing with succulents. The apartment is inexpensive and private; the neighbors keep to themselves and the landlord likes her checks in the mail. It took a little while, but now I feel safe enough here that on hot nights I don't close the patio door, leaving my bedroom open to the breeze whispering up from the city streets and to the phantom intruders that used to haunt my dreams.

I love this apartment the way astronauts love their ships. My only complaint is the display in the window of the pharmacy downstairs, which I pass every day on my morning run. It features three female mannequins with rounded onyx surfaces where their faces should be, their arms and legs cut off at the biceps and thighs. They've been arranged in come-hither poses, hips torqued out as though they were modeling bikinis—but instead, they model first-aid equipment. The one closest to my apartment door has a black lumbar support belt strapped around her waist like a corset and a blue sling for a broken arm draped around her neck. Perched in a wheelchair to her left, another has a knee brace attached at the thigh. The third leans stiffly against the far wall, a sleep mask covering the place where her eyes should be.

For months and months now, this display hasn't changed. Try as I might to look away, I can't help glancing at it as I pass, the way a woman in a horror movie can't resist going upstairs. Don't take this the wrong way, but whenever I look at the mannequins I think of you. My oldest friend, you have always stood by me in the face of casual misogyny and bad taste.

WHEN YOU CAME TO BARCELONA, I really did intend to meet you at your hotel, as I'd said I would. But then I got to the street and found myself walking in the opposite direction. I needed time to think. It was one of those abundant late-summer days, and I walked in a wide arc, under orange trees ruffling their leaves in the sun. I passed old women walking arm in arm, families pushing children on swings in clean public playgrounds. I walked all the way to the Parc de la Ciutadella, where green parrots bobbled around, mingling with pigeons on the paving stones.

I didn't mean to stand you up. I told myself I was circling around to approach your hotel from the opposite side, but then I just kept circling.

Eventually I walked back to my apartment. I turned off my phone, then went out and sat on my wide patio in the afternoon sun and finished a mystery novel whose ending I'd guessed from the start. I fell asleep for a while, and when I woke up I cooked a more complicated dinner than I usually bother to—pasta with olives and artichoke hearts, an endive salad on the side. It was delicious. Only when the dishes were clean did I finally call your hotel.

I'm sure you thought I was still angry. The truth is I was embarrassed. You've always been the one who was brave—no, the one who was *sure*. You've always been so sure of the story you want me to tell, the story you've been asking me for since we were seventeen: the story about the things that happened while I was asleep. "It's *your* story," you would say. "If you don't let it out, it will take over your life." But the story is mine only as the victim owns the prosecution, or the whale the harpoon. Telling it has always been the privilege of the perpetrators, who have the actual facts, and of the bystanders—like you—who believe they know.

Back then I wasn't ready to explain. So I told the receptionist not to call your room, just to give you the message that I'd been summoned to London on short notice by a demanding client. "Tell her not to wait for me," I said. "I'm not sure when I'll return." Then I turned off my phone again and went back out to the patio. I watched the lights blinking on across the city like eyes, a constellation of night watchmen. I hoped you would accept my excuse, though I knew it was obviously false.

Now I hope you'll accept this instead.

SATAN'S BRIDES

by Alice Lovett

& Haley Moreland

9/1/95

FADE IN:

INTERIOR. A ONE-ROOM CABIN IN THE WOODS — NIGHT

LISA is sitting alone with a bottle of RED WINE and a
PINT OF ICE CREAM. She's been CRYING. Her makeup is
all SMEARED.

>   LISA
>   I can't believe that bastard!

Lisa GULPS down an ENTIRE GLASS OF WINE.

She WIPES her mouth. She THROWS the glass across the
room. The glass SHATTERS.

>   LISA
>   Fifteen years of marriage! And he
>   leaves me for . . . Francesca!!!

Lisa flops forward facedown onto the table. She WAILS.

>   LISA
>   Why, Jim? Why? Why?

She reaches over and takes a big bite of ICE CREAM.

>   LISA
>   (wailing)
>   This ice cream isn't even that good!

Suddenly: There is a LOUD THUMP ON THE DOOR!

Lisa JUMPS. She stands up. She stares at the door.

>   LISA
>   (hesitantly)
>   Who . . . who is it?

Lisa slowly OPENS THE DOOR and sees: There is a LARGE
KNIFE stuck point-first in the face of the door.

Lisa SCREAMS and SLAMS the door closed.

THEN: She hears the sound of A WOMAN LAUGHING EVILLY.

Lisa SPINS around.

> LISA
> Who's there?

There's no one else in the room.

But: The ICE CREAM PINT has been knocked over. There's
a puddle of MELTED ICE CREAM on the table.

> LISA
> Oh my god.

Lisa sees that someone has DRAGGED A FINGER THROUGH
THE MELTED ICE CREAM, spelling out:

SATAN STILL LOVES YOU

Lisa SCREAMS.

Lisa RUNS to the door and flings it open.

She GRABS the KNIFE.

Then she FLEES.

EXTERIOR. THE WOODS AT NIGHT — CONTINUOUS

Lisa RUNS through the WOODS, panicked. Looking back
over her shoulder . . .

She TRIPS! She FALLS! The KNIFE flies out of her hand!

> WOMAN (OFF-SCREEN)
> (evil)
> Hi, Lisa.

Lisa looks up. It's FRANCESCA. A beautiful woman with
heavy red lipstick and thick blue eye shadow.

                    LISA
        Francesca?!

                    FRANCESCA
        Happy to see me?

                    LISA
        No! You stole my husband!

Francesca is witheringly condescending.

                    FRANCESCA
        I didn't "steal" your husband. I
        distracted him. I really want YOU.

Lisa scrambles backward. She's edging closer to THE
KNIFE.

                    FRANCESCA
        I stole Jim so that you would come to
        your vacation cabin alone.

                    LISA
        Why did you do that?

                    FRANCESCA
        Because I want you to join us!

                    LISA
        Join who?

                    FRANCESCA
        The brides of Satan!

                    LISA
        What?!?!

                    FRANCESCA
        Your husband is tied to a tree back
        there. All you have to do is sacrifice

him with that knife, and then Satan
will make us both all-powerful!

Lisa leans over and picks up the KNIFE, considers it.

> LISA
> So all I have to do is kill Jim . . .

> FRANCESCA
> Think of how easily he left you!

> LISA
> . . . Like this?

Lisa LUNGES forward and STABS Francesca in the heart.

Francesca SCREAMS and FALLS to her KNEES.

> FRANCESCA
> We could have been . . . all-
> powerful . . .

Francesca DIES.

Lisa stands, catching her breath. She looks up and off
into the woods. She REALIZES.

> LISA
> Jim!!! I'm coming!

FADE TO BLACK.

PART I

LAX WORLD

1999

n the fall of our senior year, my buddy Max Platt was arrested for shining a laser pointer at an airplane. We didn't even know this was illegal. It was one of the least bad things Max ever did, and it was hilarious that it ended up being the thing he got in trouble for. (This was still a few months before the whole thing with the private school girl.)

We were at Denny's when we heard the story, of course. The lacrosse team practically owned Denny's. But that night it was just Max and me and my old buddy Richard Roth.

Been doing it since August, Max said. He'd cut class, go out to the empty field behind the auditorium, and lie on the sandy grass, pointing the red light at the sky, slowly waving it back and forth. *Like the Bat-Signal.*

Really? Richard said.

It always got under my skin how Richard was so impressed with Max. So I said, *But why, Batman? What's the point?*

Fucks with the pilots, Max said.

Max did a lot of things we wished we had the balls for. But this one, personally, I never understood the appeal.

He told the story again at practice. The story was better with all of us there. Max stood up and did his impression of the cop who caught him. *"What are you doing?"* he said, in a big Yosemite Sam voice. He waddled around with his hands out to the side, like he was too fat to put his arms all the way down.

"I slipped and fell," I shouted, Max said, *or I tried to shout, I dunno, I was so fucking high, who knows. I put my hands up over my head, they felt like jelly, like I was moving them through jelly.*

We all nodded like we knew what he meant. Like we'd all been too high to raise our arms. Even though I knew for a fact some of those guys had never smoked.

The cop goes, "Get over here, son. Put your arms down." I just leave my bowl in the grass, he never checked, too lazy to walk a hundred feet, Max said. *He had no fucking clue.*

We were all cracking up listening to the story. The cop had no clue Max was high! We shook our heads.

Cops are such dumbasses, I said. Everyone laughed.

But the next Monday, Max wasn't at practice. He was suspended. Coach told us the laser pointer thing was actually a federal crime. A $250,000 fine and up to five years in prison. We were all super low that day. The state championships were only eight months away. We wondered if Max would be in prison then. We wondered if he would tell the FBI that we smoked weed. For a while we discussed nothing else, jogging in anxious circles around the track.

But in the end nothing really happened. We were only seventeen. And Max's dad was a CPA, so maybe he knew a good lawyer. Max didn't even have to do community service. He was put on probation and had to check in with a cop every month for a year. That was basically it. The only other thing was that he had to get up in front of the whole school and give a speech about the dangers of laser pointers. It was, of course, hilarious.

Say it with me: watch where you stick your pointer, Max said, pointing his thumb over the podium like Bill Clinton. And everyone in the auditorium said it with him: *WATCH WHERE YOU STICK YOUR POINTER.*

Mr. Kaminsky, the English teacher, tried to step in—"Thank you, Max, that's enough"—but the whole school just kept chanting it: *WATCH WHERE YOU STICK YOUR POINTER! WATCH WHERE YOU STICK YOUR POINTER!*

In the end it took two administrators to quiet everyone down, Max grinning onstage the whole time. We sat in the back and cheered him on. We knew that he was with us again.

The only thing was, now he had a record, so he couldn't get caught again. But we didn't think that would be a problem. If we could get out of a felony, we could get out of anything.

I MADE VARSITY SOPHOMORE YEAR, a year earlier than Max. Richard and I had gone to lax camp and we were pretty good. Only two other sophomores made varsity that year, Ham Tierney and Alan Byron.

The four of us got buzzed in together the first week, right after last period on a Friday. There was only half an hour between last period and practice. It wasn't much time. And you had to do fifteen push-ups for every minute you were late to practice. I wasn't that good at push-ups and doing more than ten was humiliating, so I made sure I was never late. I always went to the locker room right away after chemistry.

That day, I was thinking about something a girl had just said to me at the end of class. She'd said, "Nick, for a guy, you've got such pretty hair." I couldn't understand why she'd said it. We weren't having a conversation. We were standing at our desks, packing up our stuff, and she just said it, out of nowhere. But she said it in a really nice way. Maybe she meant it as a compliment, and I should have asked her out. Maybe she was being sarcastic and insulting me, and I should have said my hair was pretty like my dick, and *then* I should have asked her out. The point is I failed.

This is what I was thinking about when I opened the locker room door and saw like six of the juniors and seniors sitting silently on the benches. This was strange. Usually I was the only one there so early. I let the door swing closed behind me. Then, all of a sudden, I had a funny feeling. I had this sense that I should get out of there. But they were already up. They grabbed me and then I was on the floor.

When you play lacrosse, you get used to being under a lot of weight. We always pile up after a goal, to celebrate. We even did it at camp, where the goals don't matter. The weight freaks you out at first, like you're drowning. But you get used to it. I was used to it by then. It was kind of a familiar feeling, actually. It helped me stay calm. I just breathed and tried to play it cool.

One senior straddled my chest and someone was holding my legs and one guy was tugging on my hair. "With this long hair, you're just too pretty," someone said.

I wondered if I was really so pretty. Between the girl in chemistry and now the team, I wondered if people were going to keep saying this to me forever.

"So pretty she's turning me on," someone said, and they all laughed. I was pissed off, but I didn't want to seem like a jerk. I hoped I didn't look pissed off. The guy on my chest was pulling his dick out over his shorts waistband. That freaked me out. But I stayed still. I knew that as long as I didn't resist, it would be over soon, and then they'd leave me alone. There was a buzzing sound. "Hold still, my pretty," someone said. "Wouldn't want to slip."

Suddenly, I understood what the girl in chemistry had meant. She hadn't meant anything. She'd only said it because the lacrosse team told her to. They put her up to it, to get me ready. It was part of the ritual. They were all shouting and laughing and the senior sitting on my chest was waving his dick around. It was limp, of course, we weren't gay. I closed my eyes as he waved it in my face. I kept my mouth shut. I thought about the fact that the girl wouldn't even have talked to me if I wasn't part of the team, and how she wasn't actually saying anything to me. She was just the messenger.

Then I felt someone rub my head and they said, "Like a monkey ready for space," and the sound had kind of died down, and the weight was lifting off of me, a little bit at a time, like pulling yourself out of a swimming pool, and everyone's dick was in their pants, and everyone was playing it cool.

"I thought he was gonna piss himself," someone said. They were all walking out.

Then someone else said, *You're all right, Nick. You're cool. We'll see you on the field.* Their voices had changed. Like they respected me all of a sudden.

I got up onto the bench and sat there for a second. I felt a little better. Then I stood up and looked in the mirror. My hair was gone, shaved off in uneven patches. My face looked strange—bigger. I stuck my tongue out at my stupid face.

They'd left me the buzz cutter. I ran it over my head until I was clean. It left a few spots of blood, but I wiped them on my jersey. A little blood on your jersey looks tough.

When I walked onto the field I was very late. The team was stretching as usual. But it seemed that I was not going to have to do any push-ups.

Sit down, Nick, Coach said, with a nod of approval.

I folded my leg and felt the stretch all the way up my thigh. I looked at Richard. His hair was gone, too. Ham and Alan wouldn't look up from their knees.

Richard told me later that they'd gotten him in the bathroom outside the gym. After they shaved his head they stuck it in the toilet. His face wasn't in the water, though. Just the top of his head. It wasn't like they were trying to kill him. They stuffed toilet paper in his mouth and made him learn one of the sacred team songs. Every time he messed up, they added another wad of toilet paper. He had to get through the whole thing without gagging. This made sense. Richard was a little soft.

But I didn't say that to Richard. I just said, *That's crazy! All they did to me was put me through the paddle wheel.*

Ham said, *Same with me.* And Alan said, *Me too, just a paddle wheel.*

It was the first time I had ever caught a friend in a lie. I looked at Ham and Alan a little different after that. I wondered what the team had actually done to them.

But the important thing was that we had all been buzzed in, and together. I felt warm whenever I thought about that. It was humiliating, but at least we were humiliated together. Not like the usual humiliations, girls or parents or whatever. We had been through something important. We'd probably go to state again this year.

I wanted to play well on that first day with my hair buzzed. I wanted them to know that I was tough. The cold air around my scalp and neck felt strange as I ran, but I played well. I played maybe better than ever. I wondered if maybe, all this time when I felt humiliated, when I was alone and lonely, when I didn't know what to say to a girl, maybe all this time it was my hair that was holding me back.

AFTER PRACTICE one of the seniors, Dean McGarvey, said, *Hey. You maggots wanna hang out?* So Richard and Ham got in his car, and Alan and I rode with Matt Komen and Sam Simpson. We threaded back through the neighborhoods to one of the guys' houses. We parked on the street and walked around back. The lawn sloped down to a dock that stretched into the Chesapeake Bay. The sun was starting to set behind us and the sky was all pink. The dock stuck out like a middle finger.

It's Coach's, Dean said to someone.

"What?" Richard said.

I was annoyed at Richard for reminding the others that we were newbies. *It's Coach's house*, I told him, trying to play it cool, like I'd known all along. I hoped I was right.

I was. The seniors explained that Coach's son was a senior when they were sophomores, and they were still allowed to use the dock, just not to go into the house. *So if you gotta pee, you gotta pee in the bay. It's nature's toilet*, Gary Wooten said. We all laughed and sat on the weathered wood and marveled: we were at Coach's house.

I got a little nervous when Komen said, *Take your shoes off, gentlemen. Relax.* Gary was pulling on a slimy rope. We were all playing it cool. We were all laughing and joking. We didn't feel nervous, we were part of the team. I didn't have to worry that Gary was pulling up a crab trap. I didn't have to worry that they were going to make the crabs pinch our toes. We'd been buzzed in. We didn't have to worry anymore.

And I was right again. It wasn't a crab trap. It was a blue cooler, secured with a bungee cord and covered in barnacles. I felt that something incredible was about to happen.

Nature's refrigerator, Gary said, gesturing toward the bay. He unhooked a rusty carabiner on the bungee cord and opened the top of the cooler. It was filled with rows of golden cans. *Sunken treasure*, Dean said. We all laughed.

Dean tossed beers to the others, one at a time. The smell from practice drifted away over the slow-moving water. We dipped our bare toes in the bay. Our feet were hot and tired, and the water felt good.

I wasn't sure if we sophomores were going to get beers or not.

Greg Morrissey and Matt Iglehart didn't want beer. I was confused, but I didn't want to look stupid, so I didn't say anything. But they told us anyway. *We're on Oxy,* they said. *Can't drink on Oxy.*

Shrivels your swimmers.

Which is why I don't mess with Oxy.

Me neither. I save them for girls.

Yeah. It's better that way. When the girl takes the Oxy. We all laughed at that.

"What's Oxy?" Richard was my oldest friend, but I really wished he wouldn't be such a dickhead. Dean still hadn't tossed us beers. Morrissey and Iglehart looked at each other and started laughing.

Oxy makes you happy about everything, Komen said.

Yeah, Wilbur got it when he broke his ankle in June, Iglehart said.

Matt Wilbur, one of the seniors, raised his beer in salute. He didn't say anything.

Komen said, *He's a true tough guy. He took, what, like one a day? Barely any. So he could save some of the love for the team.* Komen had a couple of big pits on his nose, like he'd scratched a bad batch of zits. He had a lot of freckles so you couldn't really see the scars. But I was sitting a few feet away from him; I could see. He was pretty funny looking, actually. But everyone seemed to like him. He talked for a while. *You guys can try some next time,* he was saying. *There's not enough to go around now, but it won't be long until someone else gets injured and gets a prescription. There's always injuries.*

Then Komen looked at Wilbur. Wilbur nodded. He seemed to be the resident expert on injuries. He seemed to be a true tough guy. He hadn't said a single word yet. And then he said, *If it's you? You know what to do.*

We nodded solemnly. We agreed with all our hearts. We'd take only the minimum Oxy. We'd save some of the love for the team.

We never got beers. We worried that we had failed, and we were right: on Monday after practice the seniors got into their cars and drove off without us. We felt humiliated, and we blamed Richard, mostly. He shouldn't have asked what Oxy was. He should have played it cool.

But the next Saturday we won our scrimmage, and we were invited to the party after. Everybody drank. I had a beer even though I didn't normally drink back then because I was an athlete first. Ham and Alan drank a lot. Richard drank a little. We sang the sacred team songs with our arms around each other in Wilbur's backyard. When Alan threw up on the driveway we all helped hose off the pavement. We hosed off Alan, too. It was hilarious. After that we were invited to all of the parties. We partied whenever we could.

THE MOST LEGENDARY PARTY happened the summer after our junior year, right after school got out. We had just won the state championship, our sixth in a row. The Matts Wilbur and Komen and Iglehart and all the other seniors from our first year on the team had graduated the year before. McGarvey and Simpson and those seniors were on their way out. We were the rising seniors, and we were running things now.

The party was at Dave Campbell's house. He'd made the team junior year, along with Max and five other guys. They were all good guys. But Dave and Max were the best, next to Ham and Alan and Richard and me. We started every game, we played goalie and attack, and I was the face-off specialist. The six of us were the best. We were the heart of the team. We were the rising seniors running things.

The party was a lacrosse party. But it was open to everybody. There were all kinds of people there. There were kids from the swim team, who were usually too preppy and uptight to drink, and from the soccer team, so even the German exchange student and Mateo, the guy who was born in Mexico, were there. There was a group of three girls who ran the school arts magazine who had shown up in matching wifebeaters. They all had Sharpies in their back pockets. As soon as they walked in the door they were telling people to write on them. So there were all kinds of people there. But everyone knew it was a lacrosse party.

Early on, some people were looking for Solo cups. Max had them. He wouldn't give them out. He got up on the dining room table and held the stack of cups like a megaphone. He bumped into the ceiling fan. It was hilarious.

He shouted to everyone to be quiet. *Gentlemen—and you know what I mean when I say* gentlemen.

We were all cracking up. Then some guy heckled Max. *Squeal like a pig!* It was one of the younger guys on the team, shouting, *You got a pretty mouth!*

Max wasn't fazed. He stuck his middle finger up in the air. He shouted louder. *Gentlemen!* And then he sang, *We are the champions, my friends!*

Max was hilarious.

He shouted, *We are the state champions all year!* Then he got serious. He almost looked like he was going to cry. For a second we worried. Then we realized he was faking it. He closed his eyes and bit his lower lip. He pulled himself together and said, *We are state champions all year. And then next season?*

He paused, pretending to sniffle back a tear. This time we all cheered. Our voices joined in. We lifted him up. We all said together, *WE WILL BE THE STATE CHAMPIONS AGAIN.*

Then he handed out the cups and everybody got beer and the legendary party began.

At the legendary party, four guys vomited and Max hooked up with three different girls in the same night. At the legendary party we all ate cherries that Ham's brother's fraternity had been soaking in grain alcohol for a month. At the legendary party we did our best impressions, and Richard was pretty good at Nicolas Cage, but I won with my Jack Nicholson. At the legendary party we drew a hundred dicks on one of the art magazine girls' tank top, the girl thought it was hilarious, and she got back at us by tricking Seth Marcus into letting her draw a dick on his cheek. At the legendary party, Max's dealer showed up, and like magic everyone came together with the cash, and we hotboxed Dave's entire bedroom.

The cops broke up the legendary party before midnight. It was too legendary to last.

One of the art girls was smoking on the front porch, so she saw the cops first. She came into the house yelling, *Cops cops cops!*

We all ran. Everyone was pushing, trying to get out the back door. A bunch of kids jumped off the deck. It wasn't so high. Dave's house was back in the woods. We all got away.

My car was parked down the street. I ducked through a neighbor's yard and got in, then drove the other way. I drove around alone for a while, too amped to go home.

But the magic of the legendary party was still with me. Because just when I thought I'd have to go home, that there was nothing else to do, I stopped for a Slurpee and found Richard, Ham, and Alan at the 7-Eleven. They were just leaving. Alan had a cell phone and Dave had called him to find us all and meet him at Denny's.

(After that, it was tradition. We always knew to meet up at Denny's after a party got broken up.)

Dave and Max were already eating pancakes when we got there. Dave grinned. *Sit down, gentlemen, I have a story.*

The man has a fucking story, Max said. He was grinning, too.

Dave had gotten out through the basement and run into the woods. Then he circled back to check what was going on at the house. The cop was still there, talking into the radio on the front porch. *I freaked the fuck out*, he told us. *I could see the look on my dad's face already. The cut-me-a-switch-boy look.*

(Dave used to say his mom was a lawyer and his dad was an asshole. I didn't know if he meant the switch thing literally, but no one asked.)

So Dave couldn't go back in the house, with the cop on the front porch. But his car was parked on the curb, so he snuck around and waited until the cop had turned his back and then started the car and just fucking gunned it out of the neighborhood. He didn't think the cop got his plates or anything.

Just before he turned onto the main street, he saw a guy walking on the side of the road. It was Max. For a while they drove around together.

Dave kept whining about his dad, his dad, what am I gonna do, Max said.

Dave said, *But then Max gets an idea.*

They went to the movie theater and waited until a couple of cute girls came out. They were private school girls. Dave and Max told them what had happened and got their ticket stubs from them.

What movie? we wanted to know.

Get this: it was the nine o'clock showing of Gone in 60 Seconds.

We all burst out laughing at that. *It's a sign*, we said. Richard did his impression of Nicolas Cage again.

The story continued: Dave and Max drove back to Dave's house, to all the beer cups scattered on the lawn. Dave called the police. He said someone had broken into his house while he was out at the movies on a double date. He wanted the cops to come and make sure it was safe.

We laughed and laughed at that. *It's true*, Max said. *I had no idea Dave had such big balls, but it's true. I watched him do it.* The cop who showed up was the same cop who had broken up the party. Dave played it perfectly. He acted like he was scared and upset. Max backed him up. The cop was skeptical, of course.

"You're saying to me," Dave said, doing the cop's voice as Nicolas Cage. *"You're saying to me that you're a senior in high school and you have no idea who might have broken into your house to throw a party on the Saturday night your parents are out of town."* And I just flash him my big baby blues and say, *"No, sir!"*

No way he believed you, I said.

Probably not. Richard shrugged. *But it's nearly one in the morning, he wants to go home, he doesn't actually care about a party.*

Plus we had the ticket stubs, Max said. *Said we were on a double date, gave him one of the girls' numbers if he wanted to check out our story.*

She's my alibi, Dave said. *I think she likes me.*

Of course Dave's parents didn't buy it. We found out later that he got in big trouble. But at Denny's we were impressed. It was a really good lie. We were impressed with Max for having the idea and impressed with Dave for pulling it off.

We all ordered pancakes to celebrate. And then we started talking about what had happened during the party. Hotboxing the bedroom. Max's three girls. All the incredible things that had happened that night. We hadn't realized how legendary the party had been until we told the story together. As we talked about it, we realized we'd been through something amazing. And we couldn't wait to do it again.

FOR A WHILE THAT SUMMER, Dave hooked up with his alibi. *Life imitates excuses,* Richard said (he was always quoting *The Kids in the Hall* like we were still in eighth grade). Dave's alibi loved comedy movies and she went to fifth base, so Dave didn't hang out with us as much and we understood why. It was summer, anyway, and some of us were at the beach or in Europe with our parents, and a lot of us went to different lax clinics, especially if there was one at our top-choice school. Richard was at the Naval Academy, for example. I didn't have a top choice so I went to one at the University of Maryland. I also got a retail job at the lacrosse store, Lax World, where I spent afternoons talking to kids who were just getting started. When I told them I was a face-off specialist and that my average was over 50 percent, they looked at me with real respect in their eyes, and I remembered what it was like when I was just a freshman, watching the team from the outside.

Which is all to say that we were busy, we didn't really miss Dave. And our parties were smaller on the whole, just a few guys hanging out and drinking and telling stories about the legendary party and how we'd throw an even more legendary one in the fall.

By August, Dave and the girl had kind of drifted apart, so he was back with us in time for conditioning. Around then our parties started picking back up, too. Dave said all of the private school girls wanted to hang out. Even though he and the alibi had broken up, they were still friends.

Private school girls were like that. They never put any pressure on you. Not that they were the kinds of girls you wanted to hang out with all the time or anything. Our public school was a really good school. My mom said that kids in our town only went to private school because something was wrong, like a learning disability, or like they'd been kicked out of public school. We didn't know exactly what was wrong with the private school girls, but you could just tell something was off. Like one time, I was talking to one who said that she loved to get a six-pack of beer on a Friday and just drive around all night, drinking and listening to the radio.

When I heard that, I thought to myself, *That's a little much.* I mean, sure, maybe sometimes I drove myself home from a party when I was a little too buzzed to drive. But I wasn't going to have that be my whole goal for the evening. I kept talking to her, to be nice. But I couldn't really respect her after that.

The thing you had to respect, though, was that the private school girls knew how to party. They always brought a bottle of something. They shared their pot. They danced, whether anyone else was dancing or not. They had good advice about the college admissions process. Most importantly, they always showed up.

That August, just before school started, we were eager for another legendary party. We thought all parties should be legendary. We tried hard. We shouted *Here's Johnny!* when we walked in the door. We made party mixtapes. We got so good at beer pong it wasn't fun anymore so we made up new games; we set up empty bottles and shattered them with a bowling ball Richard bought at a thrift store (we called it Bowling Rock), we chanted the sacred team songs. Everything was exactly right, but something was always wrong.

One night, at Ham's, I found a bottle of whiskey in Ham's dad's office and I took it outside. I went and stood at the edge of the yard. I wanted to think about how I was watching my life more than living it. I looked at the sky and it felt true. It made me feel sad and kind of restless. It was like sitting next to a girl and the movie is boring, but it's making her cry and you feel like you're not supposed to touch her, until you realize maybe she actually wanted you to touch her. But by then it's too late.

The feeling never really went away. It was there at all our parties. It was there when I drove home with the radio loud so I wouldn't pass out and when I stared at my ceiling because I couldn't sleep. We never talked about it, but I felt like a lot of the other guys were feeling it, too.

The juniors partied hard, but us seniors all sort of stood off to the side. We drank too much beer and felt weird about dancing so we just watched the private school girls. They were the ones partying. We were just going through the motions. Looking back, if it hadn't been for those private school girls, I don't know if we would have even had parties that year. We would have missed those good times. And that would have been a tragedy.

IN THE FIRST MONTH of senior year I decided to get a blow job from Haley Moreland. We were eating pizza in Max's basement after the first day of tryouts. We didn't have to try out, of course. We were the team. Except there were like thirty kids at tryouts.

This is a hungry bunch, Coach said as we watched the kids lining up to get their numbers. We knew he was right, and we worried about it. The kids ran so fast and worked so hard and some of them jogged laps during breaks, showing off.

They were the ones trying out, they wanted a chance to be with *us*. But we had to work to keep up. So we were hard on them. They got hit hard in the clearing drill. Max picked out this one blond kid who was really good and kept muttering *pussy dick* right in his ear.

It actually kind of annoyed me. The blond kid would be good for the team, and I tried to get Max to lay off him. *You're an asshole,* I told Max during a water break. *Pussy dick isn't even a thing.* But actually, we all thought it was pretty funny. And we needed to blow off steam somehow, because on the whole, that day sucked.

We knew what was up. We'd had too much fun that summer. We were in shitty shape. Coach knew it, too. At the end, he clapped his hands and thanked everybody for coming out. Then he said, *I want to see my seniors.*

All of the new kids left, heads down, hopes high. They still had two more days to try out, years of high school ahead of them. We only had this one year left.

Sit down, gentlemen, Coach said. We sat in a circle around him. The best seniors, the six of us, were right in the middle. Coach was looking right at us.

You worked hard today, Coach said, *I know you worked hard. But . . .*

As he let that word hang in the air, I got cold. Even though I knew what was coming, I listened to his speech with my whole fucking heart. *I remember the pressure*, he said, *college staring down the barrel. And this is the best time of your life, your golden years.*

I felt a little lighter at that. It wasn't all bad. Coach wanted us to have fun, to enjoy this time. I sat up straight. I glanced over. Max and Dave were smirking on my left. Ham and Alan looked bored and angry. On my right side Richard was watching Coach seriously, his face calm, nodding slightly. I tried to make my face look like Richard's.

But I also want you to be state champions. And this is your last year to do that.

When he said that, it was the first time I realized we might not win that year, that things could be taken away from us. *I have faith in you*, Coach said, and I felt both cold and hot in my chest, and my lungs felt so big I worried my eyes were gonna water. They didn't. But it was a good speech.

Then Coach made each of us set goals, going around the room saying them out loud. I said I wanted to get my face-off percentage over sixty and Coach said, *Good man*, and I knew he meant it.

Coach had done a good job. He was right. He just needed to motivate us. But still we were all annoyed after. So we went to eat pizza in Max's basement, and Dave imitated Coach's voice and said, *Let's all set goals, gentlemen*, and then we went around and said which girls were going to blow us before Christmas.

All of the other guys listed three or four girls. Max named five, and two of them had already blown him, which shouldn't count. I only said Haley Moreland. *I'm a one-girl kind of guy*, I said. Everyone had to respect that. I wasn't just some follower, bragging about his conquests. I was a one-girl kind of guy.

But it was a mistake. A couple of days later it was obvious I was fucked. Haley and I had first period together, BC calc. She was a junior but she was a year ahead in math. I kept looking at her all through class. She was supposed to give me a blow job. I kept trying not to look at her and then looking at her anyway.

I had known Haley since we were little. Her mom was friends with my mom. There were pictures of us playing basketball together when we were seven or eight. Sometimes we talked between classes. So it shouldn't have been weird when I tried to talk to her that day. I had to get a blow job, was all. I'd heard she'd blown one of the seniors last year, a guy who ran track with her.

But whatever I said didn't work. I made a stupid joke. She kind of laughed but mostly groaned. I wanted to punch myself in the face. I had set Haley as my goal because she was easy. And I had always liked her. I'd always thought she was pretty. But as she walked away, I felt my chest tighten and that's when I realized that I had fucked myself over. I had it bad for her.

I MADE A FOOL OF MYSELF around Haley for months before I got the balls to ask her out. I didn't want to ask her to a movie or anything in case she thought I was lame. So I just asked if she was going to the party at Dave's house.

It was December, the last day of exams. Dave called it The Party WAGLER. It stood for The Party Where We All Get Laid (Even Richard).

Obviously we couldn't tell people that, so we said "the Waggler" was a new dance. *But we can't show it to you*, we told people. *It's way too sexy. If we dance the Waggler, you will be overcome with lust.*

It was funny, but it wasn't as funny as it should have been. And not just because Richard got pissy about it. Jokes just weren't that funny anymore. Our first seeded game was in March and my face-off percentage was still hovering around fifty. College applications were due in January. Some of us had applied early decision and been wait-listed. One guy got flat-out rejected. There was a weight on our chests that wouldn't lift no matter how fast we ran at practice.

But, there was a glimmer of hope. The Party WAGLER was at Dave's house. It was the first party at Dave's house since the legendary party.

Dave's parents didn't trust him anymore. They'd hired a house sitter, a girl from the community college. So we all pooled our money to pay her off, and Dave promised we'd keep the noise down and clean up after, that it would stay under control.

We had high hopes. We wanted this party to be great. Of course we all acted like every party was great. But we really spread the word about this one. We wanted everyone to be there. Haley had already heard about it when I invited her. But she said she hadn't decided whether to go or not. She told me to convince her. I told her there would be beer and not just vodka but good vodka. *I don't drink*, she said.

Yeah, but you smoke weed, I said.

She said, *So?* And I said there would be plenty of weed, too.

I hear there will be dancing, she said. *I hear we're gonna do the Waggler.*

Well, some people might do the Waggler. If they're feeling reckless. It's a powerful dance.

Will you do the Waggler?

If you come.

She smiled at me and kind of squinted, like she was thinking hard. She didn't say anything. I said, *So. Will you come?*

She said, "Nah, sounds boring."

I must have looked like an idiot.

I'm just teasing, she said. *I'm going. Could you give me a ride? I was gonna ride with Georgia but she's grounded.*

When I got to Haley's house I had to go to the door and say hi to her mother, of course, and her mother had to go on and on about how tall I was now. She asked whether I knew Haley had been selected to be the teen columnist for the local paper starting in the spring.

Mom, Haley said.

"The column is called Teen Scene, and she even gets paid."

Mom! Haley looked at me, rolling her eyes. *It's no big deal.*

I thought again how cool Haley was, how smart.

"Lee, come on, you should be proud," her mom said.

I wondered if I'd ever get to call her Lee. *That's really great,* I told Haley. And it was great. *We should celebrate. Want to get a milkshake before the—*

Haley jumped in and said, *Before the movie? It's a ten-thirty movie, so we've got time, right?*

Right, I said. *Before the movie.*

I shook Mrs. Moreland's hand as we left, which made her laugh. "You've always been such a sweetie, Nick," she said. She still saw me as a little boy. I wanted to say something back to her, prove myself, but I didn't know what. So I just smiled and we left.

The milkshake thing was a good idea, it turned out. I wanted some time alone with her anyway. We went to the Greek diner, and Haley complained about her mom. *It seems like she's really proud of you,* I said.

It's suffocating, she said. She asked if my parents were a pain, too. I said I guessed so.

I felt, as we finished our milkshakes, that things were going well. As she wiped her mouth with her napkin, I thought about her blowing me. It was going to be great. There was no reason to worry about it. I ran my hand over my head. My hair was getting long. I needed to buzz it again. I needed to get Haley high. I had a joint saved for her, in an Altoids tin in the glove compartment of my car. I wanted us both to relax, so we could talk more, better, about real things.

She let me pay and then touched my arm when she said *thanks*. When we got to the party, she went over to say hello to some friends, but said that I should find her later. It was okay. Things were going well.

I guess it was around ten at that point. I went over to talk with Richard and ask what had happened so far. *Nothing much*, he said. I nodded and looked around; one of the private school girls was dancing, all by herself in the middle of the room. She was really out of it. *Hey, pussy dick, out of my way*, Max said, right in my ear. *I've got a new goal.* He slapped my butt and pushed past, approaching the private school girl to dance with her. He raised his arms in the air, beside her but not touching her. Slowly, like he was raising them through jelly.

How about you, I said to Richard. *Got any goals for tonight?* I said it to be encouraging. No judgment. Richard was my oldest friend, but part of me always wondered if he was gay. Not like he acted gay. He just never made a move.

I'm going to see what turns up, he said. Which was what he always said. Which was why he never had a girl. Girls didn't just turn up. I was no expert, but everyone knew that.

Cool, cool, I said. We both took sips of our beers. It's not like I could judge Richard anyway, with Haley on the other side of the room and me trying to figure out what I was going to say when I went over to talk to her again.

The party was fine. Of course, it wasn't legendary. Dave kept running up to people and making jokes about the Waggler. He kept trying to get people to do shots. Some of the private school girls were really drunk. The girl who had been dancing stopped being able to dance. She had to sit down. She was laughing, but her eyes were closed as Max rubbed her shoulders on the couch. (He was the exception to the rule, I guess: girls turned up for Max.)

Mostly people were just talking, though. I realized I was hanging back, watching. I felt suddenly urgent, like I was once again letting a good time get away. I resolved not to let my life be that. I went to find Haley.

She was talking to some private school girls. I touched her shoulder. When she turned and saw it was me, she smiled. I said something, I don't remember what. Then we were walking to the edge of the woods behind Dave's house. We went to sit down but the ground was cold, so I grabbed a couple of cushions from the chairs on the deck and set them down for us, and Haley sat right next to me, the arm of her jacket touching mine. As I dug the joint out of the plastic bag in the Altoids tin, Haley said that she only ever needed a single hit to get high. *I always stop after my first hit. So this is your lucky day, Nick. I'm a cheap date.*

I lit the joint for her. Just like she said, she took one drag and then passed it back to me. It drove me crazy in every direction. I took a hit. She exhaled, the smoke curling around her face. She put her head down on her arms on her knees, her thin body folded in on itself. She made me want to take a train trip through Europe. She was a long-distance runner. All state. I realized everything about her was that feeling. Only needing one good hit. Running forever. I wished she would just let loose. And I wished I could be more like her.

She was talking about what she thought about while running. She ran for hours at a time. I must have asked her about it, because she said, *No, it's not lonely. It's peaceful.*

I felt the moment as it was happening. I leaned forward and kissed her. It was just the right thing. I pulled back a little, testing her. She leaned forward, kept our lips together. The feeling of her lips on mine was strange. To be totally honest about it I hadn't really kissed anyone before. I'd said I'd done it with girls so many times I guess I believed it, so it was super weird, actually kissing her. Wet and soft and different. Then I was on my back and she had both hands on my chest. She was kissing me. I opened my eyes and saw that her eyes were closed. I looked up, higher, at the sky, and the lights of a plane blinking by. I felt myself floating. I tried to stay focused. I worried she would get bored. I worried I wasn't a good kisser. I wondered if this was when she'd give me that blow job, or if I'd have to make her my girlfriend first, how long that would take.

She pulled away, then rolled over and lay on her back beside me. The night sky wagged back and forth over us. I was crushed by the many meanings of what might or might not have just happened.

So, she said. She looked at me for a second. Then she said, *We should get back?* I didn't know if it was a statement or a question. Her thin body was curling up off the ground. She rested her head on one hand. I didn't say anything. She stood up. I was angry. I had bored her after all.

She stood over me and reached out a hand to help me up.

"I'm too high," I said.

"Should've stuck to just one drag," she said.

She kind of kicked my thigh. I didn't know what that meant, either.

"Whatever, Nick," she said, and walked away. I lay on my back and looked up at the sky.

After a while I got up and went back to the house. I found Dave's mom's office and lay down on the couch. On the opposite wall I saw one of her diplomas was from the University of Maryland, and I thought about how many girls were there, how jealous Haley would be when I was dating them all.

After a while Haley came in and woke me up. "People are going to Denny's," she said.

"Okay," I said. I waited but she didn't say anything.

"Guess I'll see you later," I said.

She said something like *okay*. Then she left.

WHEN I WAS STRAIGHT enough to drive I got in my car and went to Denny's. It was a little after midnight. Ham and Alan were there, and some juniors, and Haley. I saw them through the window, all laughing. I pretended I had forgotten my wallet. I mimed checking my pockets in case anyone was watching. I walked back to my car and vomited all over the front wheel. Then I felt a little better. I went straight to the bathroom when I went inside. I washed my hands and splashed water on my face and then sat down with everyone. Dave had showed up in the meantime so there was only one seat left, across from Haley. She glanced at me and then down, and then back up and kind of smiled. Like she was back to leading me on, or maybe she really was shy.

Everyone saw it. Everyone felt bad for me. We all knew I had it bad for Haley. We all thought she was cool, and it was true, it was fun having her at Denny's, she was like one of the guys. But she acted like she didn't know how I felt. She must have known. Everyone knew. I wondered if maybe she was using me. Maybe she actually had it bad for one of the other guys.

Couple of pussy dicks rolling up late, Dave said. Max and Richard were walking in. They were laughing. They had left the party with Max's private school girl, the one who was too drunk to dance. She wasn't with them anymore.

She was really out of it, Haley said, shaking her head.

That's for sure, Max said.

You show her your pointer? I asked.

Nick, you're obsessed *with my pointer*, Max said.

We all laughed. *Watch where you stick your pointer,* we all said in unison. I laughed and glanced at Haley. She wasn't really paying attention. She was curling the wrapper of her straw around and around itself into a tight little tube.

Dudes, you will not believe. Richard was pulling up a chair, Max was politely asking the waiter if he could take a chair from another table. *Her mom freaked out and yelled at us.*

No!

Yeah. And she chased us down the street. Max was sitting in his chair backward. Behind his back, the waiter was watching him and frowning. Max didn't notice. The girl had been too drunk to walk, he said. He and Richard had carried her to the front door, one under each arm. They had argued about whether to leave her on the stoop or ring the bell. Max had been on the side of leaving her.

Haley looked up at that. *Assholes,* she said.

It was a comfortable stoop, Max said. *There was a bench.*

And I gave her my jacket, Richard said.

Max and Richard told the story together. They passed it back and forth. The girl's mom opened the door. The look on her face. *I thought she was going to pull out a shotgun.* The mom screamed her daughter's name. She grabbed at her. *But she wasn't strong enough to hold her up, and the girl slumped on the floor.* They didn't know what to do. What were they supposed to do? They said they were sorry, ma'am. They said they were lacrosse players.

"What did you do?" she kept screaming. "What did you do?" She was crazy!

What could they do? They backed away slowly. Then they turned and ran.

The waiter interrupted. All anybody wanted was a coffee refill. The waiter was pissed, but what could he do? Coffee refills were unlimited. He refilled our coffees and left.

So there we were: running across the lawn. And the woman screams, "I know your last name!"

How did she know your last name?

Richard left his team jacket on the stoop!

It's cold out. I put my jacket over her, to cover her up. The woman was crazy anyway.

I know. She ran after us, screaming, "I know your name!"

She couldn't keep up, obviously.

Obviously.

We raced to the car, we got away.

But she was still behind us the whole time.

In the street!

In her robe! Carrying Richard's fucking jacket!

It was hilarious. We laughed hysterically. And as we were laughing, we realized together: Had the Party WAGLER been legendary?

Haley sighed and leaned back in her chair. She let go of the straw wrapper and it unspooled into a loose coil on the wet table. *You're such assholes*, she said.

But we were all looking at each other. We were realizing that we hadn't yet told each other everything that had happened that night. It was the same as the legendary party. No single one of us had experienced the entire thing. It was too legendary for one guy alone to see. We had to tell each other about it. Maybe the Party WAGLER was about to become legend. We just had to tell the whole story.

I don't blame the mom, Haley said. We all looked at her. She shrugged. *I'd be pissed if I caught my daughter with you.*

I'm a good guy. You can trust me with your daughter.

Maybe you, Richard. But Max, if I see you around my daughter, I'm definitely getting my shotgun.

We laughed.

Not so fast, Haley. Before you take shotgun, you should try the back seat with me.

You're a creep.

Max lifted his hands, innocent. *The last girl didn't complain.*

He was being an asshole. But Haley was asking for it. She had already called him an asshole like three times. You couldn't do that with Max. He was like a pit bull: once he latched on, he would never let go. After I told him *pussy dick* wasn't a word, he'd started saying it all the time, he said it so much that we all said it now.

I wanted to get Max off Haley. I wanted to get her away, outside, take her home. But she was a pit bull, just like him. She wasn't letting go, either.

The one who was totally out of it? she asked.

She was totally out of it, Richard agreed. Max shrugged again.

Then Haley's voice changed. "You didn't." She narrowed her eyes at Max.

Didn't what? Max said. And he kind of licked his lips.

"That's disgusting."

Relax, Haley, I didn't bone her, Max said.

She stood up. "Can someone who's not Max give me a ride home?"

I will, I said, and stood up quickly. Maybe too quickly. Everyone looked at me. Max smirked.

Haley looked away. "I gotta go to the bathroom first."

I sat back down and said okay. Haley was already walking away. Everyone waited until she was out of earshot to laugh.

Max got her all worked up.

You're welcome, Nick.

What?

She's all worked up, she's ready.

Shut up, pussy dick.

Maybe you'll get luckier than Max did.

We all laughed.

Who says I didn't get lucky? Max said.

You did.

I said I didn't bone her.

Oh, fuck off.

Swear to God. Max reached over and took a creamer packet out of the little dish in the center. *I sat in the back seat with her. She needed someone to keep her sitting up straight.* He looked sideways at Richard. *And to help her get her panties off.* We heard the sound of the wrapper peeling off the top of the creamer, because none of us were breathing. Max tilted his head back and drank the cream like a shot of Jäger.

No shit, we said.

Max wiped cream off his mouth and smiled. *Swear to God, soft as melted butter. Poor Richard sitting up there had to just smell it.*

Not true, Richard said.

I knew it, everyone said. *Max, you're full of shit.*

Richard was looking out the window.

Richard, come on, Max said. *We're among friends. We can tell them what happened.*

Yeah, Richard. You can tell us.

What happened, Richard said, *is I stopped the car and beat Max's ass.*

Richard don't take no shit, Ham said, and we all laughed. Max held his hand up to stop us.

It's true, he said. *Richard was angry. And rightly so! I was being an asshole.* We all watched Max. Even Richard was watching him. *So I said, "Come get a piece of her, too."* Max smiled at us, looking around. He spread his arms and lifted his hands, like a king. *I always save some love for the team.*

No. We waited for the punch line. But Max just looked at Richard. We waited.

Max said, *You guys think Richard is a complete gaywad, but I know the truth. We went behind the 7-Eleven, parked in a dark corner. Right, Richard?*

Richard looked out the window. *Yeah,* he said

Then Haley was back at the table. "Parked in a dark corner for what?"

Everyone shut up.

"Seriously?"

We looked at each other. We burst out laughing. How could we help it? Even I laughed. It was too much. *To smoke some extremely stanky weed,* Max said, and this made us laugh harder.

Haley turned and walked out of the restaurant. I got up and followed her. Everyone gave me a thumbs-up behind her back.

They told me the rest later. How the waiter interrupted, said our unlimited coffee refills had run out, he was going to call the cops if we didn't get out. How Dave said, *Unlimited coffee can't run out, that's a paradox.* They all laughed but it was no use. The waiter was not gonna budge. They were just about to get up and leave when Richard suddenly ordered pancakes for the table, a large stack for everyone.

How the waiter hesitated. "You have to pay first," he said, his voice rising. "You have to pay before I bring them."

How Richard whipped out a credit card, defeating the waiter, which maybe, more than anything, made us think the whole story with Max and Richard and the private school girl might actually be true.

So they told the whole story over pancakes. Richard had climbed into the back seat, and they had both fingered her. The guys still didn't believe it, but then Richard said that he was going to eat her out, but he found a piece of toilet paper stuck in her pubes. That's when everyone knew the story was true. We were all bullshitters, but who would make *that* up?

I was nervous walking to the car, there were still some chunks on the front wheel from when I'd gotten sick earlier. But luckily Haley just walked right to the passenger side. I realized too late that I should have opened her door for her. Instead I just hit the automatic locks and she got in.

On the ride home we didn't talk much. At one point she said, *Max is a douchebag, huh?* I laughed and agreed. It felt good. Then we were quiet until I pulled onto her street.

Her house was dark, just a single lamp on in the front window. She said, *Uh-oh.*

Are you in trouble?

Don't worry about it, she said. She paused, her hand on the door, her purse in her lap. She bit her lip. I felt like I should kiss her, but I wasn't sure, so I made a joke. *I could carry you to the front door?* I said. *Leave you on the stoop?* I just wanted to keep talking, but I knew right away I'd said the wrong thing. She looked at me like she'd been catching whiffs of a bad smell for an hour and had only just realized what it was. I thought about the vomit on the wheel of my car. I didn't know what to say.

Then she was out of the car. She floated up to her house, taking slow, long strides. Her legs were so long. She took fewer steps than seemed possible, her feet barely seemed to touch the ground. I watched her go. It felt like panic but there was nothing I could do. She closed the front door behind her. Then I saw the single lamp go dark.

WE TALKED ABOUT IT for weeks. It was so good. We got every detail out of Richard and Max, her face as it leaned back on the seat, how the smell of tuna fish was so strong Richard worried it would be in his car forever. How they both jizzed on her, like champions.

We asked if they had talked to the girl since. We kept asking, and finally Max said he had. She was grounded for being drunk but other than that she was fine. He said she would do it again. *Maybe with more of us.*

No way, we said. *You're lying.*

I'll show you. When's the next party? But none of our parents were leaving town anytime soon.

When we got back from winter break, we found that other kids were talking about it, too. It was suddenly a thing people knew. When they asked, we said nothing. We were gentlemen. But somehow all of the details became known anyway, and it was a joke everywhere. *How do you find a private school girl in the dark? Just follow your nose.*

It kept us going through the worst time of our senior year. It was a welcome distraction. Something to talk about besides when the next party would be. Something to think about other than our college essays. We were already supposed to have turned the final drafts in to our English teacher, Mr. Kaminsky. We hadn't even written them. We had nothing to say for ourselves. The example college essay was a kid who had lost a leg to cancer and had learned to play soccer with a prosthetic. He had made the all-state team. His essay was about overcoming adversity.

That wasn't really fair.

All we had to overcome was pressure, school, our state championship, and the sinking feeling that we weren't good enough. But writing about playing lacrosse, even when you worried that you weren't good enough, wasn't good enough.

And then, at the end of that very long first week of January, we learned that Richard and Max were in big trouble.

THE HALLWAY OUTSIDE of Coach's office was painted bright blue, with a yellow stripe at shoulder height. The stripe traced the inside of the office, like a pothole painted along with the road. It crossed the locker room door, dipped into Coach's office from the left, and then exited on the right side. From there it traced behind a long glass case holding all our school's trophies. State championships stretching back five yards and five decades down the hall.

Have a seat, Nick, Coach said. *Have a candy. I don't know what the flavors are. Take a yellow one. School spirit. It's probably butterscotch.*

The office was tiny. Coach had told us once that the architect had forgotten to account for an office for the gym teacher and so they'd had to convert a closet. We assumed he was joking but his office really was tiny. When you sat down, your knees nudged up against his desk, and your back was nearly touching a bookshelf piled with binders that was about one sneeze away from tipping over. It was not usually good news when you went to talk to Coach in his office, and the smallness of the space just added to the pressure.

Even Coach seemed nervous as he asked, *How's your family, Nick? How're your folks? Everything good?*

I took a yellow candy. It turned out to be lemon. *All good,* I said. I tried to think of any recent fact about my family worth sharing and couldn't.

Coach was leaning back, his hands folded across his stomach. He kind of squinted, like he had a headache. There were a couple of things I was afraid he was about to bring up. The first was a scholarship I was hoping to hear about from the University of Maryland. Then there was my game, which was not so good. There was also my face-off percentage, hovering now definitely under fifty. I was working on that, though; that very morning I had decided to stop drinking, to get back in shape. There was also half a joint in a plastic bag in the Altoids tin in the cup holder of my car, which was now sitting in the school parking lot. I'd put it there the night before, on a trip to the grocery store. I was hoping to run into Haley, and I wanted to have something to offer her. I did not see Haley, and I forgot to take it back out, so now there was a joint in my car and maybe drug-sniffing dogs had found it and Coach was about to tell me that I was caught. Coach looked down at his folded hands, and I knew it was bad.

You're a good kid, Nick. I know you and Richard are good friends, and I know that you care about this team.

I nodded, trying to keep the right expression on my face. I wanted to look serious, but not guilty. Coach was talking about our weekends, and about how what we did once games ended on Friday nights was our business. *Boys are boys,* he said. Then he laughed to himself, looked up at the ceiling. *Believe me, I know what it's like to be a boy.* He shook his head and didn't say anything for a second.

Yeah, I said, to remind him I was there.

He squinted again, and exhaled. *Okay, Nick, here's the thing: an old buddy called me this morning.*

Coach was a retired police officer. At the end of sophomore year, when I got my learner's permit, he'd asked me to come with him to pick up the new uniforms for the spring and had let me drive his car, and all over town he had pointed out the places where the cops like to sit to give tickets to high school kids. I never got a ticket, thanks to him. All of Coach's old buddies were cops.

Seems two of my guys allegedly drove a young lady home after a party last month.

I said, *Oh.*

We both know who. Hold on, don't say anything yet. You don't have to get anyone in trouble.

The story that Coach told me, that his cop buddy had told him, was the same story that I had heard from Ham and Alan and Dave and everyone else at school, although Coach slid quickly over the specifics. *When you're a cop, you see parents sleeping on the job,* he was saying. *All the time. Parents want cops to do their jobs for them. This mother—I want to ask her why she'd let her daughter get like that? What kind of parent is she that her daughter is out drinking at all hours?*

Yeah, I agreed. *Most things can be traced back to the mother's fault.* This was something my mom liked to say, but the way Coach laughed when I said it, I saw that it meant something different to him. I didn't really have time to think about it, though. Because then he told me something new: the girl had attempted suicide.

It took me a second to understand what Coach meant by *Tylenol and vodka.* He said, *She seems to need some kind of psychiatric-type help.*

When I understood, I had to say it out loud to be sure. *She killed herself?*

No! No. Just an attempt, he said. *Still, it's a hell of a thing.* He leaned forward and folded his hands on the desk in front of him. *The kind of thing that can derail a young man's life.* He looked me right in the eye. *Nick,* he said. I sat up straight. *Richard left his team jacket on the stoop.*

I was slow to understand, I'll admit that. But once he said that I got fucking pissed. I couldn't believe it. It was like they'd been set up.

But—that doesn't mean anything, I said. *They just drove her home. It's not a crime to leave a jacket.*

Coach nodded. *I know,* he said. *That's exactly right.*

We talked about it for a while. We talked about Max, a little, but Coach knew that Richard was my oldest friend, so mostly we talked about Richard. *Richard's got a bright future serving our country,* he said. *I talked to Representative Patterson's office about him just this week.* Richard had to get a letter of recommendation from a local congressman for his application to the Naval Academy, and he'd been stressing about it all fall. I couldn't believe that he might lose that just because he'd hooked up with a crazy drunk girl. But Coach was serious as a heart attack. *It's politics,* he said. *But that's how it works. They're gonna come out of the woods. And not just for Richard and Max. For all of you boys on the team.*

They were coming after us because she'd hooked up with a couple of guys? They wanted to punish us for her drinking too much, for her being easy? When there were assloads of kids doing stuff like that every night of the week. Just because Richard left his jacket behind, because she was too drunk to get inside and he didn't want her to be cold. It was worse than the laser pointer, which was just an arbitrary rule. And maybe Max deserved it, karma-wise. But Richard didn't. Richard was my oldest friend, and he was a little soft, and whatever he did it was only because the girl wanted to hook up with Max—she had let him rub her shoulders, she had gotten into the car. And anyway, if she'd tried to commit suicide, didn't it only prove that she was unstable, the kind of person who drank too much and regretted it after?

I didn't understand this world, I thought, where everyone just wants someone to blame, when all of us have enough to deal with as it is.

The crazy thing was, the girl didn't even want to get Richard and Max in trouble. It was her mother, Coach said. *She did the whole cry-for-help thing because people wouldn't stop teasing her. So really, we're all on the same page. We want the same thing the girl wants. We all just want this to settle down.*

Right, I said. I leaned forward and put my fist on the desk. I wanted Coach to know that I was serious. I wanted him to see my commitment. I wanted to do the right thing.

I felt like a man. I said, *What do you need me to do?*

THE NEXT AFTERNOON, Saturday, Haley called and asked if I'd give her a ride to the mall. She had to buy a birthday present for her dad.

And I was thinking maybe we could talk a bit, she said.

Sure, I said. I was so nervous I worried my voice was going to crack. I hadn't talked to Haley in weeks, and I thought she didn't like me anymore. *Yeah, I was going to the mall today anyway,* I said. *I was thinking about seeing a movie.*

Oh, cool. Yeah, Scream 3 *just came out,* she said. *I'm dying to see it.*

That's so awesome, I said. *Amazing. Yes.*

I could barely speak to her on the drive there. She looked out the window. A song came on the radio that I liked. *I like this song,* I said, but Haley just kind of said *mm-hmm.* I was sure I was fucked.

But in the mall, it was a little easier. We walked by racks of T-shirts and flip-flops. We went to the bookstore and to a store that sold only teapots. I saw guys look at Haley, then at me, then away. I made myself look them in the eyes. *Yeah. She's with me,* I said to them, in my mind.

We had a good time. Haley was a good time. She made fun of this stupid T-shirt and the kind of person who would wear it. I made a joke about a teapot, I did the I'm-a-little-teapot arms, it made her laugh. She bought a book for her dad about the Civil War. *Does your dad love the Civil War?* she said. *My dad is crazy about the Civil War.*

Yeah, I said, but only to keep her talking.

In line at the movies I asked what the first *Scream* was about. *Is there anything I need to know before I see this one?* I said.

Haley stared at me. "You haven't seen *Scream*?" she said.

So I laughed and said I was joking. *Of course I saw* Scream, I said. *I saw it twice.*

Haley laughed and kind of punched my shoulder. *God, Nick, you fooled me. For a second I don't know what I thought,* she said.

Ha ha, I said. *Yup. There's no way this one will be good as the first,* I said.

They're all good, Haley said. She kind of punched me on the shoulder again, in a way that let me know *we* were all good. She even let me buy her a Mountain Dew.

So you like scary movies, huh? I asked her.

Yeah, I love them, she said, and I loved the way she shrugged when she said it. I loved how she drank soda, she wasn't one of these girls who always make a big deal about calories. She was easy to be around. She was so pretty.

I've been wanting to ask you something, she said. Our elbows were almost touching on the armrest between us. An ad on the screen was trying to sell us another Mountain Dew.

I want to ask you something, too.

Oh, okay. You go first.

I panicked. For a wild second I thought she was about to say that she was falling in love with me. I thought about saying something emotional first, maybe that's what she really wanted. Something like *I really like you.* But I chickened out. *No, you go first.*

No, you. Then she laughed. *I'm just kidding. I'll go first. It's this whole thing with Max and Richard. I've been really wanting to talk to you about it. I know Max is a jerk, but what about Richard?*

The lights in the theater went off and a trailer started playing. I leaned closer to her, smelled strawberries. *Yeah,* I whispered. *Richard is a good guy.*

So he didn't really . . .

Didn't really what?

She was looking at me, but it was dark, so I couldn't read her expression. *Richard is my oldest friend,* I said.

She didn't say anything. I thought she just needed me to explain. *It's not like everyone is saying,* I said. *That's just a dumb story. You just can't understand the pressure he's under, that we're all under.*

She laughed. I decided that maybe, yes, okay, what I said could have been a joke. I forced a laugh, too, but then her eyes were wide. It had been a sarcastic laugh, I realized.

You think I don't understand pressure?

Yeah, you know how it is. I turned to face her. I thought about taking her hand but didn't. *I know you do. We're scrutinized for every little thing. Every little thing gets all blown out of proportion.*

What do you mean?

I just mean, people are coming out of the woods for Max and Richard.

Wait. She looked away. She pushed her hair out of her face. *Wait.*

She was quiet for so long I wasn't sure she was going to continue, and then she said, in a different voice, really agitated now, "What you're saying is, you're saying they're allowed to rape a girl because of pressure?"

"What?" I sat up straight. "No. Haley, you can't just throw that word around."

"She tried to kill herself."

She was sitting up stick straight. I remembered what Coach had said: that I couldn't talk about it, that I shouldn't say anything, except that nothing had happened. I tried to think of what to say to Haley that would fit the bill.

"But the rape thing. Where did you hear that? Who said that to you?" I felt myself getting agitated.

"Max and Richard said it. At Denny's. You were there."

"They didn't say *that*." I was surprised how nice it felt to be angry.

"They said they fingered her while she was passed out."

I asked how she had heard that.

"Alan told me," she said.

The idea that she'd been talking to Alan made me furious. What if she was the one who told everybody? I hated Alan. I hated her. I imagined him telling her, betraying Richard and Max and all of us—I'd always known he was a liar—and it felt right to be angry, it was like finally finishing a run and drinking an entire bottle of water in one go. Haley didn't understand that we were just trying to have a good time while we could. We had to be able to run three miles in twenty-five minutes. We had both legs and nothing to write about in our college application essays. When we broke our arms, we couldn't even take the Oxy because our teammates might need it to give to girls. I didn't even want a blow job from Haley. Not if I had to feel this way to get it.

I stared at the screen. I was so angry I couldn't look at her. But I didn't have to put up with her anymore because the movie started. I couldn't decide if the timing was perfect or terrible. On the screen, a guy was careening through Los Angeles trying to get home in time to save his girlfriend from a murderer. I looked over at Haley once and she was looking away from me, toward the door. Just when the girl-friend got out of the shower—and the killer was right there, ready to strike—Haley got up and walked out.

I went back and forth but finally decided to follow her out. Even then she wouldn't let me drive her home.

"I need some time alone," she said. "I'll get a ride with Georgia when she gets off work."

Her arms were crossed. Behind her, kids were blowing up plastic grocery bags and setting them in a shallow fountain, giving them a little push, watching them float. I realized I would have to tell the team about this. I would have to tell Coach. Who else was Haley talking to?

I touched her for the first time since the party. It was just my hand on her elbow. I was surprised she let me keep it there. *You can't tell anyone what you said in there*, I said. *That bullshit about Richard and the girl. You can't say that to anyone.*

My hand was still on her arm. Her eyes softened, and her mouth opened just a little bit, and for a second I thought that I had cracked through. She was sorry, she was going to apologize. She uncrossed her arms and took the smallest step backward, just enough to step out of my reach.

"Everyone knows, Nick," she said, and walked away.

COACH WASN'T WRONG: they started coming out of the woods for us, and hard. The second week in January was the worst. It was my first experience with injustice. We were no longer individuals, talented young men with hopes and dreams. We were the lacrosse team that had raped that girl.

On Monday they had a moment of silence over the loudspeaker for suicide awareness. Some sophomore did it during morning announcements. But the loudspeaker stayed on the whole time, you could hear the kid breathing. It wasn't a moment of silence. It was a moment of spittle in the corner of some mouth breather's mouth. I watched the second hand on the clock, and the "moment" only lasted thirty seconds, which seemed cheap to me.

Also that day we missed fifth period for a special presentation about suicide. A bunch of people were wearing black on Tuesday. By Wednesday it was almost everyone. Then on Thursday some girl got up during lunch and shouted that she was organizing a boycott of lacrosse games and asked people to come over and sign up. Dave wanted to go over and rip her sheets into shreds, but I told him to stop. I felt myself standing tall even as I said it. I told him what Coach had told me: that we had to keep our cool. And I was right, because then some random guy yelled *suck my dick!* and the girl got all red in the face and ran out of the lunchroom and no one signed her stupid boycott anyway.

Richard had stopped coming to school the day before. When I called his house, his mother said he was sick and that she'd have him call me soon. Over lunch Max said they had both talked to the police.

The police had treated him like shit, he said. *They kept asking the same questions, like I was an idiot.* And none of us said, *You are an idiot*, because things were different now, we weren't joking around anymore.

One of the cops said they talked to this other girl. This random girl told them I pushed her on a bed last summer. At some party. Max looked at us as he said this, like he was daring us to agree with the girl. *She said I made her uncomfortable.*

We couldn't look at Max. We weren't sure what to say. *So the ladies' man gets rough,* Dave finally said, and sort of laughed, then stopped. None of us were laughing.

Anyway, it was months ago, Max said. *What does it matter.*

And we all agreed: *They're coming out of the woods for us, is all.*

On Friday, Ms. Lomax gave us the whole class just to write about our feelings. "I know a lot of you are probably feeling upset, maybe confused, maybe even afraid. Writing can help. It's not graded, and you don't have to share."

Dave folded his arms and refused, said he didn't have anything to say about *recent events*. "This is calculus," he said.

"You kids' lives are more important than calculus," she said. "But if you don't want to write, you can excuse yourself and go sit in the library."

I was the only lacrosse player left in the room but I wasn't going to bail. We spent a silent half hour bent over our papers. The sound of everyone's pens going was like ants chewing up a man buried alive to his neck. I stared at the blue lines in my blank notebook and wrote nothing. When thirty minutes were up, Ms. Lomax asked if anyone wanted to share. Haley volunteered. She walked by my desk without looking at me and stood up in front of the class.

What is a boxing ring for? Climb the velvet rope. Shrug off your robe. You can't complain about getting hit. What did you expect,

we might say, when you climbed into the ring, wearing those gloves?
When you heard the bell? If you get hit on the street, one-two, by a
stranger in silk shorts? Okay, we might say, not your fault. Or
maybe we'll bring out a coil of velvet rope, to wrap and wrap
around you, so that when you wake up, hit and upset, we can
explain what a boxing ring is for.

I didn't totally get what she was trying to say, but I knew it was good. She sounded good reading it. Confident and smug. I hated her. She hadn't looked at me all week. She walked by my desk and still didn't look.

Dave threw a party that Friday. No one came but us. We sat in the basement together and got drunk, except for Richard, who we still hadn't seen. We slept over, splayed out on the floor. I couldn't sleep, and I got up and drank the last two beers by myself. I stood looking out of the sliding glass door that went out onto Dave's deck. There was a spotlight on, and I watched the moths flutter around it.

The next morning we went out for egg-and-cheese bagels. There was a group of private school girls at the bagel place when we got there. They must have seen us before we saw them. They were sitting there silently, staring at us. We thought that we should probably leave, but no one made the move. The girls all stood up at once. I heard one of them say, "Two, three," and then they screamed, "Rapists!" in unison. We backed out, trying to act like we'd just decided to go somewhere else. We went out to the parking lot and sat silently in my car, each of us looking out our own windows, hungry, with nothing to combat our hangovers. Eventually Max said, *Bitches.*

All week, I just tried not to think too hard about it. I tried to focus on playing well. I was waking up earlier and earlier in the mornings anyway, so I would go to the track and run twice as far as we were supposed to during the off season. It was dark and cold, and my breath would puff out ahead of me as I ran. I'd get to the showers first and stand in the hot water, alone. After school I ran more. If I wasn't running I was drinking. So I ran as late as I could, because I wanted to play well, and to play well I couldn't drink too much. So I ran for hours. I ran farther than I'd ever gone before. I tried not to think about Haley when I ran. She was wrong. It wasn't peaceful.

RICHARD SHOWED UP at my house on Sunday morning. I ran downstairs when the doorbell rang, because I didn't want my mom to wake up. I hadn't told her anything about Richard and Max. I didn't want her to hear it for the first time from a cop.

But it was just Richard. I hadn't seen him since lunch on Tuesday. His hands were folded behind his neck like he was stretching. He looked tired. There was a spray of pimples on his chin, and he'd missed a couple of hairs shaving. *Poor guy*, I thought.

We went to the basement to play video games. Neither of us wanted to think about anything for a while. But when I turned on the system, Richard said, *Wait.*

He was sitting on his knees, looking at the ground. The theme music for the game played on a loop; behind him, the screen asked us to choose between one player or two.

Nick, we made the whole thing up.

What whole thing?

The thing with the girl.

The thing with the girl?

Nick, quit it. You know what I mean when I fucking say the thing with the girl.

Richard had never talked to me like that before. I reminded myself of what Coach had said: no matter what, we couldn't turn on each other, we would make it through as long as we stayed loyal to each other. So I said nothing.

The private school girl. All we did was drive her home. We didn't touch her, we didn't finger her, we didn't jizz on her tits.

I thought you said you jizzed on her stomach.

Well, not that, either. I'm telling you, nothing happened.

The music from the video game system was making me crazy. I grabbed the controller. I selected TWO PLAYERS. Richard picked up the other controller. We started playing. I was trying to think. Mostly I was just shocked because I realized I'd never heard Richard actually say it before. I'd heard the story from Alan, from Dave. Richard almost sounded like he was Mr. Kaminsky or something when he said the words *finger her*, like the words disgusted him. I wondered again if Richard could be gay.

Tell me the whole thing, I said, finally.

I was glad to have the screen to watch as he talked. *Max was in the back seat, basically passed out with her. If he even put an arm around her, I didn't see it. She was more awake than he was, actually. She told me where she lived. But then by the time we got to her house Max woke up, and she had mostly passed out. We drove straight from the party to her house. Ten minutes. I never touched her.*

But you carried her up the lawn.

Well, except for then.

But you guys were gone like an hour.

We went to the Giant parking lot after so Max could get high. Then he spent like an hour trying to talk this slutty girl behind the counter at 7-Eleven into locking the doors and taking him up on the roof. Richard was mashing the controller. Aliens died in splatters of blood. *Which she didn't. I don't think Max gets half the girls he says he does.*

But, what about the thing about the toilet paper. You said there was toilet paper in her pubes.

Because then in Denny's Max starts shitting on me. The way Max always shits on me. His guy had died. I thought about how it wasn't just Max, it was all of us who gave Richard a hard time, but only because Richard never hooked up with anyone. I kept playing. Richard kept talking. *So I started agreeing with him: Yeah I pulled the car over. Yeah I got in the back seat. Yeah we're basically porn stars.* Richard shook his head. *I didn't think it would get around like that.*

My guy died and I let the game sit for a minute, my guy's dead body on the ground under the words GAME OVER. I looked at Richard. I felt this was important. *I believe you,* I said. And I did.

Richard was shaking his head. He didn't say anything. He was upset, I knew. But to be honest, I was starting to feel kind of good. And not just because it meant that Richard wasn't ahead of me, that I wasn't the only guy on the team not getting laid. It was because he had told me. Of all of us, I was the one he came to talk to. I was the one he trusted.

We were each other's oldest friends. I felt like I was realizing for the first time how important this was. I'd let my own shit get in the way. But we were *friends*. This was what mattered. Not girls and parties. Loyalty. When your friend got into a bad place, it was your job to back him up. That's what mattered.

I said, *Not to sound like a cliché, but I think we need a drink.*

It's Sunday morning.

What do you care, aren't you Jewish?

Richard followed me upstairs. My dad was at church, and my mom was still asleep. She had worked overnight at the hospital and was no doubt in her room with the blackout shades pulled down and her earplugs in. We went into the kitchen and dumped the water out of our Nalgenes, then filled them up with white wine from a box in the fridge. This had been my trick for a little while. My parents didn't drink beer or hard liquor. When I could get a bottle of vodka, I hid it in the basement, in a box marked TAXES, which I knew my parents never touched. But when I ran out I'd go into the kitchen and put some boxed wine in my Nalgene. Richard was the first person I shared this with—I guess, in my own way, I was trying to show him that we could trust each other.

The wine tasted like sheet metal, especially at first, but I found that it was a good kind of drunk. It was better than vodka for sleeping. It kind of lulled you under. And there was always a box in the fridge. It was like a limitless fountain of booze. As I filled my bottle, I tried to ask, casually, *So the thing about the toilet paper stuck to her. Do you think that could really happen?*

Richard looked at me.

You said that there was a piece—

No, there wasn't—or, I don't know, I didn't see.

I know, I believe you. But where did you get that idea?

I guess I heard it in a porno or something.

I kind of laughed and shook my head. *Fuck, that's disgusting,* I said. *I was hoping that part wasn't real.*

Then we were laughing, so I didn't realize how much I'd filled my bottle up. Then Richard put his under the tap. It hadn't occurred to me that the boxed wine would ever run out, but the stream turned into a little dribble.

I was going to make a joke—performance anxiety? But this didn't feel like the right moment, so instead I said, *Tilt the box forward.* My mom always tilted the box forward when it started getting empty.

We went back to the basement and started playing the game again. *Okay,* I said. *We'll figure this out.*

Thanks. He took a sip, then scrunched his face up. *This tastes like shit.*

I know. But I promise it's a good buzz. Give it a second. I took a deep gulp of my own bottle to show him. I felt the burst of excitement it always brought in my chest.

The thing I don't understand is why she tried to kill herself, I said.

I know. It's like she's bipolar or something. Who wants to kill themselves just for being teased? It's not like we're twelve.

I guess what I mean is, why does she let them tease her, why doesn't she tell them it didn't happen? We played for a minute.

Then Richard said, *She was passed out. Maybe she thinks it did happen.*

I shook my head. *A girl would know. I'm sure of it.*

Richard's guy died again. He was no good at this game. He threw the controller against the carpet. *People are never going to stop talking about it. I wish we'd never started that stupid rumor.*

That's when I realized.

Wait. I dropped my controller in my excitement. My guy died in a splatter of blood. I didn't care. I felt giddy. I stood up, like a lawyer on TV. I had cracked this motherfucker. And I was going to get us out of this. All of us.

It's just a rumor! I said. *And who spread the rumor?*

Richard was staring at me. *Everyone,* he said.

No, pussy dick, I said. *Haley. She was there at Denny's. She was so mad at us, remember?*

Richard nodded slowly.

She was mad at us, so she told the story to everyone. She must have spread the rumor; it wasn't us, right? It's her fault.

But you like Haley, Richard said.

I shook my head. *She's not who I thought she was.* I took a long gulp from my Nalgene. *Richard, old friend. I know what to do.*

WHEN THE COPS FINALLY CAME to talk to us, we told them what we knew to be true: How the private school girl had a crush on Max. How she got herself so drunk, really early on in the party, too. How she danced alone in the middle of the floor. That she always drank too much; we'd heard she was bipolar. That Richard offered to drive both Max and her home. They had done the right thing and gotten her home safe.

We told them how we'd met up at Denny's after, like always. And how we'd teased Max about it because the girl had a crush on him. We told them how Haley misinterpreted things. *She's a pothead*, we said. We'd seen her smoking earlier that night. She got all freaked out when Max told us about taking the girl home. We told Haley nothing happened in the car. It's not that we thought Haley would lie, necessarily. But Haley was not totally reliable. After all, she was the only girl at Denny's that night. She was the kind of girl who followed us around. We liked her, but actually, when you thought about it, it was kind of weird—kind of attention hungry, you know? To be the only girl hanging out with all those guys. At the time, before things got out of hand, we didn't say anything. We didn't want to get her in trouble. But now it was out of hand. We thought it was time she took responsibility.

They interviewed us separately, like cops on TV, trying to trip us up. But we played it cool. We told the same story, again and again and again. The more we talked, the more true it became. And soon everyone else knew the truth, too. Even before the cops dropped the whole thing, everyone had heard the girl was bipolar and knew that's why she took all those pills. It was really sad, we all agreed.

But what was even sadder was that someone could be so starved for attention they'd try to get it the way Haley had, spreading gossip that was so hurtful. Personally, I didn't think she did it for the attention; she was just angry at us, she just wanted to get back at us for something. But the attention-seeking story was the one that everyone kept telling. People really turned on her for that. I heard people saying it: she'd walk into a classroom and someone would say *attention whore*, I walked by her locker and it was written in black Sharpie, too, *whore*, and it seemed a little harsh, but I was starting to understand how the world worked. And anyway, it was Haley's fault. She'd gotten into that fight with Max. She had egged him on.

Somehow, through it all, Haley seemed fine. She won in the state championships, she had the fastest two-hundred-meter dash in the state. She sat in the front of the classroom and never looked at me. She even got that poem about the boxing ring published in some magazine. Ms. Lomax made a proud announcement about it during class. But I didn't care either way. By then, it was March, and almost time for our first seeded game, and that's what I really cared about.

We never really talked about it again. I didn't get my scholarship, but I got into the University of Maryland, and I felt good about that. I could try out for the team. And it was better that way, because it would inspire me to work hard over the summer, to get in shape, and then I would show up in the fall, and I would show them I was worth something, that I could be part of something.

Richard got into the Naval Academy. We told him he was never going to get to drink again, that he would never have fun again, and that now he would definitely never get laid. It was all military from here on out. Then a few weeks later, he said he had news for us. He'd been accepted at Princeton.

We hadn't even known he'd applied there.

My dad is pissed, Richard said. His dad was navy. He'd promised Richard a car if he went to the Naval Academy. But Richard didn't want to be in the military. He was going to Princeton.

Princeton, we said, shaking our heads. We couldn't believe it.

So things turned out all right after all. Ham got a small scholarship to Georgia. Alan and Max were going to the University of Maryland, too. We all teased Richard about the fun we would have without him. We told him that whenever he got sick of those uptight prep school pussy dicks he was welcome to come to our dorms and party with us. Princeton wasn't so far away.

Things had turned out all right. We had been through something together, we agreed, and it had made us stronger.

On the day we heard that the investigation would be dropped, Coach canceled practice and invited us all to his house. It was a bright and cold Friday at the end of February. The front door was open, and there was a sticky note on the storm door telling us to come on inside and take off our shoes. Coach was on the back porch in his winter coat, starting up a gas grill. There was soda in the fridge and chips and Cheetos on the kitchen table. He told us to help ourselves and to meet him in the living room.

Coach's wife was a dermatologist and his house was big. There was a big, wide window over the sink in the kitchen, and from it I could see the dock, at the end of the sloping lawn, where we'd gone that day our sophomore year, right after we were buzzed in, when we first became part of the team. We'd never actually been back to that dock. Matt Iglehart was the one who was friends with Coach's son, and when Iglehart went to UVA, none of us really felt right going to hang out there. But as I stood in the kitchen, I remembered the weathered wood, the smell of early fall, the feeling of just starting out. And now I had made it into the house. More than anything else, coming back here, as seniors invited in our own right, made us feel that things were going to be okay.

We sat in the living room, on the couch or the floor, and ate burgers and chips on paper plates. Coach stood in front of the TV, a professional pool game on mute behind him.

My buddy called me personally last night to let me know that they're totally expunging the investigation. It's over. He reached down and picked up a plastic grocery bag from the floor next to him. He held it in his fist and looked almost like he was thinking of crying. He said, *I'm proud of you boys. You stood tall.*

Then he looked at each of us. We remembered past speeches he'd given us. When we had smirked or ignored him. Today we were all looking at him seriously, with great respect. *You were gentlemen*, he said, and we knew that he meant it.

But it turns out you're also little boys, he said.

We laughed and looked at each other nervously. We weren't little boys. Of course not, Coach was just lightening the mood. Then he explained: *In some of my conversations with you all about these rumors, I realized you all haven't been prepared for the birds and the bees.*

Those of us closest to him saw that the grocery bag was filled with condoms. We laughed. We turned to tell the others behind us. Soon we were all laughing.

Gentlemen, Coach said, holding his hands up to quiet down our laughter, but smiling, too. *It wouldn't have been appropriate to hand these out in the middle of the investigation. But now. You all are going to be back at your parties—as long as you win all your games.* We laughed. Of course we would win our games.

*I know you've learned a lot. You'll keep yourselves safe from here on out, right? Because there are gifts girls will give you, you can't give back. I'm talking about herpes. I'm talking about babies. So, gentlemen—*and now Coach was chuckling, we were all laughing—*remember these!* He reached into the bag and started throwing the condoms at us. He threw handfuls at a time, like confetti. We laughed and caught them. We joked that we needed more; we joked that we needed a larger size. We stuffed our pockets with them.

Then we got down on our hands and knees and searched the floors and the couch cushions and made sure we got them all. We joked that we needed every last one. But we also had to make sure that Coach's wife didn't find one of them later and get the wrong idea. Coach didn't have a son in the house anymore to blame for a stray condom. We were still laughing. We laughed and laughed. We laughed at the thought of Coach trying to explain the condom in the couch cushions to his wife; we laughed at all the silly ways a misunderstanding can occur.

PART II

FINAL GIRL

2000

DRAFT 1

For this college application essay, I'm supposed to write about a "significant experience" that's "had an impact" on me. But I'm *not* supposed to write about when I was raped. And . . . I just did. Shoot.

DRAFT 2

For this college application essay, I'm supposed to write about a "significant experience" that's "had an impact" on me. I don't know what that's supposed to mean. My tutor Ms. McConnolly says not to worry too much, the prompt doesn't really matter.

How the heck do you write a good essay based on a question that doesn't matter?

It kind of reminds me how everyone says "How are you," but they don't really mean it. People ask me how I am all the time, but they don't actually want to know. Probably because they suspect

I'm probably not all that great, after my accident. Which . . . ha ha, I'm not supposed to write about, either.

DRAFT 3

For this college application essay, I'm supposed to write about a "significant experience" that's "had an impact" on me. My tutor Ms. McConnolly suggested I just start writing and see what comes out.

So: Ranch dressing and swiss cheese. Michael Stipe. Lampedoodle. Freak out. Hang ten. Power down. Whistle stop. Cry for help.

Game over. Try again.

DRAFT 4

For this college application essay, I'm supposed to write about a "significant experience" that's "had an impact" on me.

To help me think of a good topic, my mom bought me a book of sample college essays to read through. They were all freaking terrrrible.

In one of them, a guy who wants to be an engineer writes about the time he took the family microwave apart. In another one, this girl goes through the etymology of a bunch of interesting words that have been important in her life, because she found words so *interesting* and wanted to be an English major. In the worst essay of them all, another girl talks about the time her mom took her on a very, very, very special shoe-shopping trip.

All of them made me feel like a monster.

DRAFT 4.5

For this college application essay, I'm supposed to write about a "significant experience" that's "had an impact" on me. One such experience was the time I took the family microwave apart. The impact was that it exploded. The end.

DRAFT 4.75

For this college application essay, I'm supposed to write about a "significant experience" that's "had an impact" on me.

I think the word "impact" is really *interesting*. I looked it up in the thesaurus because that's more *interesting* than starting an essay with a dictionary definition. The synonyms for impact are: 1) effect, influence, consequences, OR: 2) crash, smash, bump.

It's *interesting* to think about how that second one applies to my life.

So here's a short list of some crashes and bumps in my life. When I was eight years old, Gretchen Langeloth pushed me off the swing set. The impact was two bones in my elbow against the ground. My cast was hot pink. Everyone wanted to be my friend the next day. By the end of recess, there was no pink left on the cast, it was covered in Sharpie signatures. That was the last time in my life that I felt popular.

When I was ten years old, I was the only girl on the baseball team, and I made contact with the ball during a game one time. I hit a double. The impact was my heart exploded. (My feelings have been in a million pieces ever since.)

When I was twelve years old, I snuck out of my bunk at camp and swam across the lake. Because my friend Madeleine had chickened out, there were two boys waiting for me on the other side. So I had both my first and second kiss in the same night. The impact was the slap of our lips. The first boy, especially, kissed too hard.

When I was fourteen, they found a serial killer in the neighborhood next to mine. They found him out because his wife was in a dumpster, cut into fifteen pieces. I couldn't figure out where you would cut a body to make fifteen pieces. The husband told the police that a burglar had broken into the house and kidnapped her. Later they found out he had told the same story in a different state about a different cut-up wife. I tried to be a lesbian after that but couldn't do it. I kept chasing boys, and then when I was sixteen, two boys took advantage of me in the back of a car after a party, and everyone at my school knew about it, and they were so mean to me about it, I basically wanted to die. A month later, I had an accident where I almost did die. I drank a lot of vodka both times, I was unconscious when they both happened. So I don't actually know the impact of either one.

If a tree falls in the forest and you're passed out, does it have an impact?

I guess the impact was these wads of wet toilet paper Tonya Simpson used to throw at me in the hallway back when I was still in school. They'd stick to the lockers above my head with a sound like *crash, smash, bump*, or more specifically, *schlop* (an accident, she said, when one of them hit me in the face). I guess the impact was my dad, breaking the window of the car where I was sitting in the driver's seat after I took too much Tylenol (an accident, he said, an accident).

DRAFT 4.9999

For this college application essay, I'm supposed to write about a "significant experience" that's "had an impact" on me.

But what does "significant" mean, anyway?

My thesaurus says: Of consequence. Uncommon. Momentous.

73

Momentous is a strange word. It should mean "full of moments," since usually a word ending in "-ous" means a thing that is full of itself. Like: "Nervous" is full of nerves. Or how "sandwicheous" is full of sandwiches.

Aliceous is full of Alice. And what does it mean to be full of Alice?

It means you have boring, straight brown hair that only looks okay if you blow-dry it. It means you wear a ponytail most of the time, and wisps of hair fly out over both of your ears and make you look like you're wearing a weird pilgrim's hat.

It means you are pretty good at physics, but you really love writing. It means you want to be a journalist when you grow up.

It means your goal is to go to the University of Virginia. Your mom took you to visit and you saw people lying on blankets reading Joan Didion in the sun on the grass and they looked like they could be your friends.

It means you've been working so freaking hard this year, as hard as anyone has ever worked. You dropped out but then you went back and completed junior year with summer courses at the community college and even brought up your GPA. You're working on your GED. You're proving you are UVA-ready. You are ready for all of the acronyms.

A.L.I.C.E.O.U.S.: Artistic Lovable Intelligent Creative Elegant Original Unique Smart

It means your fifth-grade drama teacher cast you as Grizabella in *Cats*, but another girl came onstage to sing "Memory" instead of you because you can't sing. It means wolves are your totem animal. It means you love horror movies.

Does that sound weird? It's true, though. I really love horror movies. My favorite is *The Silence of the Lambs*, but I will watch any horror movie, and I won't close my eyes. I've seen the scariest ones, like *Se7en*, and *The Shining*, and *The Blair Witch Project*, and even the really awful ones like *The Texas Chain Saw Massacre*. The worst I ever saw was *The Last House on the Left*, which was just *awful*. You might think that one is a weird one for me to watch, because it's a rape revenge film. But it was my friends on the Horror FanGrrls message board who convinced me to watch it, and they're all survivors of sexual assault, too, so I figured . . .

Oh wait. Okay, new try.

DRAFT 5

For this college application essay, I'm supposed to write about a "significant experience" that's "had an impact" on me. One significant experience in my life was seeing *The Silence of the Lambs*. It was the first horror movie I ever saw. The impact on me is that now I love horror movies.

What I love about *The Silence of the Lambs* is that it's about a strong woman, not just one running away all the time—a lot of horror movies are just women running away (and getting hurt anyway).

I love that when you first see Jodie Foster, she's jogging through the woods alone. She's like any woman in any horror movie—running, running, running—but you can tell immediately that she's not running away from a murderer or anything. She's doing an obstacle course; she's training herself.

Later, you realize that the thing she's running from is inside herself.

Jodie Foster is not afraid of Buffalo Bill, the serial killer on the loose. *He's* afraid of *her*. She's *his* monster. (Actually, I feel bad for Buffalo Bill. The movie is pretty mean to him. The camera spies on him in his room. You get the sense he got teased badly in school.) Jodie Foster is also not afraid of Hannibal the Cannibal, who is stowed safely in jail. What she's afraid of is Dr. Lecter the psychiatrist. And it doesn't matter that he's behind glass and can't physically harm her. The scary thing is inside of Jodie Foster, and Dr. Lecter the brilliant psychoanalyst has the key to let it out just by talking to her.

I could keep going—I could spend this entire essay describing the plot of *The Silence of the Lambs* and what it means. For the past year, I've watched the movie at least once a week. I could probably reproduce the whole script from memory! But this is a college application essay, not a fan grrl message board. So what I'm going to tell you about is what it feels like to be Jodie Foster.

Like Jodie Foster, I've been working really hard for what I want. I didn't grow up on a ranch and was never traumatized by the spring slaughter of any farm animals. But I do want to get away from the place where I grew up. And I do have big ambitions: I want to be a journalist. And I'm willing to work hard for it. Like Jodie Foster, I'm driven, and like Jodie Foster, I'm not afraid of any serial murderer. What I'm afraid of is that I'm not good enough.

Alice Lovett
9/30/2000
505 words

Let's explore your POV on sexism a bit more.

College Application Essay DRAFT 1

One significant experience in my life was seeing *The Silence of the Lambs*. It was the first horror movie I ever saw. The impact on me is that now I love horror movies.

We need a stronger opening. Maybe "in medias res"?

What do I love about *Silence of the Lambs*? There are a lot of things, but the big one is that it's about a woman who is strong and powerful. In most horror movies, women are just running away all of the time. *Silence of the Lambs* challenges that cliché from the beginning. When we first see Clarice Starling (played by Jodie Foster) on screen, she's running through the woods. But you can tell immediately that she's not running away from a murderer or anything. She's just doing an obstacle course, and she's a strong woman. Still, you can tell by the look on her face that she is running away from *something*. It's something that is inside herself.

Then she's given an assignment to talk to Hannibal Lecter, and we realize that Clarice is going to have to face that thing.

Everyone knows Hannibal Lecter, whether or not you've seen the movie. Say "Hannibal the Cannibal" and basically anyone is *funny!* going to say, "Yeah, sure, that guy who chews faces and likes fava beans." But the thing a lot of people don't know about Hannibal Lecter is that he's the perfect monster for Clarice, specifically. He is *her* worst fear. She's not afraid of the serial killer Buffalo Bill (actually, *he's* afraid of *her*; she is *his* monster). She's not even afraid of Hannibal the Cannibal, who's in jail. What she's afraid of is Dr. Lecter, the psychiatrist. It doesn't matter that he's behind glass; the scary thing is inside of Clarice, and to let it out, all Dr. Lecter the brilliant psychoanalyst has to do is talk. *I'm surprised you love horror movies . . . I want to know*

I could keep going—I could spend this entire essay describing *WHY.* what *The Silence of the Lambs* means. I could probably reproduce *Can this essay go* the whole script from memory. For the past year, I've watched the *deeper?* movie at least once a week. Instead, I'll stick to what's important, which is what it feels like to be Clarice Starling, because I identify closely with her.

This is funny, BUT it doesn't tell me anything exciting about YOU.

Like Clarice, I've been working really hard, training myself, and working for a big goal. I want to go to the University of Virginia and begin my path to reaching my dream of being a journalist. Like Clarice, I'm driven. Like Clarice, I'm willing to work as hard as I have to. And like Clarice, I'm not afraid of any murderer. I'm afraid of what's inside me.

But I think I might be ready to face it.

EEP!

Let's chat. I almost feel like going to UVA will be like interviewing Hannibal Lecter. At UVA, I'm going to meet new friends and professors who—like Hannibal Lecter—will have the key to letting the monsters inside of me out. I believe that if I keep working hard, I can learn to wrangle those scary things and overcome them and keep reaching for my dreams.

Alice: you're a v. strong writer. Your essay is going to be great. BUT we need to figure out WHAT you want to say. This first draft feels like you're just warming up. We'll brainstorm at our next meeting!

— Ms. MC

DRAFT 2 V1

People are often surprised to learn that I love horror movies. I'm a teenage girl with straight brown hair. I'm not goth or anything. I seem really normal at first. But I watch at least four horror movies every week. I've seen *Se7en* twice as many times as the title.

Why do I like them? It's kind of like the Apple Jacks commercials: *I JUST DO.*

I guess one reason is the adrenaline. I love the tight, excited feeling I get when the first image flashes up on the screen. I love the suspense. It's like being at the top hill of a roller coaster. And it's like a roller coaster when you're done, when you get off, you feel so alive!

Most people want to know what I mean when I say horror movies. Like, slasher films like *Halloween*? Or even like *Texas Chain Saw Massacre*? My answer is *all of them*. I even used to want to be a horror filmmaker; my middle school best friend and I used to make silly scary movies together on her dad's camcorder.

It's not because my life is like a horror movie. Although maybe it is! Bad things happen to all of us. Even on a normal day you can turn on the television and see a man, who lives in the neighborhood next to mine, giving an interview because his wife's body was found mutilated in a dumpster. The world is scary. It's not hard to imagine Pennywise from *IT* hiding under my bathroom sink. It's not hard to imagine a *Poltergeist* in the walls of our house in these weird sterilized suburbs. It's not hard to imagine that this is *Invasion of the Body Snatchers*; there are times where I definitely feel like everyone around me is in on a secret conspiracy, and I'm the weird outsider who didn't get the memo.

DRAFT 2 V2

Sometimes I feel like I'm living in *Invasion of the Body Snatchers*. When I saw that movie in middle school, I thought—that's just like my school! I feel like the last person who hasn't been killed and replaced with an automaton of myself.

And I'm kind of afraid that writing this essay is making me fall asleep.

DRAFT 2 V3

Shelley Duvall is walking through the kitchen, checking to make sure the Overlook Hotel is running, checking all the machines and everything. Note, *she's* doing her *husband's* job. Jack Nicholson is the star of *The Shining*, but it's actually his wife who's taking care of everything. Sexism!

What do I have to say about sexism?

I feel kind of like Jack right now. I'm sitting at my desk trying to write this essay. It's making me a dull grrl.

DRAFT 2 V4

What do I want you to know about me? I want you to know that I should go to UVA. But why should I go to UVA? I don't know the answer to that myself.

In a horror movie, when someone doesn't know the answer to something, it's usually time to go to the library.

DRAFT 2 V5

Morgan Freeman walks into the New York Public Library. He banters with the night security guard, an old friend. The guard lets him into the reading room, even though the library is closed. Morgan Freeman is Detective Somerset, and he's come to the library to read about the seven deadly sins, because the serial killer Kevin Spacey is using the sins as a script.

The movie is set in a city that is so dark, grim, and violent that most murders and assaults pass unnoticed. At the beginning of the movie, Somerset has given up. He doesn't want to try to help anyone anymore, and he's leaving the city. The movie is a running argument between him and his replacement, Brad Pitt, about whether it's better to keep trying or to give up.

The serial killer complicates their argument because he agrees with both of them, in a way. On one side, Kevin Spacey agrees with Morgan Freeman that the world is lost. He commits these truly violent, grotesque murders because he knows that the world is so bad nobody will pay attention otherwise. But on the other side, he's like Brad Pitt, in that he's committing the murders because he thinks he'll sledgehammer everyone out of their complacency, he thinks he will change things, he thinks change is possible.

I used to argue with my middle school best friend about this movie. We both watched it together for the first time, and Haley was on Brad Pitt's side. She believed that there's such a thing as right and wrong, and that those of us who know the difference have to fight those who are evil—she believed it's possible to make the world a better place. She seemed so sure of things so I went along with her at the time. But now, I've gotten older, I've seen more . . . (plus Haley and I haven't really talked since ninth grade so she isn't around to convince me otherwise) . . . and anyway now I understand that Somerset didn't really disagree with Brad Pitt. It's just that he has given up on the fight.

Maybe that's why I'm having such trouble with this essay. Ms. McConnolly says that it's good to talk about overcoming adversity. But I don't think you ever really overcome adversity. I think you just figure out how to carry it along with you and continue on your way.

By the end of *Se7en*, Morgan Freeman and Brad Pitt switch places. Brad Pitt, who kills Kevin Spacey because he killed his wife, Gwyneth Paltrow (Wrath!), has lost all hope and realized that the world is a bad place. Morgan Freeman ends the movie by reclaiming his hope. He says that the world is a bad place, but worth fighting for. I agree with him. I think. Although on a lot of days I still don't know.

My favorite scene in the movie is in that library, though. It's a beautiful scene, quiet and soaring, even though Somerset is diving into the horrific research about hell and the seven deadly sins. This scene, to me, is the answer to life: When everything seems like too much, go to the library. The best way to confront horror is through study.

Brad Pitt's character is the one who goes to Kevin Spacey's apartment and nearly catches him, he is the one who chases him down, he is the one who kills him in the end. He is the one who strives for justice. But Morgan Freeman is the one who figures out the code, understanding it through study at the library. His journey is to understand evil. Through understanding, he learns to live with it.

Is it lame if I say that's why I want to go to the University of Virginia?

There's one more thing I want to say, which is that I think horror movies can bring people together. Maybe this is what I really want to write about.

I'm part of a group of girls who all meet on a message board online. We all pick the same movies to watch on Saturday nights, and we chat about them the whole time. We're all survivors of sexual assault. It's not true that all survivors are horror fans; there are lots of other message boards on other topics. We just happen to be horror fans who have found each other.

I think talking about horror movies is an escape that lets us talk about our real feelings. There is only so much you can say about your own disgust and worry and guilt. I'd much rather talk about whether or not Morgan Freeman had a chance to stop Brad Pitt from killing the serial killer at the end of the movie or not.

Alice Lovett
10/12/2000
586 words

Start with something about YOU!!

College Application Essay DRAFT 2

Morgan Freeman walks into the New York Public Library. He

banters with the night security guard, an old friend. The guard lets

him into the reading room, even though the library is closed, because

Freeman is a police detective. He's come to the library on a mission.

He needs to stop a serial killer who is using the seven deadly sins as

a road map.

The film *Se7en* is filled with horrific scenes of gore and the

aftermath of murder (one interesting fact is that there are few scenes

of actual violence in the film!). But this moment, in the middle of the

film, is pure beauty: a night in the library, reading and learning.

Not sure about this transition . . .

That's what I hope to find at the University of Virginia.

ha. yes.

It might seem strange to you that I talk about ~~my dreams~~ for

college in the same breath as I talk about a horror movie. People are

often surprised that I love horror movies at all. I'm a good student,

a normal girl with straight brown hair, I smile politely. But I watch

88

like four horror movies every week. I've seen *Se7en* twice as many times as the title. !

One reason I love horror movies is the adrenaline. I love the tight, excited feeling I get when the black screen first flashes up an image. I love not knowing what's coming. It's like being at the top of a roller coaster. And I love when the movie is over, I feel like I faced the monster myself and come out victorious. You really feel alive at the end of a horror movie.

But the biggest reason I love horror movies is that I'm part of a group of girls who all meet on a message board online to talk about the movies we love. I love to share movies with my friends. We all pick the same two movies to watch on Saturday nights, and we chat about them with each other online as we watch.

Those friends on the message board are the first friends I've had where we found each other because of our intellectual interests. Before, all my friends were just people at my school, we were forced together. Most of those friends didn't last when things got tough. My horror friends are my friends because we share a passion.

Their friendship is the first taste of what I want the rest of my life to be. I dream of being a journalist and a writer, and I want to work and spend my time with other people who share my passions. Most of the people at my old school reminded me of the aliens in *Invasion*

Funny . . . BUT it's a little immature. This essay needs to be about what makes YOU unique!

of the Body Snatchers. They seemed like they were just doing what everyone else wanted to do.

That's why I started this essay by talking about Morgan Freeman in the library. Like him, I know that the world is full of evil. Like him, I feel pretty sad sometimes when I think about all that evil, but I still want to fight. I want to be a journalist, to learn and explore and study, and work for what's right. I know that I can't do it alone. I want to go to the University of Virginia to meet other passionate, hardworking people.

I want to have deep conversations. I want to study hard. I want to find new ways of looking at horror movies, and politics, and everything. I'm thirsty for knowledge. I can't wait to find it at UVA.

A little muddled at the end . . . I know you can do better than this! Let's try again ☺

DRAFT 3 V1

Last night, I was awake until three o'clock in the morning, chatting with my friends on a message board about whether or not I should write this essay. These friends are my closest friends in the world, although none of us have ever met. We have two things in common. The first is that we are all fans of horror movies, and we watch them together while chatting online every Saturday night. The second thing we have in common is that we are all survivors of sexual assault. Through their friendship and support, I've learned to be grateful and maintain a positive attitude even on the hardest days, and I've learned to focus on building a positive future for myself. I see that positive future at the University of Virginia.

My friends have always given me great advice. But when I asked them whether or not I should write this essay on this topic, they were of two minds.

Some of them believed that I should steer clear of the topic entirely. Friends like AlaskaWitch and Blink1982 reminded me that their guidance counselors and parents told them to write their essays about constructive experiences and not traumatic ones. Like learning a new skill, or being proud even to be on a losing sports team, or the lessons taught to us by a parental figure. Talking about your rape is too easy to turn into a pity party, Blink1982 told me, which she said a guidance counselor told her.

Others of my friends, like JillyBean16, believed that I could write about it, but only as long as I was careful. They argued that it was a serious and weighty experience and also that I did need to explain the dip in my grades in the spring of my junior year, and the nontraditional academic path I've taken since.

But they agreed with the others on one point—everyone says that if I do write about this, I should focus not on the trauma itself, but on my recovery, and the way it has changed my outlook and my character, rather than on how bad things were for me last year.

So: I've been working hard and taking good care of myself this summer and fall. After dropping out, I went back over the summer for community college classes to catch up, and I'm on my way to a GED. I'm sad that I won't be walking up at graduation with everyone else. But as my real friend RedHotChiliSarah put it, Why would I want to walk with those people anyway?

What I learned from the experience is to find constructive ways of dealing with my emotions. Like I have learned to be optimistic, and handle my emotions in healthy ways. And . . . I can't think of anything else actually.

DRAFT 3 V2

Last night, I was awake until two o'clock in the morning, chatting with my friends on a message board about whether or not I should write this essay. These are my closest friends in the world, although we've never met. Like me, they are all survivors of sexual assault, and their friendship has helped me get through a very dark time in my life. Most of them say that I should not write this essay. Their guidance counselors and parents have told them to write about constructive and character-building experiences instead of trauma.

But, UVA, I keep going back to your question. You asked me to "evaluate a significant experience" and its "impact" on me. Nothing in my life has had as much impact on me as this, and I feel like I have to tell you about it. Plus, I do have to explain the dip in my grades last year, and why I'm taking courses at the community college.

In the middle of my junior year, I passed out in the back of a car after a party, and two boys took advantage of me. The thing you might not expect is that the worst part of the experience was the months afterwards, when rumors flowed all around my school about me, and I was bullied viciously. At the time, I didn't know how to handle my emotions. That was part of the reason I went to the party when I wasn't supposed to, part of the reason I got so drunk, why I was so vulnerable. It was the reason I couldn't handle the teasing and ostracizing afterwards. It got so bad, I even tried to kill myself. My grades fell so far that spring because of all that.

I was on a bad path for a long time. But it turned around when I found my friends online. If it weren't for the internet, I don't know if I would be here to write to you today. At first, they helped me just by understanding what I was going through. It was so nice to settle in and talk to them about what I was feeling. And they knew exactly what to say because they felt it too.

The other thing that helped is that we are all horror fans. We all pick the same movies to watch on Saturday nights, and we talk about them the whole time. It's a kind of escape for us. There is only so much you can say about your own disgust and worry and guilt. It's fun to switch over and debate, instead, about whether Morgan Freeman should have stopped Brad Pitt from killing Kevin Spacey at the end of *Se7en* or not. (I hope I didn't just spoil the movie for you.)

But through these conversations, these friends have helped me find a way to talk about what happened to me to people who haven't had the experience. I feel them now, standing beside me as I try to write this essay and explain.

The part that is hardest about it is that I don't really know what happened. So how can I explain? I was unconscious for it. I'm almost jealous of my friend JillyBean16, who says she told her story so many times, to family and police and eventually in court, that she feels like the thing didn't even really happen to her. It's turned into just this story she tells; whenever she wants to not think about it, she just has to tell herself the story, and the memories settle back down into this kind of blank feeling. I've told her I'm jealous of that, because I don't even have a story to tell. I start out with that blank feeling, and sink lower from there.

So I don't know what else to tell you. I guess, to conclude, I'll just say that I've already been through an incredibly hard experience, but I survived. And I've gotten better. I've been working hard at my classes. I feel strong. I feel ready for UVA.

Alice Lovett
10/27/2000
588 words

GREAT opening!
I'm hooked!

College Application Essay DRAFT 3

Last night, I was up until two o'clock talking to my friends on a message board about whether or not I should write this essay. Most of them said I should not.

These friends are my closest in the world, although we've never met in person. But we have two things in common. The first is, we are all fans of horror movies. Every Saturday night, we all pick two movies that we watch together, pressing Play at the same time and then chatting as we go. It's not only fun, but I learn so much.

For example, one thing I learned from my friend JillyBean16 is that in the book *The Shining*, the family drives a red punch buggy. In the movie *The Shining*, when Hallorann is driving up to save them, he passes a red punch buggy crashed on the side of the road, impaled by an 18-wheeler. It's a foreshadowing about Hallorann (who's about to get smashed himself), but also, because Hallorann doesn't die in the book, it's also Stanley Kubrick's way of saying to Stephen King, this is *my* movie, I'm smashing *your* book.

I include that story because I want to tell you something similar: this college essay is not going to go the way you expect. *Wow. Yes! You have my attention.* :)

Because the second thing my friends on the horror message board and I have in common is that we are all survivors of sexual assault. I was assaulted last winter. Afterwards, I was bullied so badly, I had to go on medical leave from school and had to work hard to repair my grades and get to the point where I am today. I was only able to do it because of the support of my friends online.

Most of them say that I should not write this essay. Their guidance counselors and parents have told them to write about constructive experiences instead of their trauma. But this isn't the first time I've disagreed with them.

We have another running argument, about a famous Stephen King quote, which they all love. King wrote, "Monsters are real. Ghosts are, too. They live inside us—and sometimes they win." My friends all agree that the worst monsters are our own internal demons, like jealousy and anger, and that those demons torture us much longer than it would be humanly possible for any real person to do.

I think that's a very mature way of thinking about the world, and it's a good way to help yourself recover. But I disagree. I think that there are real monsters. They cheat, and lie, and cause injustice. And I believe it's we have to stand up to them.

That's why I decided to write this essay. Terrible things are possible. I don't want to have to smile and write a sweet essay pretending that I've overcome some kind of adversity and reached a happy ending. I'm doing better, but I still have a long way to go.

I want to be a journalist. And as a journalist, you have to tell the truth. You tell the world about the monsters, so that everyone knows to watch out.

And that's why I want to go to UVA. I know I can't reach this goal alone. I've learned that I need the support of other passionate people. I know that with the new friends I will make in Charlottesville, and with my own hard work, I'll be ready to reach my goals and stand up to all of the monsters, inside and out.

Alice: Let's talk.
— Ms. MC

DRAFT ONE MILLION

Stephen King once wrote, "Monsters are real. Ghosts are, too. They live inside us." I'm a member of a message board of other horror fans who all debate this quote a lot. We are also all young women, and we all have seen examples of sexism in the world.

We talk to each other about how we're going to overcome sexism. That's the biggest adversity young women face today.

DRAFT ONE MILLION AND ONE

One time my mother took me on a very special shoe-shopping trip. We bought shoes, and I can't wait to wear them at UVA.

See? Everything has been fine in my life. The end.

DRAFT FORGET THIS STUPID THING

Stephen King once wrote, "Monsters are real. Ghosts are, too.

They live inside of us—and sometimes they win." My mother and I debated this quote once on a very, very, *very* special shoe-shopping trip.

Alice Lovett
11/21/2000
535 words

College Application Essay DRAFT 4

My mother stands in the doorway, still wearing her work outfit and the white tennis shoes she wears to commute. "I'm taking you to the mall," she says.

I clean up my physics homework, shuffling papers and textbooks into a pile, and wonder why we're going to the mall. We've always been close. But my mother works long hours at her job, and I've been studying nearly nonstop this year, catching up and finishing my high school diploma after an illness took me out of school in the spring of my junior year. We don't have a lot of time for mother-daughter shopping trips.

But in the car, I knew that this day was special. She turned down the radio and told me a story about the importance of shoes.

Could be a good opening line?

After college, my mother moved to Philadelphia and got a job at the city's planning department. When she had interviewed, she didn't have anything to wear except for a pair of sensible, flat brown

Can you show this?
Maybe with a quote?

loafers that were hand-me-downs. The interview didn't go well. The boss was brusque and cruel. This was in the seventies, when women still had to fight for respect in the office. The boss even put a hand on her lower back as he walked her to the door. He insulted her and gave her the job in the same sentence: "Our top candidate took a better-paying job already." *Wow. Great (& terrible!) line.*

What my mother hadn't realized was that she wouldn't get her paycheck until she had worked two weeks. She ate nothing but peanut butter that whole time, stretching out the last of her graduation money.

And when she finally got that paycheck? She felt so good. She was the first woman in her family to go to college, and most of her aunts and female cousins had never even worked. Delirious with the pleasure of having earned her own money, she spent the entire paycheck on a pair of new shoes for herself.

We looked for the same pair of shoes at the store, but of course they don't make that style anymore. Instead, we bought a pair of black Mary Janes.

Like my mother's shoes, I know this pair is going to help me stand tall. Because my mom said that her shoes were like magic. Even though the heels were only an inch high, she was amazed on Monday morning when she found herself in the elevator, standing next to her intimidating boss, and discovered that they were eye level. All along, he'd only been an inch taller than her. But that tiny difference was invisible until she'd overcome it.

This story inspired me. I won't have to face the same kind of sexism when I get a job, but as an aspiring journalist, <u>I know that there are still hurdles I'll have to face. I know UVA will</u> prepare me for them. *Let's get specific.*

And I know that my mother prepared me for them. I'm saving the shoes she bought me that day, a pair of nice black Mary Janes, for my first month at UVA. I want to wear them at convocation. That extra inch of height will remind me that I'll go far, because I'm standing on my mother's shoulders.

Alice: I'm so proud of you. This is a <u>GREAT</u> essay! One more draft to iron it out and make it sing—plus a proofread!—and we'll be there! You're going to do big things—I can tell. :)
— Ms. MC

STEPSISTERS

WHITE DRAFT: 3/21/96

BLUE DRAFT: 4/14/96

PINK DRAFT: 4/23/96

Written by Alice Lovett & Haley Moreland

Directed by Haley Moreland & Alice Lovett

Cinematography by Alice Lovett & Haley Moreland

Special effects by Haley Moreland & Alice Lovett

Starring:

Haley Moreland

Alice Lovett

FADE IN:

INT. CORNWALL HOUSEHOLD — THE TV ROOM — DAY

A normal TV room in a normal house. Two girls are
standing in the middle of the room: CYNTHIA CORNWALL
and MARGARET RUSH, both thirteen. They're in a tug-of-
war over the REMOTE CONTROL.

>   MARGARET
>   I hate you, I hate you, I hate you!

>   CYNTHIA
>   Not as much as I hate you!

They keep STRUGGLING over the remote. Cynthia PULLS
and the remote goes FLYING, breaking against the wall.

>   CYNTHIA
>   You broke it!

>   MARGARET
>   No, you broke it!

>   CYNTHIA
>   Ugh, I hate you!

Both girls FLOP onto the COUCH with their arms
crossed.

>   MARGARET
>   I never wanted a stepsister.

>   CYNTHIA
>   You think I did?!?

>   MARGARET
>   Well, at least we've got that in
>   common.

Cynthia CHUCKLES despite herself.

                    CYNTHIA
          It's like that "Breakfast at Tiffany's"
          song.

Margaret CHUCKLES, too.

                    CYNTHIA
          Also, we both hate my dad.

                    MARGARET
          You hate your dad?

Cynthia nods.

Margaret thinks.

                    MARGARET
          What about my mom?

Cynthia looks slyly over.

                    CYNTHIA
          I hate her, too.

Margaret sits up straight, looking at Cynthia.

                    MARGARET
                    (excited)
          Me too!

Cynthia sits up straight.

                    CYNTHIA
          Are you thinking what I'm thinking?

Margaret holds out her hand to shake.

                    MARGARET
          Friends?

                              CYNTHIA
          Friends.

They shake hands.

FADE TO BLACK.

                              TITLE CARD: Three weeks later

INT. CYNTHIA'S BEDROOM

Cynthia and Margaret are sitting on Margaret's bed,
looking at magazines. They are drinking ORANGE JUICE.
They are wearing GREEN FACE MASKS.

                              CYNTHIA
                    (pointing to the magazine)
          He's cute.

                              MARGARET
          Not my type.

They laugh.

Cynthia rolls on her side and looks at Margaret.

                              CYNTHIA
          I can't believe we're friends now.
          Like, real friends!

                              MARGARET
          I've never had a real friend before.

                              CYNTHIA
          Me neith . . . .

Suddenly Cynthia puts her hand on her stomach.

She GROANS in pain.

                    MARGARET
                  (hesitating)
      What is it?

                    CYNTHIA
                  (groaning)
      I don't . . . feel so . . . good . . .

Cynthia PUKES all over the bedroom.

                    TITLE CARD: Three days later

INT. CYNTHIA'S BEDROOM

Cynthia is LYING IN BED. She is DEATHLY PALE, her hair
is stringy and wet. She can barely open her eyes.

Margaret comes into the room and CLOSES the DOOR
softly.

                    CYNTHIA
      Margaret? Is that you?

Margaret doesn't say anything.

                    CYNTHIA
      I can barely see you . . . come . . .
      closer . . .

                    MARGARET
      Cynthia. I hate seeing you like this.

                    CYNTHIA
      It's okay. I'll . . . get better . . .

Cynthia leans over and VOMITS.

Margaret CRINGES.

                    MARGARET
      No you won't.

                         CYNTHIA
              What are you talking about?

Margaret takes a step closer.

                         MARGARET
              I wish I could save you . . . but it's
              too late.

Margaret turns her face away and SOBS.

Cynthia struggles to sit up. She reaches for Margaret.

                         CYNTHIA
              It's okay. It's just . . . the flu.

Cynthia COLLAPSES back into bed, EXHAUSTED.

                         MARGARET
              It's not just the flu.

Margaret comes over and sits on the edge of the bed.
Cynthia doesn't move.

                         MARGARET
              I have a confession to make.

Cynthia still doesn't move.

Margaret LIFTS Cynthia's hand. She LETS the hand GO.
The hand DROPS.

                         MARGARET
              Oh.

Cynthia is DEAD.

                         MARGARET
              You were . . . my only real friend!

Margaret THROWS herself onto the bed.

MARGARET
(sobbing)

I'm so sorry! I killed you! It's
because of my mother! We do this . . .
we go around and she marries single
men and then we poison them and take
their money . . . she's a black
widow . . . she said we had to poison
you, too! But you were my friend!

Margaret SOBS.

Margaret STUMBLES out of the room, still SOBBING.

INT. CORNWALL KITCHEN — CONTINUOUS

Margaret STUMBLES into the kitchen, sobbing, thrashing
around.

MARGARET

What have I done?!?!

Margaret WAILS, tearing open cabinets, tearing apart
the room.

MARGARET

I'll kill my mother! I'll kill her!!!

Margaret FINDS the BOTTLE of POISON. It's a large
bottle with a SKULL AND CROSSBONES on the label.

Margaret OPENS the FRIDGE and pulls out a GLASS of
ORANGE JUICE.

Margaret adds the ENTIRE BOTTLE of POISON to the
ORANGE JUICE.

MARGARET

She made me kill my friend! I'll kill
her!

Suddenly . . .

JUMP SCARE: A figure is standing in the doorway behind Margaret.

Margaret turns and SEES the FIGURE and SCREAMS.

IT'S CYNTHIA STANDING IN THE DOORWAY!!!

Cynthia is a GHOST. She is wearing ALL WHITE, she is VERY PALE, she is wearing HEAVY DARK EYE SHADOW.

Margaret COLLAPSES in FEAR. She nearly DROPS the glass of poisoned orange juice, but Ghost Cynthia catches it.

Ghost Cynthia crouches down, holding Margaret's head in her lap.

Ghost Cynthia holds the orange juice to Margaret's lips.

> GHOST CYNTHIA
> Join me, sister.

Margaret sleepily DRINKS the poisoned orange juice.

Margaret DIES.

A LONG, DRAMATIC DEATH.

Finally, she lies STILL. She is DEAD.

A long beat.

JUMP SCARE: MARGARET STANDS UP!!!

MARGARET IS A GHOST.

Ghost Margaret is wearing ALL WHITE, she is VERY PALE, she is wearing HEAVY DARK EYE SHADOW.

Ghost Margaret STARES at Ghost Cynthia.

> MARGARET
> Cynthia?

                    CYNTHIA
        Welcome to the land of the dead!

Margaret looks around.

                    MARGARET
        It looks just like our normal house.

                    CYNTHIA
        True. But now that we are dead, we can
        do whatever we want!

                    MARGARET
        Aren't you angry that I killed you?

                    CYNTHIA
        I killed you, too.

                    MARGARET
        I guess that's one thing we've got.

                    CYNTHIA
        Just like "Breakfast at Tiffany's"!

The two ghosts LAUGH and HUG.

FADE TO BLACK.

PART III

LOST WEEKEND

2008

Nick was parked at one of those backwoods gas stations that haven't even installed credit card readers on the pumps, it was Thursday, two hours into the drive and he was already bored, so when the CHECK ENGINE light had clicked on, he'd stopped at this gas station to check the oil in his mom's car, pretending he knew how, saying to himself in his head, *See, Lindsey, I'm responsible,* but then apparently he didn't properly latch the bar that holds the hood open, and it lost its grip and slammed down on the fingers of his left hand.

He anticipated the pain before he felt it, a sharp tingling and then a numb ache, and he knew it was going to be bad, and then, *Jesus,* he felt it, suddenly bad and getting worse, he jumped up and down a little bit, trying to push through the pain to its peak and out the other side, trying to tackle it head-on, because the whole point of this weekend was to build up the discipline to look at pain straight in its ugly face.

Still, his fingers hurt, but it was too early in the drive to start drinking, he'd never make it all the way to Lindsey's cousin's cabin if he started drinking now, so instead he grabbed his backpack out of the back seat and pulled out the seventy-dollar bottle of bourbon he'd bought special for this trip and just held it against his left hand to see if the proximity made the pain better, and when it didn't, he opened the bottle and sniffed, which didn't really help either, except in the way that pregnant women learn to breathe.

He thought about taking a little sip, just to get his brain to slow down a bit and stop chattering like this, on and on and on, but it really was too early to start drinking, and there were people around, so he tucked the bottle into his backpack, congratulating himself on his discipline, and went inside the gas station and bought a pack of cigarettes and a lighter and a package of cookies and a big waxed paper cup of Mountain Dew as reward for not drinking. He stood just outside the door with the sun in his face, set the soda and the cookies on the lid of a big red trash can, and unwrapped the plastic from the cigarette pack. Using his right hand to flick the lighter, holding the cigarette between his left thumb and pinky (because all his other fingers were still hurting), he lit up and inhaled.

A beefy man with leathery skin walked past and gave Nick a look, like Nick was wearing a clown suit or something, even though he was just wearing jeans and an old Metallica T-shirt. Maybe the man was frowning because of the way Nick was holding his cigarette, or maybe it was because of the way his hair was cut, or maybe it was some essential thing about Nick, the air of a comfortable white suburban middle-class upbringing that Nick would never be able to hide. Nick tried not to let it bother him, what did he care what that redneck thought, all he cared about was how good this cigarette felt and how great this trip was going to be, how great this trip already was. He pretended that his bender had already started, that the journey was the reward, that the drinking he was getting ready to do was just an excuse to be alone in the woods, instead of the other way around, and he switched the cigarette to his right hand and held it with his first two fingers like all good Americans, looking at the road ahead of him, and at the sparse woods beyond the gas station, where old cans and piles of trash were scattered all around. When his cigarette was almost gone he pulled out another and lit it with the first, and it was delicious as he inhaled, but then he realized that if he didn't stop himself now, he was going to smoke this whole pack of cigarettes in the next half hour, and he was seized by an impulse to be good, to be better, to be strict with himself, and also to be wild: he started throwing cigarettes away, three or four at a time, enjoying the recklessness of it, the discipline and masochism, plus the sheer wastefulness, he really was *such* an asshole, wasn't he, *Yes, you're right about that, Lindsey*, and this was truly going to be a weekend of nonsense and chaos, a Personal-Pan-Pizza-size performance art piece.

"Hey. Asshole."

Nick froze, the nearly empty packet of cigarettes in his left hand and four cigarettes in his right, holding the lid of the trash can open and the lit cigarette balanced on his lip, the ash lengthening delicately off the burning end, and Nick looked over his shoulder and saw the beefy man again, walking out of the store, leading with his belly, which was pronounced and firm, and he walked up, his belly uncomfortably close to Nick, and said, "That's not how you smoke a pack of cigarettes."

Nick pulled the four cigarettes away from the can and held them in front of his chest in a closed fist and wondered if this was the start of a fight, he had never been in a fight with a stranger (especially not such a large and leathery stranger), and he felt terrified and wondered if he could give this man one of his pints of cheap whiskey as a peace offering, which would be totally fine, he could stop by another liquor store, and so he smiled at the man with all of his teeth, telegraphing how little of a threat he was, and tucked the four cigarettes back in the pack. "I'm trying to quit," he said. "So I can't keep these all, I'm throwing most of them away, but I'm going to keep just one, and I'm going on a trip to the woods, this way I can only have one more."

The man, squinting at him, asked, "What woods you going to?" and Nick wondered, was there something in the guy's mouth, was he chewing something?

"Just outside the state park, over yonder in Youngs County," he said, embarrassed that he had said *yonder*, worried the man had noticed the affectation, and also worried that he was wrong about his landmarks, because he had only been to this cabin once, with Lindsey, more than a year ago, and he didn't know which state park it was close to, he just knew the state park was a thing they had talked about visiting.

"Well, you should be careful," the man said, his eyebrows up, real serious. "There's killers in the woods." Then his face changed as he laughed to let Nick in on the joke, a deep laugh that stretched his mouth open wide, and Nick smiled again with all of his nonthreatening teeth and kind of went *ha* in a way he hoped was noncommittal. The man was shaking his head to himself, laughing at his own joke, as he pulled a cigarette pack out of his shirt pocket and opened it to show Nick the single cigarette left inside, then closed it and held it out, an offering.

"Here, I'll trade your sins away," he said. Nick struggled to understand the deal for an embarrassing second but pulled himself together and took the man's pack with the single cigarette and traded it for his own pack, which was now half-empty (or half-full, depending on the man's outlook on life). The man said, "I usually don't smoke Camels, but a little experimentation never hurt anyone," and then, honest to God, the man *winked* and kind of raised an eyebrow, and Nick smiled and made a gesture like he was tipping an imaginary hat and then turned and walked quickly back to his mom's car, trying to commit the line to memory, knowing he would tell this story over beers for years to come, maybe not to Lindsey, but maybe yes to Lindsey, maybe she would laugh if she heard. *Oh, Nick*, she might say, shaking her head but smiling at his story about the time some redneck propositioned Nick at a gas station in the backwoods that he only in that moment realized was actually one of those gay cruising spots that, for the most part, had been rendered obsolete by the internet. Nick felt the man's eyes on his back but just kept walking, walked purposefully to his car, keeping his back straight, trying not to look like he was rushing.

When he had opened his cookies and his Mountain Dew and pulled back onto the narrow highway, it was just after noon, so if he drove ten miles an hour over the speed limit, he'd get to the cabin with a couple of hours of daylight left to build a warm fire and a good buzz, but almost immediately he realized the flaw in his plan, which was that he was going to have to drive for three more hours, and it was already boring, and he'd already eaten all of the cookies.

It was deep fall and the trees on the mountains around him were burnished red and orange, but there were just so many of them, it was hard to see them as beautiful, and in fact they mostly just reminded Nick of the background photo on the computer he had used at his mother's friend's consulting firm three summers ago, before he was informed that he was no longer an intern there, because of one little nap in the handicap bathroom.

He'd left that morning on an impulse and so had forgotten to bring the cord that turned the car's tape deck into a CD player, and he had no tapes, and the radio was no good—it was more like a parody of radio, there were only three stations and all of them were broadcasting the same booming voice going on about some character that Nick guessed was biblical but did not recognize (his mom would be so disappointed) and after scrolling through the dials for an eternal half hour Nick reached over and pulled the seventy-dollar bourbon out of his backpack and held it between his legs to remind himself of the reward on its way, then he pulled into the left lane and drove a little faster, eager to get there, then cut the radio off completely and said, out loud, "I'm going to have to face myself at some point," which was actually one of the main goals of the trip—to see himself clearly, and all of his faults, the way Lindsey had seen him—which was why he was going to the cabin where she had first asked him to stop drinking and why he was going to spend three days there getting good and drunk.

Lindsey's cousin had bought the cabin years earlier with the intention of fixing it up into a nice rental vacation home, but then never did (the cousin apparently rarely followed through on plans), and so the cabin was never actually renovated but merely in a state of constant repair, fighting the entropy of the forest, and Nick and Lindsey had laughed so hard, when they'd stayed here for her birthday, the weekend she'd asked that he spend just three days with her not drinking, they kept finding tools hidden in strange places, like the power saw stored on a pile of towels in the bathroom. So Nick didn't think it would be a problem for him to head up there now, the cabin wasn't even that nice, and even if he wasn't technically invited, he knew for a fact that nobody ever used it from November to February, it wasn't winterized, so Nick's bender wasn't going to hurt anybody. On a whim he unscrewed the cap of the seventy-dollar bourbon, checked in his rearview, and when there were no police, just some indifferent trucks, he took a quick pull, just to see what it felt like to drink expensively on the highway. Nobody was surprised when it felt pretty good, or when he took another, deeper pull.

Thus fortified, time passed easier. Nick thought about the nature of inevitability. He looked at the bottle. He had drained it down by about an inch. He thought about how it was probably enough for now. He took one last swallow. He had a

It was

Nick snapped back to himself. Realized he'd zoned out for a minute. He slapped his face. Took another sip just to balance things out. Kept driving.

A little later, he needed coffee, stopped at a Waffle House. Drank two cups, used the bathroom. Splashed water on his face. In the parking lot he did a couple of half-assed push-ups. Got up and the asphalt had left pockmarks on his hands. He brushed his hands off on his jeans. Felt a little better, pulled up the map on his phone. Walked around the parking lot until he got a signal. Saw that he had missed the small, unmarked road that led from Route 237 to the cabin and felt a little worse. He'd gone twenty miles too far. Went back into the Waffle House for another coffee, then hit the road again, watching more closely this time. He kept the bourbon in his backpack but still missed the exit, stopped to pee at a gas station, headed back the other direction. On the third pass he felt sobriety creeping up on him, annoyingly, but he did the thing where you delay pleasure, like that test they do with kids and marshmallows, and drove thirty miles an hour until he finally found the turnoff, saw the blue metal mailbox he remembered from years earlier, the landmark Lindsey had looked for when she was navigating them up here. It was leaning over so far it was almost horizontal, like an old drunk. There was an hour to go until dark, the sky high above still light gray but the evening dark starting to unfold from under the trees. He took a deep, satisfying pull to celebrate. Then put the fancy bourbon away, further proof of his discipline. Replaced it with a pint of the cheap stuff.

The house was fifteen miles off the highway. The first stretch of road snaked through what could loosely be called a neighborhood. The dirt road was so potholed, so lined with trailers and cinder blocks and barking dogs and other signs of rural poverty that he almost turned back. He didn't remember it being this depressing. Then he entered a stretch where the houses were set back in the woods, and bigger, their windows dark. Vacation cabins, used when the season was warm. Then the houses stopped, and he drove alone through the woods.

The feeling of adventure helped him relax, along with the booze. The sun had set now but the light was still even and gray. He kept his headlights off, enjoying the dusk. It drained the color out of the woods around him.

Then he came around a bend and saw three men standing on the side of the road.

They had just crossed the road. Hearing Nick's car, they'd stopped, and turned, and now they were standing still, watching him approach. Then one of the guys lifted a flashlight and pointed it at Nick's windshield. It wasn't that dark out so he wasn't blinded, but he was offended. He flashed his high beams back. Worried he was going to have to get out of the car. Didn't want to talk. Thought about the guy from the gas station. Had already dodged one fight today. Didn't want to fight these guys either. Was relieved when they turned, continued on their invisible path into the woods.

They were headed up the hill. Going roughly the same direction as Nick. But he was sure it was fine. They were probably hunters. Although they were wearing these weird brown robes. But maybe there was a monastery or something up somewhere. Anyway, they were definitely headed somewhere else. He knew for a fact that nobody used the cabin in the winter. He knew because he had begged Lindsey last winter to take him up here, this was a month before she left for good and two months after she had started threatening to leave, and he'd said he could do it this time, he'd said, *Let's go to the cabin and not drink for three days.* She'd refused. There had been multiple reasons for that, but the cold weather had been one of them. The cabin wasn't winterized, so nobody went up in the winter. He was not going to interrupt anyone at the cabin. Took another sip of whiskey. Started driving. Kept getting flashes of the movie *Deliverance.* Kept drinking to shake the dumb fear away.

Top of the hill, the road curved and opened onto a wide-open meadow. The cabin at the far end, with its red porch. He recognized it with a thrill. Then his stomach sank. He missed Lindsey. He took another sip of whiskey, drove across the meadow. A herd of deer looked up and watched his car as he passed. They struck him as unconcerned. Cool guys, those deer.

He remembered that Lindsey had pulled the spare key from the belly of a ceramic deer on the porch. As he parked in a patch of dirt and got out of the car, he saw the same menagerie of ceramic animals lining the porch. But the key was not in the deer. He checked a frog, three bears, a flamingo, two ducks, and a gnome. Finally found it under a second frog. It was a funny thing to misremember. As he fit the key into the door he ignored the NO TRESPASSING sign nailed into the wood right at eye level. It didn't apply to him. He let himself in to the smell of old fires and dead bugs.

The inside of the cabin was a series of punches in the gut. The mustard-colored couch where they'd cuddled around a movie on Lindsey's laptop. The table where she'd taught him cribbage. The kitchen where she'd made him a grilled cheese. It wasn't even a kitchen, really. Just some stained white plug-in appliances and a narrow chopping block. She'd made the sandwich on a George Foreman grill, but the George Foreman was now gone. There was the thick fireplace at one end with a black woodstove jammed in its mouth.

There was the horizontal row of antlers displayed along one wall where he'd hung a pair of Lindsey's panties as a joke. She had laughed so hard. She had the best sense of humor. The cabin was a time capsule. Happier times. It hit him in waves. He hadn't talked to her in six months.

It was very cold. He fortified himself with a little more whiskey and reminded himself that he had a job to do. He was here to drink and face his faults. So he kept settling in. He went back to the porch and found some logs. There were a few piled by the door. He carried them all in. He piled them all in the woodstove. They were long dry and lit easily. He rubbed his hands together. The logs were burning quickly but hopefully would last through the night. There were no more logs. But he could chop some tomorrow. A massive ax hung over the fireplace like a trophy. He would use it tomorrow to chop more wood. He would make it three days in the cold. *See, Lindsey? I got this*. He was just fine.

Outside it was suddenly dark. Like a curtain draped over the house. Flicked switches until the porch light came on. Slipped the whiskey pint into his jacket pocket. Pleased with how neatly it fit. Walked to the car. Grabbed his backpack and the grocery bag. The jerky and granola bars and oatmeal. He'd purchased them in his hometown. The checkout guy was some guy from high school. Nick had forgotten his name. But he remembered Nick's. "Nick Brothers, holy shit!" the guy had said. Greeted him with a smile. Clearly, he hadn't heard what Nick had been up to these past few years. "What have you been up to?" he'd asked, and Nick said he was on his way to a weekend in the mountains. Said he was going with his closest college friends. He had meant it as a polite lie. Realized the irony only now, holding the bottle's familiar hand.

Back inside, measured the oatmeal into the Crock-Pot. Three days' worth. One case of beer in the minifridge. The other case would stay cold in the trunk. Took two beers to the porch. The stars were amazing. Went inside, turned all the lights off. Then back out to the porch, and even more stars. A beautiful night. Wanted the cigarette already. Tested himself, holding it in the palm of his hand. How long could he go without lighting it? Forever. He was reckless and disciplined. An artist of chaos. He sat for a long while, looking at the thin moon. The beer was delicious. He studied the delicate black weave of the tree branches. The richly blue night sky. Admired his own eloquence. And his powers of perception! They really could have used him at that consulting firm. Their loss.

Then across the field he saw something. No, it was trees. No, it was people. In a circle.

It was an odd hallucination. He watched. Waited for it to change to something else. It stayed a circle of people. They lifted their arms. All at once. And clapped. The sound echoed across the meadow. They were maybe a football field away. Or maybe not quite that far. Anyway. They were pretty far. Their hands were still raised. They were totally still. Like trees, again. It reminded him of something. He remembered the men he'd seen in their weird robes. Some kind of weird backwoods cult? He wanted to shout at them. *No trespassing! Can't you see the sign?* But he was too creeped out.

Out of nervousness he went to light the cigarette. Then stopped. He was afraid. Which was stupid. But there it was. Didn't want the pagans to see him. He put the cigarette in the pack. Like a soldier in a trench. Too afraid to light a match.

His second beer was empty. Maybe that was the answer. This little extra buzz of fear could be easily fixed. Stood up slowly. Kept his eyes on the figures, slowly lowering their arms now. There was a new sound reaching him. A low hum. He walked back to the door. Opened it gently. Latched it behind him. Walked quickly to the fridge. Drank the beer in three long pulls. Focused on the alcohol rinsing out the veins in his arms. Took another beer back to the window. Looked out.

The temporary absence of fear made its return sharper. The circle was moving now. Uncoiling. It was no longer a circle but a line. It was pointed at him. He could see each person's shape. He counted twelve of them. He was embarrassed by his fear. But couldn't move. Frozen at the window. They were heading toward the cabin. Not going to come all this way. A football field away. Not coming for him. Just going to pass by.

But they were getting closer. He realized they reminded him of

He must have fallen asleep on a pile of blankets and sheets on the unmade bed in the bedroom, because that's where he woke up, cotton in his mouth and the day outside bright with false promises, his car-hood-bruised hand hurting, the familiar hangover knocking on the inside back of his forehead like a landlord, he would need a beer fast, and a glass of water, but first he had to pee, his mornings were always so busy and complicated, so urgent in contrast to the rest of every day.

The cold was sharp and prickly, so he wrapped one of the old blankets around his shoulders as he stumbled into the bathroom, where he found a wet towel on the floor and the smell of vomit, and also his bottle of sleeping pills on the floor, he didn't think he'd taken any, but then again he'd slept, but then again no need to dwell. He tried not to think about the dreams he'd had, the pagans coming for him across the field; it was just his subconscious trying to scare him into leaving, and he wasn't giving up so easily, he was really committed to this weekend. He splashed water on his face, filled his mouth with it, splashed more, and dried his chin on a corner of the shirt he'd slept in.

He got dressed and put on his jacket and gloves, at least until he could start a fire, and then went into the small kitchen and put water on the hot plate for coffee and scooped himself a mug of tepid oatmeal, and he decided to sit on the front porch to eat. But when he opened the door he saw that the hulking red ax was buried in the front, the business end sunk deep into the sign that read NO TRESPASSING.

Someone had tried to chop down the front door with the ax, and there was nobody else in this cabin, so it must have been Nick himself, blacked-out drunk, who had tried to chop down the door with an ax.

It was so strange and shocking that he closed the door immediately, walked back to the bathroom, and vomited up the three bites of oatmeal he'd eaten, then went to the kitchen and ate some jerky, which he managed to keep down with the help of a beer. He slowly let the idea come into his head that he must be crazier than he thought, that he had taken the ax down from above the fireplace and taken it to the front porch, maybe to chop wood, maybe just to do his impression of Jack Nicholson, just to shout, *Here's Johnny!*, but either way it was legitimately suicidal, he could have chopped off his leg, he could have bled to death, and it's not even like Lindsey would be the one to find him dead, no one would find him up here, not for months.

He grabbed a second beer and tucked the pint of whiskey into his jacket pocket, then went out the side door, through a mudroom stacked with old tools and flattened cardboard boxes, and it was a little warmer outside, the late fall sun gently baking the meadow, and he made a point to enjoy it as he walked around to the porch and stood looking at the ax, sunk directly in the middle of the NO TRESPASSING sign, cleaving the N and the O.

He took a step back and tried to think about this thing rationally, because this situation was definitely a first, he had never before done something so legitimately suicidal as swing an ax hard enough to embed it three inches deep in a solid wooden door while blacked-out drunk. This made him think about finally getting around to attending Alcoholics Anonymous, which was not something he felt he could do with a straight face, but it would at least give him a venue to tell this story. They would all say, *Hi, Nick!*, and then he would say, *Well, I woke up, my first morning on a bender I had planned for myself, alone in the woods. I had borrowed my mom's car (you know what I mean by "borrowed,"* he would say, and the crowd would laugh supportively). *I'd gone to the woods to drink so much that I wouldn't want to drink ever again. Yes, even I knew that was stupid, even at the time,* he would say, and all of the other alcoholics would laugh and be impressed that Nick was so honest.

But the truth was that he was still far away from any kind of twelve-step program. It was his understanding that most people had to hit rock bottom before they signed up for AA, and he maybe wasn't in the greatest shape but he wasn't at rock bottom yet, he was still on his way down. Ha ha, he thought, yes! He *was* on a twelve-step program. He was on the twelve steps down. Equal and opposite to the other twelve steps. When you thought about it that way, everything he did was on his way to redemption.

He finished the beer, then felt in his jacket pocket and found the packet of cigarettes. He opened it and was delighted to find the single cigarette still inside. What a pleasure, a reward in his future. He was so happy he almost lit it, then was proud when he again decided to wait. This pride gave him the returning urge to smoke, which was harder to resist the second time. Anxiety crept up along his neck, and he looked up and saw again the ax embedded in the door, and he thought how dumb it was, it was just a stupid ax, and here he was feeling all afraid of it and letting it ruin his morning. He crumpled up the beer can in his fist and threw it, missing the ax handle by a mile, but it still made him feel a little better, he was the boss around here.

He walked over and grabbed the handle with both hands and pulled, but it was wedged in so deeply that he couldn't get it out, which freaked him out all over again. He let go and closed his eyes and tried to think about this rationally, because he needed to chop wood, he would freeze to death in this cabin without wood. He couldn't get the ax out of the door, but he didn't really want to touch it again anyway. He took a sip of whiskey. It was weird that it was wedged so deep. He didn't know his own strength. Maybe he should leave. Yes, he should definitely leave. He would sober up a bit and then pack up and go.

But maybe there was a smaller ax in the cabin. Like a hatchet that he could use. This house was full of old tools, right? There had to be something. He could even go out and just hack some thin branches off of some trees in the woods nearby. He didn't have to split those whole big logs. He just needed a little fire.

He went inside and decided not to have another beer just yet, in case he decided to leave. He wasn't sure yet. Either way he would chop wood, though, he should at least replace what he had taken. So he went back to the mudroom and found a plastic case of tools tucked under a bucket, with a hammer, some screwdrivers, and an inexplicably short length of rope. Under the rope he found a soft pair of leather work gloves. He checked for spiders and pulled them on. He opened and closed his hands a few times, flexed his fingers. He felt like a complete and total badass in these gloves. He felt that he could go out with these gloves and just grab the logs he needed from the woods. He could rip the trees up by their roots. Who needs a hatchet when you have leather hands like these.

Then he looked around and saw the power saw. *Oh,* he thought. *Well, that's an idea.*

He remembered Lindsey had put the saw out here when they had found it on the stack of towels in the bathroom. Seemed like nobody had touched it since. He imagined holding the saw was like holding her hand, or the ghost of her hand. He took off his glove, held the saw handle tenderly.

He carried the saw first into the kitchen to plug it in and make sure it worked. It worked with a metallic sheer roar. He went back to the case of tools and found an extension cord. He fed it from the outlet in the kitchen, through the mudroom door, and out and around to the far side of the house where there was a pile of thick logs and a stump set up for chopping. He grabbed another beer and carried the saw out, plugged it in, tested it again. Then he set a log up on the stump.

He cut the first round like butter. It practically fell into four neat, fire-size pieces. He shouted with the thrill of it. He held the saw over his head and swung it up and down like the guy in *The Texas Chain Saw Massacre*. He grabbed another log, cut it, and stacked the six total pieces of firewood beside the stump and put his foot on them and said, *Yeah bitch!* He dropped the saw on the ground and sat on the stump to rest. He finished the beer. The day around him was bright and sunny, and he watched a hawk swoop above the meadow, long and lazy flight patterns. And just think, an hour ago he had been planning to leave.

He carried all six of the logs inside and fed them into the woodstove. When it was roaring, he stood and watched it roar, warming his hands, and he got a little bit of whiskey to speed up the warmth. He took off his jacket as the room warmed up. He wished he had built a fire for Lindsey when she was here. It would have been romantic, a nice thing to remember. But that had been in the summer. Too hot. They had taken cold showers and slept naked on top of the sheets. They had taken a walk on the second day and come back soaked in sweat. They had fought more than once that weekend, and he remembered it had been because of the heat.

A walk would be nice, he thought. Now that it was bright outside. The fire was really going now, and the woodstove looked secure, he could take a walk now and warm his blood. He could take a long walk, and then get back in the late afternoon, cut up a little more wood for the evening, and then start drinking seriously around three thirty or four.

He put his jacket back on and patted his pockets, encouraged by the firm, friendly hand of the whiskey. He left through the side door and made a point not to glance back at the ax. He set off across the field toward the woods. He felt the sun on his face, felt his legs move. Already he was thinking about how nice it would be to go for a walk again tomorrow and the next day. His daily walk. By his third day he would know the woods like the back of his hand. By his third day he would have perfected his drunk. The bender would be in proper swing. There would be nothing to do but ride it out. That's when he would let himself have the cigarette, on his walk on Sunday, at the peak of his trip. It would be the best day of his life. He would see himself clearly. After that it would be easy, he would drink everything and sleep soundly through the night and wake up Monday morning and not have even one drink. He would be fresh as he drove back to his mother's, he would return her car with no booze on his breath. She would be pleased to see him. She would not ask about why he had disappeared with her car while she was at work.

He sipped whiskey and the walk was pleasant. He drifted downhill. He thought only vaguely about the return, the climb back up. It would be exhilarating, he reasoned. Soon he would be finished with this whole thing. He followed the road for a while. He came out of the meadow. He walked through the woods. Next to a small fir tree he saw a narrow path. It was one person wide. Probably a hiking trail. It was lined with pine needles and dappled light.

He followed it into the woods. Why not? If it took him too far in the wrong direction, he could always double back. That was life. Sometimes you had to double back. But usually it was better to press forward. You had to go all the way around to come back. Like this hike, his drinking. For too long he had been doubling back. This weekend he was going to go all the way down the hill. To rock bottom. Then he'd be ready to go all the way back up. He was on those twelve steps down.

He decided to list the steps. Then he would know how far along he was. This was the goal of the weekend, after all. To face himself. To take stock of his faults. And wasn't this one of the steps? A weekend bender. Maybe not the first time he had lost three days to alcohol, but the first time he had planned ahead for it. With no remorse. He decided that was step eight. And then step seven was probably when he lost his license last month for that DUI.

He hopped onto a log that had fallen across the path. He stood on the rotting bark and felt triumph. He was on his way to rock bottom. This weekend was one of the necessary steps! He was really committed. And just two or three hours ago he had been planning to leave! He was proud of himself, again, for his commitment.

He slipped off the log. When he shifted his weight, a sheaf of rotted bark slid off, his foot slid with it. His tailbone hit the log. He almost toppled backward. Caught himself, barely. *Whoa.* He stood up and brushed the cold wet off his ass. Laughed at himself. Felt proud that he could still laugh at himself. Kept walking. Took another swig.

Step six: The first time he'd lost a friend to drinking. He'd punched his friend Richard. A valid argument. They hadn't spoken since. They'd been friends since they were thirteen, had been through puberty together. And Richard threw all of that away—because of a little fistfight. Most men weren't even friends *until* they'd punched each other. Richard had always been so uptight. And he had changed so much at Princeton, he was snottier, full of himself. *Good riddance*, Nick thought. Still, he was not the only person who didn't talk to Nick anymore. Nick was no fool. A pattern was a pattern. You lose enough friends, you start to see that you're to blame, not them. He took responsibility again. Proved to himself, again, that he was wise and in control.

He came to the last sip of whiskey. He stopped, holding it. He leaned against a tree and looked up at the light through the leaves. He toasted the tree. Drained the bottle. Commemorated the moment. Tucked the empty bottle in his pocket. Planned to recycle it. Okay, he'd made mistakes, but at heart he was a good guy. The kind of guy who recycles.

He walked for a while. Not really thinking. Felt his breath. Felt his shoes. It was time to head back, he decided. He wasn't going to get all the way to the bottom of the hill. He had to turn around eventually. He cut off the path. He knew the general direction of the house. He was proud of his sense of direction. He climbed over logs, walking uphill. He felt time pass, and felt the whiskey burn, insistently, in his head. It was the feeling that came when too little whiskey dissipated too quickly. But he would be back at the cabin soon.

He reminded himself that he hadn't listed step five. Or four. The two were linked. They were a little tricky, in terms of order. One was his first blackout. The other was the first time he'd tried seriously to cure a hangover with more booze. Not just a Bloody Mary at brunch. A desperate cure on a Monday. Two shots of vodka in quick succession. Followed by a beer. Followed by a job interview at the sheriff's office. (Which he'd aced! And then he'd worked as a dispatcher for nearly a year! And then he only lost the job because of three little naps at the front desk!) Although that specific hair-of-the-dog cure wasn't the first. And the blackout that preceded it wasn't the first, either. He couldn't tell which had come first. There had been times he'd oscillated between the two steps for days and nights. It was a chicken-and-egg situation, really. He moved on.

Step three was the first time he tried to have sex and failed because he was drunk. It was the first time that drinking had cost him something. It was a point of no return. Who would choose booze over sex? But he had. Many times. How many times had he told Lindsey he was too tired? Many times. He took a break from walking and wished he had another sip in the bottle. He felt the peace of the woods around him and knew whiskey would help him enjoy it. He felt nostalgic, thinking about Lindsey. So he pushed to step two. It was the first time he'd been drunk with family.

It was both his best Christmas and his best buzz to date. He was nineteen, on an indefinite break from college. He'd sat up with his big brother and talked for hours. His brother was ten years older than him. Had been in the Peace Corps. Joined the Foreign Service and worked in Beijing the entire time Nick was in high school. Rarely came home. That night was the first time Nick felt like he even knew his brother. Their father had left a few years earlier for the woman from church, and they talked about it that night—for the first time really talked about it. And for the first time his brother saw him as a person. And when both of them were hungover on Boxing Day their mother had teased them about it, found it charming. She made them a giant plate of tortilla chips with black beans and fried eggs and mounds of cheese. She knew what kind of breakfast was necessary. She, too, had been hungover before. They all commiserated together, over fried eggs.

He thought back to two days ago, when he'd shown up on his mother's doorstep on a whim because he hadn't seen her in months, and she had not mentioned the fact that he smelled like a week of cheap beer and had walked from the bus station three miles away. She had just hugged him and offered him a sandwich. She was still deep in the realm of forgiveness and patience (at a time when even his brother would no longer see him on holidays). He knew she would do the same again and again. He had many more miles to go with his mother. Even the car, for example, which he had borrowed from her without technically asking, would be forgiven. It was just for the weekend. It's not like he was fencing it for drugs. He was just borrowing it for some much-needed time away. His mother would understand.

Then he realized that this was another of the steps. A step in his future, maybe it was number eleven: When his mother stopped loving him. She would be the last of the people who still loved him, but one day, even his mother would give up. Just as Lindsey had given up. The fact that he could recognize this was coming made him feel, again, that he was in control of his fate.

But no sense dwelling on that, back to step one: Was it too easy to say it was his first drink? But this was one of the core facts of his life. It was a bone-deep truth about himself that he could not deny any more than he could claim to be not a man or not an American. He had avoided alcohol in high school at first because he was an athlete above all else. Then they won their state championships and he had a beer to celebrate. He took a long swallow of that first beer, and then another. He did not want to stop. He took to drinking like a mathematician to a chalkboard, with a giddy flush of discovery. He had found the place where he would always be the most comfortable, simultaneously the most himself and the best version of himself, and he was very careful to protect that comfort for only when he really needed it, even as he started to need it more and more. For so many years it had been a thing that was always waiting for him, a treat at the end of any challenge, and then, increasingly, at the beginning of every challenge, and now here he was, alone in the woods, drinking all day.

The tide of his last sip had reached the "high-water mark" and was already starting to ebb. But he didn't worry. The woods around him sharpened, but it was probably just the whiskey leaving him, sobriety edging in, and he refused to acknowledge that this was scary. He decided he was worried about being lost. He focused on walking in a straight line, pretending that he could judge by the angle of the sun. Which was lucky because otherwise he would have fallen straight into this huge hole.

Wait. What was that. Nick took two steps backward and leaned against a tree. It was not a normal hole. It looked more like a grave. A long rectangle, sharp walls straight down, and while Nick wasn't the best judge of distance in the world, he would have bet a hundred bucks on a depth of six feet. There was a shovel leaned against a nearby tree, mud clumped on the business end. Nick let his mind do the thing where it stayed kind of blank with indecision as he stared at the hole. *This is probably just something hunters do*, he thought. *This is probably just for hunting.*

For hunting deer, he felt compelled to clarify.

It must have been old, anyway. He hadn't seen anyone up here, after all. Nothing since those men walking up in the robes. And the dreams from last night. Nick took two steps closer and crouched down next to the hole, trying to convince himself not to feel deeply freaked out. It was just a hole in the ground. Who knows how long it had been here? He kicked at a stick, sent it spinning down into the hole out of petulance. The stick landed on the soft dirt at the bottom without making a sound. Nick noticed that there were leaves on the ground all around him but none at the bottom of the hole. Which meant that it was pretty freshly dug. Or maybe leaves just didn't fall into this spot.

Nick remembered suddenly a ghost story Lindsey had told him when they were up at the cabin. But he had taken it to be a joke, or some kind of entertainment, anyway, she was trying to make him have fun without drinking, she was trying to scare him straight. The story she told was about how vagabonds and criminals used to squat in the cabin, because the former owners were almost never there, and that when her cousin had bought the house, he'd found a human thighbone in the closet. *Swear to God*, Lindsey had said, but Nick still hadn't believed her, she was just trying to keep him entertained while sober, which of course didn't work, although in retrospect he could have been nicer to her for trying. But anyway a thighbone in a closet really didn't have anything to do with this grave—if anything, it denoted a lack of graves, the closet being less optimal storage for human remains. Nick tried to make himself laugh. Instead he threw up, against the base of a tree.

He leaned against the tree with his back to the grave, wiping his mouth with his sleeve, and he had the sudden feeling that he was being watched. He had the feeling something was climbing out of the grave, slowly and steadily. Without looking back he started to run, although he was too weak to run quickly; he moved, in what he hoped was a straight line, and time did not seem to make any sense, he felt like he was running forever, he wondered if he had died and this was hell—constant movement through infinite woods, with no trail apparent. But eventually he broke out of the brush onto the dirt road, and while he didn't recognize this particular bend of the road where he had emerged from the woods, the right way was obvious—uphill—and he started the hike and then continued to hike and hike, it was a long way made longer by sobriety, both boring and exhausting, he stopped to catch his breath frequently, as the thirst steadily invaded until it became the only thought in his brain and the only feeling in his body and he could not really deny that it was the only thing that mattered to him, at least in that moment, as he crossed the field, as he ran, did not walk, to the front door, and ripped the ax out of it, leaving behind a single clean wound in the NO TRESPASSING sign.

"Fuck this," he said out loud, this was ridiculous, he was going to leave. He dropped the ax on the couch and went into the kitchen and got another pint of whiskey and tucked it under his arm and held two fresh beers in his right hand and took everything over to the wooden table and sat down. He was going to leave the cabin, he thought again, as he finished the first beer in a long swallow and then opened the whiskey and drank, workmanlike, until he was able to close his eyes and breathe again. He put the whiskey in his pocket and opened the second beer.

Everything was fine. There was nothing coming out of the grave, he had imagined that, there was no one following him. He went and stood over the ax. He felt calm. He didn't want to accidentally lie down on the ax later. He picked it up and held it by the neck, like a snake. He looked around the kitchen. He tucked it in the corner by the minifridge. He relaxed, knowing it was out of the way. While he was there he pulled out two more beers. Which he carried out to the porch. He closed the door behind him. He ignored the gash in the door. He sat on the top step and drank slowly.

The sun was sinking over the meadow. Everything was fine, there was nothing to be afraid of, but still, he was gonna leave. This was stupid, being here. He leaned back and looked at the clock inside the house. It was nearly six o'clock. He would just sober up a bit, just finish this beer slowly and then sober up, and then leave. He would call Lindsey.

He finished that beer and opened the other.

They had met during his year of college. They saw each other from time to time, she always flirted with him, he always liked her. Once they'd played pool at a frat party and he'd beaten her by a single shot. Only later that night did he realize. She had let him win.

They met again, years later. She was at a friend's party in Richmond. Nick's drinking was at a good pace then. He was working at a bar. Having left the sheriff's office. (Having been *terminated* from the sheriff's office, Lindsey would say.) At the bar he could do shots throughout the evening. Then he could join another party after the bar closed, when everyone else was drunk, too. Although it was sometimes hard to keep those parties going. Nick had to run circles to keep people drinking with him. On nights when there were no parties he stayed at the bar. Drank with the waiters. It was a party one night when he saw Lindsey. This was a Saturday night. He had two hundred dollars in his pocket, a good night of tips. He took her to a diner and bought her a milkshake. She'd never had one with malt. She loved it. He'd always felt milkshakes were romantic. Ever since high school, the first time he'd bought a girl a milkshake. The milkshake with Lindsey was the best. She made him laugh, and he made her laugh. It was too romantic, their meeting like this after all these years. It was too romantic to be real. So he made a point to really enjoy that one fake night.

The beer was gone and the whiskey was in his hand again. The whiskey was more than half gone. He was drinking too fast. But he needed it. He was thinking about Lindsey. How they'd walked home after the diner. Miles to her apartment. And he'd fallen asleep in her arms. Her soft, downy bed. Her sheets that smelled like warm grass. They'd had sex the next morning and he wasn't hungover. They ate eggs and he smiled at her. Then said he needed to run. *You need to run?* she asked. *An errand*, he said, *but I'll call you*, and he jogged back to his car at the diner. Got the bourbon out of the glove box. Only because he was so excited. And then he felt better. Felt, so this is it. This is love.

Two weeks of this before Lindsey caught on to his alcoholism. Had been on his best behavior. But didn't have the strength for more than ten days in a row. Passed out next to her. In a movie theater. She couldn't wake him up. Called the paramedics. Who, upon arrival, recognized him. From the last time something like this had happened.

He made it up to her. Sort of. He guessed she must have really loved him. Because she kept trying. It was too romantic to be real. He kept enjoying each fake night. She got angry. Then angrier. They would break up, then get back together. He would slow down his drinking. Make her happy for a while. Then it would speed up again ahead of him. Two years of this. She had tried. He had tried. It was over. He had to get over her. She was better off without him. She was right about him. She was

He woke up in bed feeling amazing, his eyes opened like he had only blinked. Sun coming in the window. He was refreshed and energetic. It was a morning like he hadn't felt in months. His head was clear. He stretched his arms above his head and yawned. Like how a cartoon cat would wake up. He was so glad to be here. And yesterday he had almost left! He would have denied himself this good feeling. He laughed at himself, wriggled back down into the sheets. He had never made the bed. The sheets were all piled around in the shape of his body. Beds should be shaped like bodies. It was like a comfortable nest. He basked in the sunlight. How silly that he had wanted to leave. Because he saw some weird hole in the woods? Okay, it looked like a grave, it was weird. But he wasn't from around here. Nick didn't know what people did for fun up here. Who was he to judge.

As he bounded out of bed he stumbled. Then realized that there was still some bourbon in his system. Which was part of why he felt good. But still, a good start to the day. He could get out ahead of the hangover. He would eat something. He wriggled his bare toes in a patch of sun on the floor.

He went into the bathroom and peed a glorious river. He went into the kitchen and was glad to see that the ax was still safely behind the fridge. He hadn't done any new crazy thing. The oatmeal was still warm and chewy.

He stood chewing and looking out the window. The sun was bright. There was something about the window that had happened last night.

It swam slowly at the edge of his consciousness, like a dream you can't look at head-on.

He remembered that he had left the power saw outside. That was stupid. What if bears got it? He laughed at that thought. But was glad. It was still out there. He could cut some more wood today. He could replace what he'd used. He would leave the cabin just as he'd found it. He was a regular Boy Scout. *Lindsey, see, I'm responsible.*

After he ate, he went to the trunk of the car and carried the second case of beer inside. Then he brought a beer out to sit on the porch. He said "Good morning!" to the menagerie of animals. The deer and the frogs and the flamingo. He looked out across the field and saw a small animal lift its head. He watched it. He watched it for a minute and found that the memory from the night before was there. It was just at the edge of thought. If he let his brain go soft and lazy it would float up. He watched the animal. It was a groundhog. It moved like a rolling egg, wobbling side to side as it moved. It would run a few feet ahead, weeble-wobbling, then stop and bend over to eat. He watched it and let his mind conjure up what had happened in the night.

He had gotten up for something. A drink or to pee, or something. Or something had woken him up. For some reason he went into the kitchen. There was nothing to see. But as his eyes adjusted to the dark, he saw a face. In the window. And another face in the other window, too. There were faces in all of the windows, men looking into the house. It was one of those dreams you can't remember if you're trying, you just have to let it float back. He had dreamed that the house was surrounded by men looking in his windows. He couldn't remember anything after that.

He felt cold. The good feeling of the morning went away. But nothing had changed, it was still the same situation. Just some dream. He stood up roughly. He decided to go chop wood.

The sun was still on its way to its peak. It was only about ten. He tested the saw and then turned it off and heard the echo of the buzz come back to him from across the field as the saw blade slowed with a metal clang. He set up a log on the stump and turned on the saw and started cutting. He'd forgotten how satisfying it was to cut wood this way. So quick and powerful. He felt that he could do this for hours. Maybe he would leave a good stack. A kind of payment for his use of the cabin.

He went inside and got two beers and set them next to him. He planned to spend at least another hour slicing wood. He would slice all of the wood he could find. Physical work is the only cure for busy thoughts. Lindsey used to say that. *Yes, you're right about that, Lindsey.*

He got into a good rhythm after the second log. It was better if he set the logs on their side and ran the saw in a straight line away from himself. It made him think of Lindsey. He wished she could see him doing this. He always wanted to impress her.

The third log was tricky to balance, so he held it with his left hand. He was comfortable enough with the saw now to use it one-handed. He just locked the safety shield up so that he wouldn't have to hold it with his left hand. He put his left hand on the log to hold it still. He had a lot of natural talent, he realized. He wished Lindsey could see this. He was a smart enough guy. He'd done well that one year in college, and he picked things like this up easy enough. She would say he was wasting a lot of potential, and he knew it. But he was still young! He was getting older, though, he was twenty-six, only four years away from thirty. Really, he didn't have a huge amount of time to set himself up for the rest of his life. But he could still do it. And this weekend was coming at just the right time. He would straighten out all this drinking, and by next month he'd have figured out what to do with the rest of his life. Maybe a small business he could start. Or maybe he'd go finish his degree in criminology. Look at how resourceful he was being, cutting wood. Maybe he would meet someone else. Or maybe he could get Lindsey back. He could ask her to marry him.

She wanted to get married. He should have married her. She'd brought it up all of a sudden. *Do you even want to marry me?* He couldn't remember how he'd answered. But it hadn't been the right thing.

He saw now that marriage would have stabilized him. He would have gotten his shit together. Lindsey saw that, too. That was why she'd asked. But he had been too dumb to see it. He had always been a step behind her.

But he had never understood what changed. It was all of a sudden. A week or two after she asked him about marriage. She had stopped drinking a month earlier. It was like she was a different person. Then one day they were shopping for a new couch. She was getting a new apartment, with two bedrooms. Nick was afraid she was going to ask him to move in. Was going to bring up marriage again. He was goofing around. Trying to distract her. Said something about cushions, about springiness, about jumping on a couch like a kid. He was bouncing on his ass on a white puffy couch when he looked up. Realized she was staring.

"You won't change," she'd said. And turned and walked out.

Nick was so shocked he didn't follow. Was angry, actually. She ran away! He sat on the white couch. Waited. Slunk out half an hour later.

Wouldn't answer her door. Wasn't allowed in her office. Waited out front but she never came. Must have seen him. Must have sneaked out the back. He was so furious. Wouldn't even give him one last fight. Had to fight her in his head. Got tired of it. Tried to forget about it. Got over it. Then relapsed. Worried suddenly: Was there another man? It was a month after, maybe six weeks. He'd followed her. Followed her to work and home. She'd gone to the doctor. She'd gone grocery shopping. She'd cried in her car. He almost went over to comfort her. But how to explain? Plus he was drunk. So he just watched her cry. There was no other man. There was just Lindsey, crying alone in her car. She'd gained weight, she looked different. She was different. Healthier without him. He stopped following after that. He tried to get over her. He was getting over her. She was better off without him.

He could be better. Better without her. Except on days like today. Or that one afternoon. Straight from the gym. Took off her shirt. Purple sports bra. Left her sports bra on while she

He had cut through the fingers of his left hand. Wait. No, not right. Not right.

He should probably let go of the saw. He did. It whirred to a stop. His brain was stuck on this odd loop, screaming *wrong wrong wrong,* but another part of his brain just wanted that screaming part to calm down and look at his fingers. *Fingers fingers fingers,* his brain screamed.

When the horror cascaded over him it was a physical coldness, not a metaphor, a real and strange sensation of being dunked in water. He could not believe it even as he realized that it had really happened, this thing that was a thing your shop teacher said to scare you, not a thing that could really happen. He felt the cold air on the wetness of the blood and wiped his hand against his pants but his hand did not touch his pants, his hand was shorter than it should have been, and he finally physically realized that he'd cut off the fingers on his hand, *blood blood blood blood,* his brain screamed and at least he knew he had to stop the bleeding so he raised his hand, like an eager child.

It was strangely calm and time was strangely slow as he wondered what to do, and maybe two seconds had passed when suddenly the pain cracked through and he screamed.

His vision blurred at the edges and he realized he was going to pass out and he sat down, his hand still in the air, his own screams echoing back at him from across the meadow. He panted. He would need to put the severed fingers on ice. He looked at the stump and they were not there, he had imagined them curled against the edge of the saw blade, like the kind of cheesy Halloween prop he imagined teasing his future children with, but the saw was on the ground and the fingers were not there, and he saw the blood spattered along the saw blade in a delicate spiral.

Blood blood blood, he had to stop the blood properly, he reached under his flannel and vest and pulled his undershirt away from his body and wrapped the mangled hand in it, so that it was cradled against his stomach, and this helped clear his mind, it was wrapped and out of sight. He looked for his fingers and could not find them. *Bourbon bourbon bourbon*, his brain said suddenly, the true and best solution to every problem, so he carefully got to his feet and grabbed the can of beer and drained it and then walked into the house and found the seventy-dollar bottle and drank, *three fingers of whiskey, ha ha ha*.

He took a deep breath and another sip and then thought, in quick succession, *keys wallet drive drive drive*. Bandage first, his undershirt was soaked with blood, he opened a cabinet and found nothing, not even a roll of paper towels, there was the towel in the bathroom but it was too big, his arm was tired, so he took his last clean undershirt and sat down on the bed and got ready to unwrap his hand.

The pain was insanity as he felt the fresh wetness of blood and forced himself to look, with one eye, at his hand, it was a horror show, still bleeding and a flat surface at the end of his thumb and first two fingers, a cutaway with bone like a cartoon steak. He gagged but controlled it (*a lifetime of practice, ha ha ha*) and quickly covered the hand with the undershirt and wrapped it, gasping, forcing himself to tug it tight. He cursed himself for not bringing a belt. He didn't even own a belt anymore. He went into the kitchen and got a pair of scissors and cut off the strap of his backpack, the scissors not very sharp and gnawing at the plastic fabric, but he got it through and wrapped the strap around his forearm and pulled it tight. Then somehow he had tricked his body into finally releasing endorphins, a flood of relief hit his head and while there was still pain it was lined with optimism. He realized this was all Lindsey's fault. But no time to dwell. It was time to drive. Outside the sun had set, the glow in the woods was getting faint. *Keys wallet go.*

He got into the car, the bottle of nice bourbon between his legs. There was one good thing, of course, which was that this would cut probably a year off of his mother's sympathy, which would get him closer to rock bottom; she had spent his entire life trying to stop him from putting an eye out and now he had gone and lost two fingers and a thumb.

Self-mutilation, he realized, must absolutely be step twelve. He'd done it without having to drive away his mother! He was purified, he had survived, he had skipped several steps and hit rock bottom without having to alienate his mother. He felt giddy imagining himself as the star of an AA meeting, telling the dramatic story of the day he finally hit rock bottom, because how many other people's rock bottom was cutting their own fingers off with a power saw?

By the time he had passed the meadow and entered the woods he was in a state of complete focus. He felt clearly every inch of car tire coming in contact with the dirt road, felt that he could anticipate every curve and that he

It was still Saturday, he was pretty sure, and he knew before he opened his eyes that it was the worst hangover yet, the deep regret and guilt were there, a feeling before he identified its cause, and his entire body felt like it was coated in three inches of nausea, a physical goo. He was also very cold, and his muscles hurt from shivering but also continued to shiver, and he didn't want to open his eyes but he was so thirsty, he had to pee, so he opened his eyes and saw, in the daylight, that he was sitting in the front seat of his car, which had run into a tree. The sight reminded him about the problem with his hand, but he decided not to look, didn't need to see it, instead he just left his hand where it was, wrapped against his stomach, maybe it was just a little broken, maybe it was just a bad dream.

He hesitated, living for a second longer in the moment of possibility— maybe his hand wasn't that bad, maybe the car would still start—and then he turned the key in the ignition and the engine made no sound at all, only the CHECK ENGINE light clicked on. He turned the key several more times, it didn't work but he felt too weak and sick to feel angry about it, then he looked around with no real purpose other than to find something to make him feel better and then, huzzah! There was the bottle on the floor with some nice bourbon left in it. He drank it all. Felt it course through his veins. He leaned his seat way back. Closed his eyes, tried to relax. His body tried to shiver and couldn't. His muscles hurt. So cold. He counted to three. Then again. The third time he was able to force himself to open the door and get out.

He had driven the car a few yards off the road. Tracks through the dead leaves, over a log. He looked beyond the hood. If the tree hadn't stopped him, the car would have kept going. Would have hit the steeper part of the hill. He would have picked up speed and maybe died. Small mercies. Or maybe that would have been better.

He wished he had a little more whiskey. He already knew what he was going to have to do. The highway was fifteen miles down the road. But he could see the porch of the cabin through the trees. He could make it there. There was water there, and another pint of whiskey. Someone would come and help him.

He kept his left hand against his stomach and reached out for the nearest tree, fell into it. Leaning against the trunk he got his pants unbuttoned and peed, it was a weak little dribble, he tried not to wonder but couldn't help wondering if his dick was broken, but hopefully it was just his kidneys.

He straightened up and turned, reached for the next tree, fell forward to lean on that one. Leaning heavily against it, he got his feet under him again, and in this way he started moving. He got a little steadier as he felt his blood flow, was able to walk a little farther between falls.

He had no idea how long it took him to get back to the house, if he had to guess he would say that he'd walked for three years, but eventually he stumbled onto the porch, falling forward up the steps, then into the door, he fumbled with the door handle, and then felt a sharp pain in

Nick woke up with his face on something hard and gritty. There were a dozen tiny specks of sandy dirt pressed into his cheek, and his mouth felt coated in gravel. He heard himself moan. He pushed himself up onto his right elbow and with his hand brushed off the grit that stuck to his cheek. He felt tiny pockmarks dug into the flesh, and worked his jaw.

He was in the cabin. It was dark, but as his eyes adjusted, he saw the dim shapes of the couch, the pile of logs by the fireplace, the low dorm-room refrigerator of the kitchen.

The pain in his left side was spreading along his arm. He remembered his hand.

He tried to get up. He tried again. He admitted that he couldn't. "I guess I'm just going to die here," he said out loud, coughing.

And then with a cold sensation he realized that it might be true:

This was a first. The first time he seriously considered the possibility of his own death. Was this one of the steps?

He imagined Lindsey coming up to the cabin and finding him, his body rotted away, just a thighbone in the closet. *Ha ha*, he thought, and coughed again. He imagined her coming tomorrow. His mother calling her, *Nick took the car, it's been days*, and Lindsey knowing he was up here, the way she always knew—she knew him! She knew him so well!

He wanted to cry, thinking about her. He thought about how he had seen her crying in her car. Why hadn't he gone to her? He would go back. This was why he had come to the cabin. Where he really wanted to be was with her.

He would go back to her. He would show Lindsey that he could be a good man. He would make her understand.

He tried to get up again and this time he succeeded a little bit. He made it onto one knee. With a Herculean effort he wrenched his other leg over and flipped his body around and then pushed with his right hand and found himself standing, a low crouch, in the dark. Progress!

He leaned over and held on to the back of the couch and steadied himself. Then he looked up and saw a face in the window. He froze. There was a man right outside the window, standing at the end of the porch, looking in. Then he looked and saw another man standing in the next window over. Nick spun around and saw another face looking in the side. There were dozens of them, looking in from all the windows. They were holding shovels by their faces, like pitchforks.

"Wait a second," Nick said. But the door handle was rattling.

The men were opening the door, they were coming into the cabin.

"Wait," Nick said, but his vision was swimming and narrowing, a roar swelling up in his ears, and he turned and threw himself toward the mudroom. He hit the wall and pulled himself in, then lurched to one side, knocking over the case of tools, screwdrivers flying. He lurched to the other side and grabbed the handle of the side door. He wrenched it open, took two steps into the yard, and then froze.

The yard surrounding the cabin was filled with graves.

Nick's brain clicked several times over the fact. He saw irregular rows of graves winging out like seats in an auditorium. He heard banging sounds coming from the cabin behind him, the men with shovels coming for him. This must be a dream, this must be a dream. He could feel the grit in his cheek, the pain in his left hand, he felt real. This was real. He was going to die.

And then for the first time he realized he wanted to live.

He put his hand over his heart and he thought about Lindsey. *I love you*, he thought. *I'm coming.*

He imagined himself running. He focused his mind, and then he counted down, *One two three go*, and then he really was running. He traced the narrow gangplank between the graves, he dodged from side to side like he was playing lacrosse again, and then he realized that if he closed his eyes he could go even faster, his feet were barely touching the ground, the trees were whizzing by on either side and it was

Nick opened his eyes like Ziploc bags. He saw the guardrail of a highway rolling by in a continuous stream.

He lifted his head and flopped it over to his left side and saw a strange man driving a car. It was the car that Nick was riding in. Okay. So Nick was in the passenger seat of a car.

The driver was in his sixties and wearing an orange hunting cap. Nick tried to say hello and let out a sound that was like a dying frog. "Hey," the man said, glancing over. "It's okay, buddy."

"Izz thizz a dream," Nick said.

"Hey, buddy, you were in a car crash. I found you this morning on my way to my hunting blind. You hit smack right into a tree. You're lucky to be alive."

"Ay'z dreamin," Nick said.

"You were *driving*," the man corrected him. "You were in a car crash."

Nick cleared his throat. "You know anything," he said, very slowly, enunciating as well as he could, "about holes in the ground? Like graves?"

The man glanced nervously at Nick, then kind of reached over and gently punched Nick's shoulder. "Hey, buddy! You've had a hard time. Don't worry, we're just a little more ways from the hospital now."

Nick tried to rub his face but his left hand wouldn't move. He looked down and saw it wrapped up in the dirty shirt against his stomach, and the skin at the edge of the shirt was swollen and shiny. "Ohhhhhh ssshhhhit," he said, remembering his hand.

"It's gonna be okay," the man said.

"I was up there," Nick said. "Graves everywhere. Do you dig graves? To hunt people?"

The man looked at him and kind of laughed, a quick exhale. "Listen, you've had a hard time, just relax now, okay. There's water if you need it." He gestured toward a bottle in the cup holder.

Nick shook his head, looked out the window.

He felt like shit, but his brain was starting to clear. He was starting to see what had happened. He'd really gone off the deep end this weekend. He'd cut off his own hand, crashed a car, had some serious hallucinations. But then again, he had to hand it to himself. No pun intended. He'd really managed to punish himself these past three days, hadn't he. He'd really seen the worst of himself. And hadn't that been the whole point?

He glanced over at the guy who was driving. "Sorry. I've been hallucinating," he said. And then, for the first time in his life, Nick said, "I've got a problem with alcohol."

The man looked uncomfortable and said, "We're almost there."

Suddenly Nick wondered what he was going to tell Lindsey. About his missing fingers. I did it for you, he could say. I wanted to prove that I hated myself as much as you hate me. I wanted to prove that I'm not what you need. And now that he'd done it, he would go back to her. He would track her down and explain everything. He would marry her! Hope rushed in. He wanted to celebrate.

"You got a cigarette?" Nick asked.

The man laughed. "Guess you'll live after all," he said. He patted his flat pocket. "Sorry, I quit."

Nick carefully patted his own pockets, his jeans, and then his jacket, where he felt a surge of joy: his cigarette.

Thankfully, the man's old car still had a cigarette lighter. Nick leaned over and pushed it into the dashboard, waited while it got hot.

Then finally it was time. Nick lit his last cigarette. He inhaled. He felt the good energy rush through all of his joints, even as his stomach heaved. He shouldn't be smoking, he knew. But the cigarette tasted so good. It was the last bit of his weekend. He'd be in the hospital soon, a great place to start getting sober. He'd have to get ready for Lindsey. It really was time. This cigarette would truly be his last, and so he was really going to savor it. Why deny himself this one last pleasure? Nick felt that he had been punished enough.

PART IV

TO US

2011

Haley—

This is Alice. (Had to get a new email.)

Bad news: I left Q, then the city, in quick succession. Am broke, both in wallet and spirit. Driving south now.

Which brings me to (or rather, will hopefully bring me to): Bethany Beach.

Does your mom still have that condo? And can I stay there?

Just a couple days. I need somewhere Q won't find me.

Don't say no,
Alice

Haley—

Made it to the condo last night, late. The smell of chlorine in the lobby familiar as a favorite old T-shirt.

Front desk gave me the key, no problem (thank you for calling).

Condo itself: Total time warp. Nothing changed since my last visit (that summer trip after college, I think). I swear not a single doily has moved.

Couldn't sleep. Stayed up and counted all the rabbits. If you want to finally know: 187 total (counting figurines and decorative plates but not the bathroom wallpaper).

I'm not making fun. You know I love this place. And am so, so grateful. For your generosity; also for your mom's beach stockpile of frozen dinners, mystery novels, and lite beer. Been here barely twenty-four hours and already devoured a couple of each.

Spent most of today drinking and thinking about Q. Brought a cooler of beer down to the ocean—wanted to watch the waves and replay our relationship from the beginning. Wanted to pinpoint the moment I started lying to myself about him. Took me three beers to get through our first date.

Now I'm sitting on the balcony, late afternoon, hunched over the glow of this phone. Typing is exhausting. My finger muscles all out of shape. But writing is therapeutic. And your email was the brightest spot in my day.

To answer your question: The car is Q's. I grabbed his keys and phone on my way out the door. Middle of a big fight. He was in the kitchen. Banging open drawers. I got out before he could find whatever it was he was looking for.

Don't worry, I checked already, the phone is not set to track its location (Q's paranoid about data). I'm sure he's reported the car stolen, but it's safe in the condo garage, and I'm safe here, for now, on my own two feet.

Am fully aware that I sound melodramatic. Forgive me and I'll tell you everything sometime,

Over a Lean Cuisine,
Alice

Haley—

Do you know that you are the best? The. Best. I am so deeply grateful for the LOAN, and I will pay you back, please don't argue.

But thing is, an internet transfer's no good.

Q has changed all my passwords. (Hence the new email address.) I'm locked out of all my bank accounts. Embarrassed to say that the only thing good to me right now is cash. This kills me to ask, but . . . can you send a money order, USPS?

Or don't. Seriously, I'll be fine. Your friendship is the most important thing. Please never stop writing. I need the distraction. Q has been calling. Ringer is off, but every time I look at the screen there are twelve missed calls, all from the same number.

Can't imagine his logic. What does he think is gonna happen? That I'll answer? That he'll say something that will make me forgive it all?

The scarier thought: He can't stand me ignoring him. He'll do anything to get me to respond. He hasn't thought beyond that point.

Exhausting to think about a life on the run from a man with no concept of cause and effect. A life spent like this,

In hiding,
Alice

Haley—

Peace at last. I switched the phone to airplane mode. Q can call all he wants.

Of course, that means I also can't actually send this email you. But it's nice writing to you, anyway, even if I'm

Just pretending,
Alice

Haley—

Can't sleep. Can't shake the feeling that Q is coming for me, tonight.

Don't want to take the phone off of airplane mode. I'd rather not know. I'm
going to keep writing these email drafts to you, to distract myself. Maybe
I'll send them later.

You'd say I'm being crazy.

But you don't even know the half of what happened.

Met him at your twenty-fifth birthday party. Jake Rack's, that beer garden in Fort Greene. Was there with Andy, the musician. Met him online. Probably you don't remember Andy. Super boring guy.

Do you know how stressful that year was for me? Hope not. Spent so much time trying to hide it from you. Because we'd drifted apart before. My ninth-grade transfer to private school. After our inseparable middle school years, you grew into a track star and salutatorian, and I became the bad girl on antidepressants and remedial math, the girl who smoked in the bathroom as much as others but got caught twice as often. But let's not talk about those bad old years. Thank God we found our way back to each other the summer before college. We swore we'd never drift apart again.

But then, our twenties: we moved to New York together, and you took to it like a fish in water. With your short film at Sundance and your part-time job at Tribeca. Going to parties where you hung out with famous actors. Working on your first feature documentary (an experimental film about rape culture). Dating the guitarist of an up-and-coming band. Me, desperate to keep up, dreaming of writing a horror novel, scrambling into my first gig writing movie reviews, desperate to be fancy enough to be your friend.

Worked temp jobs to pay the bills. Pitched pop culture think pieces to *Rolling Stone* online for pennies an hour. Raised my profile, or tried to. Mostly just raised hate mail, marching steadily into my inbox like zombies. Lots of angry paragraphs about my body (too big) and my intelligence (too small). Once, I suggested an all-female remake of *They Live*; someone sent me a sketch of myself hanging upside down in a slaughterhouse between two dead pigs. It was incredibly realistic. They must have spent *hours* on it.

I wasn't really sleeping. Got angry easily. Was desperate for comfort. Met Andy online. Oh, Andy: incredibly boring, incredibly reliable. Always showed up five minutes early for our dates. Never initiated sex, always waited for me. (Which I liked at first; at that point I'd only really been with one other man, and he was just as cautious.) Andy slept on his back, snored softly, didn't move all night. Played piano in a hotel lobby. I sort of hated him. Kept sleeping with him because I didn't like being alone at night. I did like the way he smelled. And the way he never asked for anything. But I stayed on the lookout for someone fancy. Someone to help me impress you.

Also had Khloé. My one true love! Remember how Jordan Owen was always sending around photos of foster cats? Khloé came into my inbox on the same day as the slaughterhouse sketch. Read her story and cried. Seven years old and fat. Didn't stand a chance against the adorable kittens at the shelter. Came from a single mother and her two daughters in Jersey City. The mother's new boyfriend didn't like cats. I wrote back *mine mine mine* before I had any time to think about litter boxes or vet bills or the fact that cats weren't allowed in my apartment. Smuggled her up the stairwell in a backpack. She followed me around the apartment like a dog. I loved loved loved sweet Khloé.

So in summary, my life: Sleeping with a boring man just to be protected from imaginary intruders at night. Doting on a fat old cat. Reading hordes of hate mail. Going to parties where your sophisticated friends fawned over you, and you graciously tried to keep me in the conversation, and I frantically tried to hold up my end of the bargain: making jokes and opinions on the news and anecdotes from my polished life story of suburban rebellion. Q stepped into this tableau like the end of a romantic comedy, offering not just protection but confidence and warmth and compliments, everything a girl is raised to want.

Funny thing: back then, I felt happy for the single mother who had to give up Khloé. Good for you, I thought. Go after the love you deserve. Don't let a cat get in your way. Now feeling the opposite. Worried about how things turned out. How many more concessions did that boyfriend demand.

Remember the trash-can fires at Jake Rack's in the spring? When it was not quite warm enough yet to be outside. That night I was trying to impress some fancy friends of yours. Andy was off at the bar. With his hand half-raised, meek, trying to get the bartender's eye. I was complaining about how gentrifying Brooklyn fetishized old tropes about the so-called inner city. Fucking trash-can fires, I said, the prop a movie in the eighties would use to signify a gritty neighborhood. With a flourish, I pointed to the fire by the door. And then Q walked in. So that it looked like I was pointing at Q.

Q raised his eyebrows in surprise. I realized what had happened. Embarrassment made my heart lurch sideways. But he told me later it was a thing he'd dreamed about happening his entire life: walking into a room and the most beautiful girl in it would point immediately right at him: *That one. That's the one I want.*

I dropped my finger. Q looked over his shoulder, saw nobody behind him. Pointed at his own chest, mouthed, *Me?* Had an expressive, open face, with big features that don't seem handsome at first, then you find you can't look away. Like an actor. Had on a red plaid shirt and blond hair long enough to tuck behind his ears, like the grunge rockers I loved when I first hit puberty. I shook my head, *No! Sorry!* but he kept looking, shaking his head in surprise, silently saying, *Me? Me?*

Went over to apologize. Said hi to him and his friend, the friend—a good wingman—already walking away, giving us space, like he didn't even know who Q was. I turned to Q. I didn't mean to be rude, I was just talking about this— He interrupted me. I liked it, he said. And as a matter of fact I was just about to point at you.

Sick of Andy. Met him on a website where people look for dates. By definition, we wanted something from each other. Yet he would never admit that he wanted me. Would invent excuses to invite me up to his apartment. The first time he kissed me, went in for it by saying, I think there's something in your eye. Then I was standing beside a trash-can fire and Q was holding eye contact, and Andy was trying and failing to get the bartender's attention, and Q said, Let me buy you a drink.

One rare consistent pleasure of my life in those days: handing out my business card. Had never had a business card before. Had made up business cards playing office as a small child; nothing to me said grown-up like a business card. After weeks of worry about the cost, had gone online and been thrilled to discover that you could print business cards for the cost of two beers at Jake Rack's. Ordered five hundred, paid an extra ten dollars to have the ink embossed.

No, told Q. I'm here with someone. But, I said, handing him my card: Here's my card. Call me later. Took the card from me. Smiled, reading it. Ran his thumb over the embossed ink of my name.

Texted me half an hour later. Thanks for the card, now you have my number, too. Then, a second later: You have a beautiful laugh. I had just been laughing. The people I was talking to were still laughing. I stepped back slightly, set my beer on a nearby table, looked around. Spotted Q at the bar, typing into his phone. Looked up and saw me and smiled. My phone chimed at the same time: Don't let me distract you. He watched me, slightly smiling. Tried to decide what to write back, settled on: I work on the internet, ignoring distractions all day long, u couldn't distract me if you tried. Wrote a smiley face, deleted it, then hit Send.

My writing lived on the internet. The more I responded to people responding to my writing, the more people responded to my writing. So it was not strange that night for me to spend so much time on my phone. Dipping away from the party to react to my screen. But this was different. The most intimate text message conversation I've ever had. The kind of deep conversation that feels like the first of many, and also like it will never be enough. Strange how romantic I make it seem. Now, considering everything. But it was.

Shared a cab home with Andy. Told him I had a headache. Told the cabdriver two stops. Okay, the driver said. Okay, Andy said, with the same level of emotion. Last time I ever spoke to him. He finally got out. I settled into the back of the dark cab. Twenty more blocks to go. I kept texting Q, listening to the murmur of the cabdriver's ongoing phone conversation. Khloé came to the door purring. I met someone, I told her, sweeping her up in my arms. Meow, she said, supportive as usual.

We met for coffee the next afternoon. Magic. One of those days that flies by. Interrupting each other. Too many new topics. Not enough time in the world for everything you want to say. Sat through two cappuccinos, charmed him with everything I had. He held my hand, stroked his thumb casually along my wrist.

Coffee flowed into dinner. Then drinks at his apartment. A sleek building in Williamsburg, looked hermetically sealed. Evening light sliding along the glass exterior. Inside, an elevator lined with mirrors. Little black eye of a security camera right over the buttons. Smell like an expensive shoe store. Parking spot included. Had never known anyone who lived in that kind of building. Not even Andy, who was in finance, had a place like that. Wondered where Q got the money. As a PhD student. In philosophy. A trust fund, I thought, and I'm embarrassed to say it sweetened the deal.

His apartment was warmer than the building. Big windows. Framed landscape photographs in black-and-white on the walls. Fridge covered with wedding invitations from friends. There was a beautiful gray wool blanket flung over the couch. We wrapped ourselves in it naked and stayed like that until late Sunday afternoon.

Looking back, were there warning signs? Maybe there were. Getting the water pitcher from the fridge on that first night, stopping to look at all of the save the dates. Was impressed by how many. There was a gay couple in their fifties, their postcard written in French. A white man and a black woman who had gotten engaged while rock climbing. Another couple who couldn't have weighed more than ninety pounds combined, who had styled their invitation like a boxing match. Eve and Michael.

Most of the save the dates were for weddings in the past. But Eve and Michael, the boxers, theirs was close, just two months away. I immediately started dreaming of Q taking me with him. As the weeks passed, I thought about it a lot. It became the way I measured our relationship: When will he like me enough to invite me to that wedding? I worried he already had a date. Didn't want to know. Couldn't ask.

The week leading up to Eve and Michael's wedding, I was a wreck. I mangled one review so badly the editors wouldn't run it, my first postcommission rejection. Went to Q's on Saturday to make ravioli. Packed my gym bag with an appropriately nice dress and shoes just in case, feeling like a lunatic. I finally asked him at three o'clock when he was still wearing a T-shirt with holes in it. Are you not going to Eve and Michael's wedding? It's today. He looked at me. Like, *What wedding.* I pointed at the fridge. Oh, he said, We're not really that good of friends. No? I said. You get a lot of invitations to not that good of friends' weddings? I started laughing. Relief flooded through me like a stiff drink. Laughing hysterically. I didn't ask why he put it on the fridge, then. Too relieved to worry about it anymore. Never worried again.

Only realized later that Q had stolen the save the dates on his fridge. The mailboxes weren't locked in that building. Did he steal them to impress me? He was an only child, his parents were dead, I never met another member of his family. I met only a few friends for dinner, and rarely more than twice. In the three years we spent together I never saw another save the date appear on his fridge, and we never went to a wedding together, not once.

Getting ahead of myself, though. The wedding story is eight weeks in. Our first week was a whole story in and of itself.

Got home to Khloé on Sunday (she was curled up by the door waiting for me). Spent six days not texting Q on purpose. Careful discipline. Delicious torture. The feeling was so good. To have met someone and spent the weekend together. To only want more of each other. Those feelings don't last. I wanted a few more days of that. Was twenty-five and had felt that first blush of love a few times before. Was halfway ready to stay with Q forever. Which meant this was the last first week of love in my life, and I wanted to savor it.

That week, while not texting Q, went to see a psychic. Had been planning to go for a while. The Psychic Love Spiritual Advice Counselor, a narrow purple awning and the words Read the Signs in blue neon. I'd always wanted to go. Problem was, could never get a handle on the hours. Jogged by at seven in the morning, the neon sign would be on, but at eight, showered and dressed and with a spare half hour before work, it was off again. Weaving by, too drunk, at eleven thirty on a Friday night, the sign was on, but when I went back at the same time the following night, it was off again. The Wednesday night after I met Q, walking home from work, it clicked on just as I walked under it. Read the Signs, it told me.

The person who answered the door did not seem like a psychic, but perhaps my ideas about psychics were shaped by the same lazy eighties movies that misled me about trash-can fires and cities. Come in, the psychic said. He was a white man, with a thick salt-and-pepper beard, maybe in his early forties. He wore a white linen tunic and a long string of wooden beads around his neck. He spoke with a formal affectation, called me "miss," offered me water or coffee, invited me to sit at a low card table draped in a red checked tablecloth. You're here because you're in love, he said. Maybe not quite love, I said. Ah, he said, but maybe not *not* love. I had to admit that it was true. The small room was draped in bedsheets that had been spray-painted with gold streaks. Mardi Gras beads were hung all over the ceiling, stuck precariously with masking tape. The room was lit with candles. Felt like a haunted house built by Boy Scouts.

You have a great ambition in life, and you worry that you will not be able to meet your own personal needs while striving for your goals. You are struggling to balance your need for love with your need to be independent and focus on yourself. You sometimes feel like nobody really understands you, and you worry that it's not their fault but yours, because you don't know how to open up and ask for help. You're hoping this love will help you learn to be vulnerable. And also: don't trust your friend with the red hair.

I thought about that last bit, the only specific piece. I don't have any friends with red hair, I said. One of the strands of beads fell from the ceiling. Landed with a clatter to my left. I jumped. A sign! the psychic said.

Of what? I said. He looked at me with his eyes wide and his hands spread. I guess you have to interpret it, he said.

Paid my ten dollars, pathologically trying to hide my disappointment. Was raised to treat everyone with kindness and support, as if everyone's feelings were as fragile as mine. That gave me a lot to think about, I told the psychic politely. Standing in the vestibule, about to leave. He peered at me. Do you want this person to fall in love with you? I did not think about it. Yes. Of course. The psychic said, I can give you a spell. Fifty dollars. But it's very powerful. I was in no position to spend fifty dollars on anything, let alone a love spell from a middle-aged man who had decorated his psychic consultation room with spray paint and bedsheets. But I was dizzy in love, deluded.

And there was truth to what he'd said. If nobody knew me, if nobody loved me, it wasn't their fault but my own, because I never let myself be vulnerable. What was fifty dollars?

Do you take credit cards? I said. He said, How about thirty dollars cash. I hadn't realized this was up for negotiation. I've got twenty, I said. Deal, he said.

When I was little, I knew that I could probably fly. Hadn't been able to fly yet. But surely could. And would. Probably just needed to believe a little harder. Eventually realized for certain that flying was impossible. Saw my imagination was a lie. It was sad and embarrassing. At some point in my early twenties, I realized I had the same misconceptions about love. Was not going to meet an incredible man and know for sure that it was fate. Was not going to be swept away. Was going to have to choose from among the boring Andys of the world and then live with my choice.

Then: With Q on our second date. Couldn't get the words out fast enough. Kept touching each other on the shoulder, holding hands, and I thought, maybe I can fly after all.

Over our third beer, confessed that I had been resisting texting him all week. Preserving the excitement. Thank fuck, Q said. I've been terrified you were avoiding me. But I did text you once, I protested. On Wednesday. The photo from the psychic. What photo? Q said. What psychic?

The psychic ducked out of the sheet-draped room. Reappeared with a heavy wooden box. Filled with Scrabble tiles. Carved with strange circular runes. Talk about this man, he said. I said, Handsome, smart, and funny, while the man picked out tiles, arranged them, nodding. He studies philosophy, he's getting a PhD, I said, and I think that's why he's so patient and thoughtful. His research is about whether ideas are essentially good or bad, or whether they're all neutral. Interrupting me, the psychic spread his hands. There were fifteen tiles on the table in front of him, arranged in an asymmetrical pattern. Like a finished game of dominoes. Got a phone? the psychic said. I did. Take a picture of this, the psychic said, and text it to the man, along with this message. He held up a piece of paper with some words scribbled on it. Am too embarrassed to reproduce the words for you here. Was a sentence so saccharine that an electric shock ran through my jaw, like a toothache. (Seriously, Haley, you would throw up if I typed it here.) It was like the punch line to a Hallmark card from the 1950s. I know, the psychic said, I know, but don't worry, he won't actually see it.

I did it because I'd been prepared to spend fifty dollars on it. Because I was convinced that I was broken. Because I really did want Q to fall in love with me, and if he wasn't going to fall in love with me then fine, let him think I was crazy, it will save us both time. Anyway. I did it. Texted him the ridiculous rhyming love couplet, along with the image of the tiles.

But: What picture? Q said. The picture from the psychic, I said, of the tarot-card tile thing. He looked at me, wide eyed. We both started laughing. Both thinking the other was setting up some kind of charming joke. One of those standard fake arguments, flirting. Showed me his phone to prove the point: No photo. No text. Opened my phone to prove that I had sent him something. I knew that I had typed it and sent it. I was not the kind of person who forgot things. But then: No text on my phone, either. No photo. Strange, I said. Q leaned back, satisfied. Told you, he said. I think I was scammed out of twenty bucks, I said.

But to myself, I thought: It worked!

For two weeks, we talked nonstop. Tried not to see each other too often. Didn't want to move too fast. Emailed all day long, like I'm writing now. Paragraphs at a time, picking up the stream of consciousness where the other left off. Texted in transit, talking ourselves to sleep on the phone. Broke down despite deadlines and saw each other the third Wednesday, sharing Chinese food on his couch and not sleeping. Dragged myself to work at a corporate office where I sat at a reception desk at a back door. Literally no one walked by me all day. I wrote an essay about how beautiful and true romantic comedies actually are (was never published).

I went back to him Thursday night and then Friday and Saturday, too, with breaks in between only to run home and change clothes and bring Khloé a paper bag to play with (she loved paper bags).

Two or three times, early on, Q stayed at my apartment, but usually he convinced me to come to his place. I don't sleep well in other beds, he said, and I saw it was true. I didn't push it. Was embarrassed about my apartment. Small. Cat hairs clung to your clothes, needed a tape roller on hand at all times. Shower caked in rings of rust, stained so that it looked dirty no matter how hard I scrubbed. The incessant rustle of a paper bag in the kitchen where Khloé was wallowing like a hippo in mud. Q didn't grumble too much, but on the handful of nights he stayed, he wrinkled his nose at Khloé, wouldn't set his toothbrush down on the edge of the sink. I liked being there, liked having all of my clothes to choose from. But I liked Q more. Started staying at Q's three nights, four nights, five nights a week.

Poor Khloé. Mad with grief. Started howling when she heard my key in the door, spent all of her time as close to me as possible. Followed me to the door on the way out and pleaded, her paws on my calf. At the end of the third week she peed in my laundry basket. Came home and found her hiding under the couch, ashamed. Was such a good cat. Even acting out, she only messed up my dirty clothes.

After that, tried to get home more often. Tried to see Khloé at least every eight hours. After work on Friday I'd feed her and pet her for an hour, then meet Q for a movie or a party or dinner and spend the night with him. I'd go home Saturday morning for fresh clothes and Khloé time, then meet Q again. But over the months, I relented slowly: Leaving extra food for Khloé on Friday, staying through Saturday night. Packing extra clothes. Was afraid she would tear up the couch cushions or knock over a bottle of wine in the kitchen and track it all over the apartment. But it was hard on a Saturday morning, or over a beer on Friday evening, with Q, his hand in my hair at the base of my skull, murmuring, Don't you have a neighbor who could feed it?

Four weeks in, I woke up in his bed on a Saturday morning and he was gone. I got up and showered, humming to myself. Planned to leave early, had a piece to write and wanted Khloé on my lap while I worked. Later, walked back from the bathroom, wrapped in a towel, found Q sitting on the bed with a bag that smelled of warm bagels and two paper cups of coffee on the bedside. He was frowning. Said, I wanted to bring you breakfast in bed.

I was overwhelmed. Such a simple gesture. Such an elegant image of a beautiful life together. I imagined being pregnant, him bringing me breakfast in bed. Imagined him and our children, bringing me breakfast in bed. Had never been the kind of woman who picks out her wedding dress or the names of her future children but this simple idea stirred me. Imagined being old and happy. Him bringing me breakfast in bed.

I sat next to him on the bed and put my head on his shoulder. Thank you, I said. He kept his hand on the bag of bagels, closed tight. But you got up, he said. I showered, I said. How do I bring you breakfast in bed if you get out of bed? he said. I didn't know you were coming back with breakfast, I said. You thought I wouldn't come back? he said. You thought I'd just leave you?

We kept talking about it. The bagels cooled off in the bag. Talked and talked and talked. I didn't understand the problem. I must have done something else, I thought. He must be stewing over some earlier hurt. I probed, tried to get him to tell me what was really going on. But there was nothing more—just the fact that I'd gotten up when he wanted me to stay. Finally we agreed that I would get back in bed, and we could eat the bagels together then. I guessed it was just that he really wanted to do something nice for me. I hung up the towel and climbed into bed. Q watched me. Close your eyes, he said. I closed my eyes. I felt the pressure as he sat on the edge of the bed next to me. Wake up, Alice, he said, I brought breakfast.

Grew up in a family that did not talk about it when we were angry. I often hurt my mother's feelings without realizing it, until she made a sarcastic remark three weeks later. So it seemed totally natural for Q to be channeling some kind of frustration into the breakfast thing. And hadn't I been stirred by the idea of breakfast in bed, too? It was a stirring idea. No wonder he'd wanted it to go well. He just wanted the thing he had imagined. Next time, he said, when we had finished the bagels and he was kissing my forehead and taking my empty paper cup—next time don't get up until I tell you. I laughed and promised I wouldn't.

It was incredible to be wanted so consistently and firmly. Not in a jealous way, not like boys I had dated in college who seemed terrified of time apart in case I met someone better. Q just liked me. Laughed at my jokes. Had things to tell me that he'd saved up all day. Was not hiding or playing games. I worked long hours, he did coursework for his PhD, after hectic days it was so relaxing to fall back into each other, to be with someone who was not waiting for you to say that you wanted them first.

Do you remember when I wrote a piece about Hillary Clinton and women and consolation prizes and they tried to shut the whole site down? I'd always gotten hate mail, but only email. After that they started sending packages with stink bombs to my editor's office, prank calling, ordering fifty pizzas in my name. Thank God my editor had lived through her own dose of hate. Of course I'm not firing you, she said. But I had a hard time getting back to writing, with the hate still flooding in. It took three weeks. Every night in those awful weeks, Q came to my apartment. Was waiting there for me when I got home from an empty corporate office at six or seven or eight, with comfort takeout and a foot rub. Khloé loved it even more than I did, spent the whole time in the crook of my elbow. Q tolerated her, sitting on my opposite side, nestling me into the crook of his.

After the first week of that barrage of hate mail, Q insisted I take Sunday off. Declared Sunday a hate-free day. But if I skip a day, I said, it just means twice as much on Monday. So that day he did it for me. I gave him my email password. He got up before me and went out to get bagels and coffee. Came back and sat on the end of the bed. I lay in bed naked, sipping coffee. He described the emails to me as he deleted them, pretending they were fan letters. This one says he loves your use of adjectives, he said, hitting Delete with a flourish. This one thinks you're the smartest writer working online today. Smiled at him, said, That's so kind. I don't want to read you this one, it's too complimentary, you'll get a big ego, he said, smiling at me, closing my laptop, running his thumb over my big toe.

Felt lucky to have him. Andy would not have been around in hard times. Andy would have waited for me to call. I had never even broken up with Andy. I just stopped calling, and that was that. Q was a blessing. Steady. Caring. Rescuing me during a hard time. I needed him. The hate mail felt too much like high school, like walking down the hallways and finding Sharpie scrawled on my locker. But now I had Q. It was that Sunday morning that I made this connection. As he rubbed my feet, I told him some of what had happened—the broad strokes, my accident. He listened. He was kind. Afterward I told him I loved him. It was the first time I knew it was true.

Came home Friday to find Q had made pizza. Handed me a beer at the door. Took my bag and shoes, carried me to the couch. Loved to do things like that. Often carried me around. I liked being carried. My arms around his neck. I smiled up at him. Set me down on the couch and Khloé leaped immediately onto my lap. I scratched her chin, she put her paws on my shoulder and nosed my ear. She had been delirious with happiness to have me home every night that week. Didn't mind competing with Q for my attention. Q minded. What would I do without you, sweetie? I said to Khloé. I'm the one who brought you a beer, Q said from the kitchen. I laughed. We ate the pizza and watched a movie about a woman who moved to the big city to join an orchestra. She practiced until her fingers bled. She had the love of a good man but was too obsessed with her work to see it. Q brought me a second beer. My attention drifted. I slid down into a comfortable space between the couch cushions, my legs in Q's lap, Khloé curled up inside my elbow.

Woke up in the dark. Felt like I'd just closed my eyes. Hours had passed. The television was off. Q was sitting quietly in the chair on the other side of the room. I have bad news, he said. Followed him into the kitchen. Khloé on the floor. Looked like a picture from my hate mail, the Photoshop jobs from strangers. Blood in a looping rope on the tile. Cats get into things, Q was saying, it's going to be okay. I thought that meant she was still alive. I went over to pick her up. I crouched down and held her, my hands got sticky with her blood.

Cats get into things, Q said. He was right. Showed me the bleach, spilled out from under the kitchen sink. I'd left the bleach in a paper bag. The cap must not have been fully on. That cat loved paper bags, he said. How could I? I'm so stupid, I said. I turned away from Khloé. I couldn't look at her. Q wiped my hands on a dish towel. Held my head to his chest. Things happen, he said, it's going to be okay. Took care of it. Like he always took care of things. I lay down on the couch and cried so hard I threw up. Felt a little calmer afterward. I lay on the couch, staring at the ceiling. Then Q came in with Khloé in a plastic garbage bag.

For a second I hated him. Take her out of there, I said. I grabbed the bag out of his hands. He watched me, frowning. I reached in, pulled Khloé out. He had wrapped her in newspaper, like a fish. I started yelling at him. Unwrapping her. Held her soggy stiff thin skeleton against my chest. You're really emotional right now, Q said, take a break, give it to me. I screamed, You'll throw her away! Carried her into the kitchen. Ruined my shirt. Dripped blood on the floor.

I grabbed the paper grocery bag. Laid Khloé inside it. Then burst into tears. Set the bag on the floor and would have curled up next to it, but Q stopped me. Picked me up. Put my arms around his shoulders. Carried me into the bathroom, started the shower, took off my clothes, and put me in.

Put my clothes in the trash can. Brought me a cup of tea. I was overwhelmed and exhausted. Suddenly needed to sleep; I felt my eyelids closing heavily. Got into bed, still wet and naked, and fell asleep. Slept through most of the weekend. While I was asleep, Q called the vet, and they came, for thirty-five dollars, and took Khloé.

I took Monday off work, spent the morning lying in bed reading, swearing that I would never have another pet, and scrolling through pictures of foster kittens online. Q skipped his office hours and came over in the afternoon with soup. We have to get you out of here, he said. I shrugged. Let him pack me a bag. I don't need so many pajamas, I said. You need to relax, he said. I didn't fight it. I wasn't sure I was going to go to work the next day. Was feeling the way I felt as a teenager, when despair was like a heavy jacket. Followed Q and my three sets of pajamas out the door. He had brought his car, drove me to his place.

I grieved for Khloé hard. She was my first pet. I knew I was attached to her, but had no idea that loss felt like that. My grandparents, when they died, it was sad but seemed natural. They lived several states away. I missed them, was sad about it, but it wasn't unfair. Khloé was just a stupid cat but she made me feel the unfairness of the world. Things died. For no reason. There was no way out of that. How spoiled I was to be realizing this only now, at twenty-six, over a cat. I cried because I hated myself, too. I blamed myself for her death—it was because I was working too hard, it was because I was distracted, or I never would have left the bleach in the paper bag like that. I refused to talk about her with Q, and he did not bring her up, either. I cried myself to sleep all weekend, and when I woke up Monday morning, I remembered she was dead as I opened my eyes, a fresh shock. A lot of things changed after Khloé died. But that first Monday skipping work it felt like nothing would ever change, permanent gray.

On Tuesday, woke up early. Knew I had to move. Was seized by energy. Realized I would sink if I didn't move. Up and dressed and walking out. Q just waking up. Let me make you eggs, he said. But I had a call from the temp agency and I wanted to go. I'll grab something on the way, I said, I have to go get clothes from my apartment, you didn't bring me any work clothes. Kissed him and left. Wore pajama pants on the subway home. Stepped into the apartment and the smell of chemicals. Q had scrubbed the floor for me, taken out the trash with the paper bag and my ruined clothes. Moved quickly, trying not to think about Khloé. Packed up a duffel bag's worth of proper clothes and went to shred boxes of paper for a law firm.

In the break room, someone suggested I just get a new cat. Something inside me burst, and an essay poured out. I stayed up late writing. An old idea, rolling around between "Bluebeard" and *Le Bonheur* and *The Mist*, stories that say women are interchangeable. Coined a new phrase for it: the Rebecca Trope. Fuck the trolls, I thought. You're going to hate this. Finished the piece at midnight. Next morning my editor wrote back: This is great. No edits. Hit Publish, and the piece spread. Felt like my first real success.

But you're not interchangeable, Q said. There's no one for me but you.

There was a palpable change in my work after that piece. I did a couple of podcasts. Was quoted in a local paper. I started going to a coffee shop every evening to write until late, suddenly editors were responding to my pitches. Without Khloé to feed, I worked long hours, ran on bursts of adrenaline fueled by the frenetic panic that I would miss this window of opportunity. I wrote until I was exhausted and then dragged myself to Q's apartment. Basically lived there; went back to my apartment only to leave a rent check downstairs or grab things I needed. Walked through the rooms quickly, holding my breath against the lingering smell of cleaning supplies, focusing my eyes away from memories of Khloé. The rest of the time I lay on Q's couch and let him rub my feet and fell asleep, dragged myself into bed, then got up early and watched the sun rise, writing at his kitchen table until it was time to go somewhere and temp. Q was so supportive. Wanted me to work less, to take better care of myself, but was happy that I was at his place most nights. So happy that you love me, he said, all the time.

Don't remember the first time I got sick. Once, I stayed home with a stomach flu. Once with food poisoning. Later, left a movie halfway through to vomit but felt better after. At first it seemed like a string of bad luck. Then it seemed like I was getting sick a lot. Then I was sick. Wrote down everything I ate, looking for patterns. Gave up gluten, then dairy, then sugar, then all three. Started going back to the apartment one or two nights a week to give Q a break. Was afraid of leaning on him too hard and scaring him away. Stayed home from work three days in a row. Low fever, aching body. Q found out on the second day. Skipped his classes and came to take care of me. Brought me back to his apartment on the third day. Made myself go to work on the fourth, but was tired, unfocused. Left early, got to my apartment, found Q there on the couch waiting for me. You look awful, he said, leaping up to take my bag, handing me a cup of tea.

A strange bad dream started around then. That Q's skin was sticky. Not sticky like honey or sweat but like cling wrap. Or like that plastic film that comes on a brand-new computer screen. The kind you have to get a fingernail under the corner to peel up. Waking up in the middle of the night, my face on his chest and my arm across his stomach and my leg across his legs, I was stuck to him like that plastic, I had to peel myself off, starting with a fingertip. Felt awake the whole time. And it was hard to get back to sleep after. I looked online until I found "sleep paralysis" and it seemed close enough, decided that was it. A manifestation of my fear of commitment. Decided I would get over it. Which is to say that I decided it was a problem with me.

I slowed down with the writing. A month went by without anything published but I told myself that was all right. Saw Q more. The heart grew fonder. Went to dinner when we could, saw movies we'd been meaning to see for years, drank bottles of wine and spent Saturday mornings in bed. Drove upstate on a fall Sunday for a hike. Felt that this was it: An adult relationship. A partner. Steady and reliable but also sexy and thrilling. The thing that would allow me to stop putting so much effort into dating and finally focus on what I was writing, my career, the things I cared about. Felt lucky that it had happened just when I needed it most. Felt like I was on the cusp of a real career. And not a moment too soon. I remember the week *The New Yorker* ran a short preview of your first film, Haley, and I was terrified that no matter what I did, it wouldn't be enough—that you would outgrow me, not least because I had refused (again) to tell my story as part of your film. Was so glad my career was taking off (despite the current dry spell, which I thought was temporary). Or maybe it was the other way around; maybe my writing was taking off because Q had made the space for it to happen.

Then one day my fever was 102 and my health insurance was shitty. I'd had the flu before. Didn't think I needed the emergency room. Just thought I needed to sleep it off. Haley, you had something you wanted to talk to me about, and I rescheduled dinner twice. You were so understanding. But go to a fucking doctor!!!! you wrote.

Q took me. He hypothesized that I was just overworked. The doctor wasn't so sure, wanted to do a bunch of tests. Somehow a fight started. I was delirious, couldn't follow what was happening. We were leaving. Q told me he would take me to NYU for a better doctor the next day. The next day I felt a little better, and my health insurance was still shitty. I worried about the bill we'd already run up. They never told you what you were going to have to pay until two months later. We decided it was a passing flu. Still not well enough to go to work. Turned down temp work so often they stopped calling. Seven days late on a piece I'd promised an editor, then eight. I called to explain. Found that I couldn't. Q thinks it could be chronic fatigue, I said, lamely. Because I worked too hard. Don't worry about it, the editor said. I didn't know what to do, was upset and scared. I started crying, hung up the phone. Was so embarrassed. I'll spend this time writing, I thought. I'll write something so good it will make up for it being late.

I couldn't believe Q was staying with me even as I turned into a puddle of sleepy drool wearing an old sweatshirt on his couch. I'll understand if you leave me, I told him. Shh, I love you, he said.

I kept trying to write and failing. It was too hard. I would sit on the couch with a cup of tea and a blank Word document and I would feel my mind go fuzzy; I'd start looking at the internet; then hours would pass. Kept saving blank Word documents marked with new dates. Didn't want to give up on that piece. Went to a couple more doctors, but they never seemed to have answers, just ideas for expensive tests. And I never got worse. And the couple of tests I did, early on, were inconclusive. Seemed like a waste of money. Tried fish oil. Tried acupuncture. Mostly slept.

The first time my parents came to visit they were worried. My mom had made doctors' appointments, friends of people she knew, and she was ready to pay. My dad had brought three weeks' worth of casseroles he'd had deep-frozen. I insisted that I was fine. It was the stress of my writing career, I said, I just needed to rest. They looked at Q, hoping against hope. He met their expectations: told them it was a pleasure taking care of me. Plus, I needed to stay in New York so I could keep writing, I said. This was in the second or third month, when I was still trying to write.

Haley, I know you tried to visit, too. And that Q turned you away. That you sent me emails—Q read them to me, and I dictated a response. But now I wonder: What did he actually write you? Why did you stop writing back?

I was so grateful to Q. He took care of my apartment. Went over and got the things I needed, packed up everything else. Paid for storage. Put the apartment on the internet and found a subletter. Suddenly, without my having to do anything, we lived together. Realized this on a Thursday evening after he had gone to pick up the subletter's check. I signed the check over to him. My half of the rent, I said, and then, This means we live together. Wanted to celebrate. Wanted to buy a bottle of champagne. Instead, he got a can of ginger ale out of the fridge, brought it back in two matching wineglasses. To us, I said. To us, he said.

My parents came again. They were more insistent this time. But so was Q. They liked him. They had never liked anyone I dated. Q was rich and intelligent. Nearing a PhD. Attentive and kind and brought me everything I needed, they watched it happen. I just need to build my strength back up slowly, I said. They really wanted me to come home with them, just for a little while. To give Q a break. Looking back, that was my last chance to get away. Q could not have fended off my mother. I was the one who did it. Told her I did not want to leave. The truth is that I felt that if I left New York I would be failing. Convinced myself that I would recover. Sent my parents away. Promised to recover quickly. Bargained for one more month. If I'm still sick this time next month, I promised, I will come home for a while.

Maybe there was also a part of me that always wanted to give up. Be cared for. Lie on the couch, disappear, be loved.

A little less than a month later, Q finished the last of his coursework and TA responsibilities. Time to write his thesis. I can be home with you more now, he said. Late afternoon, drifting up from a nap, smiled at him, told him how proud I was. We need to move, he said, I need more space, if I'm going to write at home. The apartment had only two rooms, not counting the tiny bathroom. He'd found a bigger space in Park Slope, a beautiful renovated condo on a top floor overlooking the park, with an office space and a big bay window. We moved the same day he told me. I remember the movers arrived while I was still asking questions. Q took me to a hotel, so the fuss wouldn't disturb me. Bundled me up and drove me there. Ordered room service. Sat in bed together. Talked about his fears about his thesis, about his ambitions and what he would write. Dozed off and on. Had quiet sex. That night he asked me to marry him. Gave me a big, beautiful ring.

I never told you we were engaged, Haley. I never told anyone. It never seemed like the right time. And I was so tired.

The new apartment had nice light, a nice cream color on the walls, a nice view of the park. No windows that opened (we were on the seventh floor, I think) or internet (so that Q could write without distraction). A parking spot in the basement close to the elevator. Q promised to drive me to the library when I needed to get online. I accepted, even though I knew that I would never go to the library. Hadn't even touched my laptop in two months by then. Didn't even know where it had been packed during the move. Q brought me mystery novels to read, we watched movies. I had nothing to write. Nothing to say. The days passed.

On our first night in the new place I dreamed that he was drawing my blood. How did you learn that? I asked him, not seeing anything wrong with him drawing my blood, just amazed at the hidden skill. I've been drawing your blood for months, he said, for your tests, and he put a Band-Aid over the cotton on the blood spot. Had that dream for months and months. And another one: Getting up for the bathroom and he followed me, for a urine sample. For your tests, he said. I sat, shaky, on the toilet, and lay my arms around his neck and my head on his shoulder and peed into the cup he was holding. Every morning, I woke up to him bringing me a cup of tea. There was no Band-Aid on my arm and I had to pee, same as always. I'm going crazy, I said. Shh, Q said, I love you.

Adored that apartment in the morning. Drank tea and curled up in the seat by the window and looked down at the park, where people were moving slowly. Like looking out the window of an airplane. Felt very much like I was in an airplane most of the time, a peaceful state. Patient. Floating. Began to recognize the same people in the park. Couldn't see their faces, recognized them by the color of their coats and strollers, or the way they walked. Or recognized them by their habitual configurations. Two cautious hunched people linking arms (elderly couple), or the person pushing the wheelchair (home health aide and patient), or the fast-moving large stroller (jogging mother). Was myself the curled-up thing in the window, barely moving, napping in the sun, like a cat.

Q's writing was going well. He sat in the office for steady hours, plowing away. Stacked books on his desk and taped notes to the wall in front of him. Came out every three hours on the dot, woke me up if I had fallen asleep, made me something to eat or drink. I'm sorry you have to take care of me, I said. You're taking care of me, he said, you're making sure I don't grow moss sitting at my desk. After a full day, nine hours and three breaks, he stopped and sat with me on the couch, rubbing my feet, while we watched movies and ate takeout.

Some impossibly large chunk of time passed. The elderly couple disappeared, perhaps died. The jogging mother bundled her stroller up in something white and puffy, like a cloud. The trees lost their leaves, I watched snow and rain. New couples appeared. The trees fuzzed over in new green buds. I hadn't spoken to you, or anyone, since summer. I hadn't been on the internet or spoken on the phone. Was amazed at how the time had passed. If you're sick for a day, it feels like a year. If you're sick for a year, it feels like a day. Every morning, I woke up telling myself I would call my mother. Kept planning to call you, too, Haley. Every afternoon I was too tired to follow through. Then I decided it had been too long. Knew that you were angry, that my mother was angry, that everyone was angry with me. Knew I had betrayed everyone. Knew I had lost your love by denying your help. It was easier just to wait another day. At least I had Q, told myself.

Can't pinpoint the moment when I understood. It was around the time the sticky dream returned. Occasional at first, then more frequent. Waking up with my skin stuck to his. Got stickier and stickier. By the time the trees were fully green again, it wasn't stickiness anymore, it was tiny burs, hooks like Velcro, and as I sat up peeling first my fingers, then my hand, then my arm from his chest, I watched a million tiny pinpricks of blood appear, in an even grid pattern. Next I would have to peel off my face. I did it fast, a burning streak like hot wax on my cheek. Then he stirred in his sleep and sighed and rolled over, spooning me, and I felt the million burs plunge into my back and shoulder. I fell asleep like fainting, heavy theater curtains. Woke up to him sitting on the side of the bed with my breakfast. I'm going crazy, I would say to him. Shh, I love you, he would say back.

In the evenings he would read to me from a page he had written, his thesis. I sat up on the couch with the gray wool blanket pulled around my chin and tried to follow. My thoughts were slow, tired. What he wrote always sounded good. His main point was that an idea is neither good nor bad inherently. An idea is like a word, accruing meaning through application. My focus drifted. He was sitting next to me, holding the pages with his left hand. His right arm was across the back of the couch, his thumb stroking the back of my neck. Remembered the way he had rubbed my hand during our first shared coffee, and I thought—not for the first time—how lucky I was to have such a devoted and caring man to be with during this strange, long flu. Listened to him reading. Tried to stay awake. Head so heavy. Leaned to the side, rested my head on his arm. And then I noticed that there was no longer any hair on his arm. It was totally smooth. But when I tried to lift my head, I felt the friction and then the tug of the million tiny burs. It was the first time I had the sticky dream while I was for sure awake. My face was stuck to his arm. I ripped myself away and felt my cheek sting, touched it and my fingertips came away bloody. I looked at him and saw that he had no eyebrows, no hair on his arms. Alice, what's wrong, you look crazy, he said. He had no hair at all, it made his eyes look wide, his bald head huge. Let me get you something, he said. He got up and turned the corner into the kitchen, and I sat and watched the place where he had been. Realized that he had been the only one helping me, the only person I had seen for six months.

And maybe—the next idea occurred in a slow fog. Like a conductor on a train had announced my station when I was not paying attention. Searching for what my subconscious had heard and stored away for me to hear later—maybe he was not actually helping.

And why was I there if he wasn't helping? But I really was sick. So what was wrong with me, if this wasn't help? Didn't even know what was wrong. Again, the train conductor announced something but I missed it. Closed my eyes. Breathed. Heard him come into the room. Took a deep breath and opened again. Looked at him. Had eyebrows and hair. Was not a monster. Was carrying a cup of tea and a plate of buttered toast. Relax a bit, he said. I'm going crazy, I said. Shh, I love you, he said.

I didn't touch the tea or toast. Aren't you hungry? he asked, and then said, You need to relax. Pretended I didn't hear him. Pretended to fall asleep. He sat beside me, stroked my hip with his thumb. For hours we sat like that. Pretending to be asleep. Watching me pretend.

It was so strange not to be asleep. Was easy to pretend, didn't get bored, because I was so amazed at the feeling of being awake. How long had it been since I had been awake for more than a couple of hours? Then at some point, in the dark, he said, I know you're not asleep. Didn't open my eyes. I'm nauseous, I said, I just don't want to move. The word is "nauseated," he said, if you're nauseous, you cause nausea. Didn't say anything else. Continued to sit and watch me.

Sat like that all night. Didn't move. Didn't move. Head cleared, felt myself able to think again. Had not had any of the tea or toast he brought me—maybe, the train conductor said, you are allergic to toast or tea. Later, as the morning opened up, a horrible headache knocked suddenly between my eyes and then rushed around my brain, and it hurt like hell. It was nauseous, I thought. It made me nauseated. Repeated those words like a mantra for what felt like a year, but was maybe only a minute. Was nauseous; made me nauseated. Kept my eyes closed and tried to bear it. Q didn't speak.

Opened my eyes. A golden fall sunrise through the bay window, over the park. Headache still bad, nausea gone. Sat up. You know, I feel a little better, I said. It was the clearest morning I'd had in months. No sleep crusted in my eyelashes. Opening my eyes did not feel like swimming up out of the deep. Felt grateful to Q for watching over me all night, but also something was wrong, something I still couldn't quite remember.

I asked Q to take me to the library. I want to email Haley, I said. (Haley, yes, at that moment you were the person I wanted to talk to.) He nodded, said, Sure thing. Let me get you your morning tea first, he said. He took away the untouched tea from the night before, walked to the kitchen. I looked at the place where the tea had been. You know what? I called. What? Q stepped back out of the kitchen. I said, I want a cappuccino. He stood in the doorway, stared at me. But dairy, he said. Please, I said, I want to try a cappuccino.

Don't know why he gave in. Maybe he knew that I was about to understand and needed to back off. Maybe he didn't have the heart to say no. Maybe he really did love me. Whatever it was, he sat down by the front door and tied his shoes and left.

That was when I realized he had thrown away all of my clothes. There was nothing in the drawers. Nothing in the closet. It was like I had accidentally walked into a bachelor's room, Q's clothes lined up in neat rows, taking up all of the space. In the last bottom drawer there was a stack of my T-shirts and pajama pants. Stripes and cotton. Couldn't even find a bra. How long had it been since I had worn a bra? I understood, then, the deal that I had made with Q, what it took for him to take care of me.

I hunted for shoes for what felt like hours. Finally settled for thick socks and Q's plastic slip-on sandals. Wore flannel pants and one of Q's button-up shirts. Pulled my hair back. *In New York, you can wear anything*, I told myself.

In the elevator I held on to the wall to stay upright. There was a mirror on the back wall; I saw a skeleton with hair dyed a deep burnished red, eyes puffy and squinting, skin very pale. When the elevator dinged, the skeleton in the mirror jumped at the same time I did. I turned away, trying to remember when my hair had been dyed and when Q had taken the mirror out of the bathroom. Stumbled out onto the street, overwhelmed and disoriented. Lights too bright, people everywhere. Kept my eyes on the sidewalk and forced my stiff legs to move.

Got lucky, walked in the right direction. Did not pass Q on the sidewalk, wherever he had gone for a cappuccino. I asked a man on a stoop where the nearest subway was. Went there and waited for someone to come out through the emergency exit and slipped through behind them. Realized people were looking at me but avoiding eye contact; I looked awful. I made my way to your place on York Street.

Stumbling up the subway stairs, I thought about the last time we had lost touch, and when you came to find me—summer after high school. Reading *Misery* on my parents' back deck. This is apropos of nothing, I said, and held up the book. You didn't laugh. We hadn't really spoken in years. But you knew what had happened to me. You handed me a box of Oreos—remember?—then stood with your hands in the pockets of your jeans. I wanted to come sooner, but I didn't know if you wanted to talk to me, you said. I'm so sorry, you said, and then you started crying. What they did to you, you said, and then stopped. Have a cookie, I said. I was glad you were there, but I didn't want to talk about the past. Struggled to open the pack of Oreos. Was crying, too. The package didn't open, didn't open, and then it burst, scattering cookies all over the deck. We laughed. We ate four each. After that we were best friends again, like magic.

I hoped this reunion would be just as easy, but I was afraid. I was sure you hated me for my long silence. I was sure you hated me for staying with Q for so long. But I needed your help piecing things together. I didn't know what I was going to do. You had always seen the truth.

You had moved. Lady, this is private property, the doorman said, as I pushed the locked elevator button in frustration. You can't stand around in here.

Woke up in a cab. The doorman had shuffled me out the door and into the back seat as I started to faint, caught myself, fainted again. Didn't want to deal with me. Leaned against the cab window and watched the doorman talking to a cop. Both men in uniforms shaking their heads. Then the cabdriver was yelling at me to get out of his cab if I didn't know where I wanted to go. The headache was back and the prospect of getting onto the sidewalk and deciding what to do next was too much. Gave him Q's address. It shut the driver up although he kept the windows rolled down. Got there and rang the buzzer. Asked Q, holding down the speaker button, Can you come pay for this cab? The driver yelling out his window, the meter running. Q rushed out. Threw a wad of bills through the cab's window and put an arm around me and walked me upstairs. Didn't have to say anything. Didn't even have to come up with an excuse. He would take care of that for me. You were lost, he said, I was so worried, you did the right thing taking a cab, I'm sorry I was gone, I won't ever leave you alone again. Thank you, I said, watching him.

We tried to go back to the way it had been. I wanted to be taken care of again. Spent the week asleep but it was no use. Suddenly so obvious that he was putting something in my tea. I was overwhelmed by nausea and exhaustion before I ever finished a cup. Q brought me more every three hours, a dutiful nurse. But I didn't want to be asleep anymore. Didn't want to feel sick. Wanted Q to take care of me the way he used to, when I was still working, not the way he was now. I wanted pizza and beer, not toast and tea. But Q had changed. His breath smelled metallic. His eyes were always wide open, staring, haunted. Finally, after six days, I refused even a drop. You have to drink it, he said. I just want water, I said. He left and came back with a cup of light-yellow liquid. That's not water, I said. It's water with your medicine, he said. Looked at him. Didn't budge. Fine, he said, if you're not thirsty. Heard him pour the glass down the sink. That night he screwed a padlock into the kitchen door. There's chemicals in the kitchen, he said. I don't want you to get hurt.

I held out only a day. Wasn't used to refusing food. Broke down. A slight bitterness to the soup, but ate as much of it as I could before I passed out. Woke up briefly, as if from a dream. Passed out again into the dark.

It is amazing what can begin to seem normal just because it happens all the time. I noticed, for example, how Q had grown. Loomed on the end of the couch, rubbing my feet, his head touching the ceiling. My feet like pebbles between his hands. His breath always smelled like blood, his arms never had any hair. Eyes wide and desperate.

Neither of us knew where we were headed. A new impasse. It almost makes me laugh, now, to write it, because it sounds like just one of those things that happens in relationships. We never talk anymore. We want different things, aren't sure how to communicate. Also one of us is poisoning me. All I could do was refuse food. Drank tap water from the bathroom, scooping it up in my hands, when I could get Q to leave me alone in there. Looked for my reflection in the backs of soupspoons, checking to see if my roots had grown in brown yet. Waited days between meals, as long as I could, feeling myself grow sharper. Enjoyed the feeling of alertness. Enjoyed having thoughts again. Must confess that I missed the old Q. The easy companionship we used to share.

I learned more about how Q lived. He had groceries and books delivered, never left the apartment. He wrote, maybe still working on his thesis, maybe just typing like Jack Torrance. Realized that he was constantly asking for my reassurance. Reading me sentences from his thesis. Asking whether or not I loved him. I learned that he was not a strong man. When I couldn't stand the hunger, I finally let him feed me, packed in as many calories as I could, and then slept for what felt like a week. Woke up to a freshly dyed head of red hair and a headache like an interminable houseguest. But at least I had the food in my system to last a few more days. Went back to the work of growing out roots.

For my part, I was making Q crazy. He wrote less. Spent more time watching me. Then one afternoon, all of a sudden, he left. I'll be back soon, he said. Didn't say where he was going. Didn't ask. Got up and walked out the door. I hadn't eaten anything in two days, hadn't had anything to drink. Felt sharp and nervous. Ran and pulled on the kitchen lock, nothing. So hungry I could have cried. Then stopped. Realized: I could leave. Walked back into the living room, stood looking at the door. It was my first big failure. Didn't want to go. Didn't know where I would go. I sat back on the couch. Hunger got the best of me. When Q came back, I let him feed me. Fell asleep halfway through the omelet. Slept for hours. No dreams.

I had so much more time to think than I'd ever had before. Even before I was sick, I never just sat and thought. Discovered new depths of contemplation, a pleasant buzz of energy in my chest when I sat still for hours. Sat in the window watching the winter outside. The jogging mother had wrapped her stroller in the same white cloud. It snowed early one day. The snow angels lying on their backs looked up at me. Thought about people I knew when I was younger. Missed Khloé. She would have loved sitting in this window with me. When she was alive, I was too busy. Now I had nothing but time.

By then I knew, of course, that Q had killed her. Understood why. She was competition. Of course he had killed her. The thing I couldn't understand was why he had let me see her. There were a hundred ways to make her disappear. He had wanted me to see her dead. I contemplated this fact like a chess move. A puzzle to worry over. I was realizing that I was in danger, but not yet feeling that I was in danger. Watched him with new eyes, wondering.

Q started leaving every day, at different times. Never said where he was going. Sometimes came back in ten minutes, sometimes was gone until night. No idea if he locked the door because I never tried it. It was a test, and every day I passed, or failed, depending on how you looked at it.

Awake more, talked to him more. Wanted to break through. He'd withdrawn from me. Our old magic was gone. But I realized that he still viewed what we had as a relationship. I had to convince him that I saw it that way, too. We never really talk anymore, I tried. Sitting on the couch with a book taking notes, my feet in his lap, thumb unconsciously rubbing my big toe. You've been sick, he said, and this thesis is killing me. Yeah? I said, tell me what you're thinking about. Sat up and put my arm around his shoulder. Looked at me sideways. Well, he said.

He'd gotten to the point in his thesis, he said, of needing to define his core concepts: Ideas, Words, Good, and Bad. Words that are the building blocks of definitions and thus nearly impossible to define. But he thought that he could do it. Rambled to me about it. Was making no sense. Sat up straighter, waving his hands. Said he hadn't talked to anyone about this in six months. I hadn't paid attention, had been asleep. Now I stared at him, increasingly worried. Q had lost it.

But could you, I said, trying to bring him back to solid ground, could you just skip the definitions and write around them? Looked at me like I'd suggested he write in Esperanto. Or you could define them by example, I said, use the idea that is at the center of your research. That our ideas change what we believe, and not the other way around. That in a way his thesis was about his beliefs, and not ideas. Just say that, I said. I'm alone in this, Q wailed, I'll never finish. I'm here with you, I said. He said, Can I trust you? Can I really trust you? He looked at me with big eyes filled with despair. I'm worried you want to leave me, he said. I can't leave, I said, you took my shoes. As soon as I said it I realized it was a mistake. He leaned his head back. I'm so sorry, I said. I didn't mean that. He got up and stood a few feet in front of me with both of his fists pressed into his eyes. You won't leave me, will you? he said. I won't leave you, I said. Promise? he said. I saw that he was honestly terrified that I would go, but that fear made it no less a threat.

It unraveled before my eyes that afternoon, as I watched tiny joggers under the first tree bursts of early spring. Why he'd let me see Khloé. It was the same reason he put drugs in my tea. My mother once told me that if a man is at his best when he's apologizing to you, he'll waste your life creating reasons to apologize. Sat up in the middle of the night. Looked at Q. Was not stuck to him. Enormous in the bed next to me, snoring softly. Feet hung off the end of the bed and rested firmly on the floor. Head twice as big as the pillow. Finally heard what the train conductor had been announcing: If a man is at his best when he's taking care of you, he'll waste your life creating reasons for you to need his care.

I left the next day. Hadn't eaten in eight days, a new record. Felt sharp and clear. Q had walked out without fanfare in the late morning, on his mysterious daily errand. I pulled on the same pair of his socks and Adidas sandals. I put on the same flannel pants and button-up shirt. Searched everywhere for some cash, or a credit card, or anything, but the apartment was filled with only books and the stupid wool blanket. Stood in the middle of the room, frozen for a moment. A plan occurred, maybe foolhardy, but enough to get me out the door. Would go to a bar, try to pick up a man with a story about getting locked out of my apartment on laundry day. An Andy; someone gentle. Would spend a night on this man's couch, get my thoughts together, and borrow his phone to call Haley. Or my parents. The first thing was just to find someone at a bar. Was already practicing my smile, trying to arrange my face into a charming come-hither shape, as I opened the door.

Q was standing in the hallway, waiting. He was both surprised and completely unsurprised to see me. Had been waiting for me to break his heart like this. He closed his eyes tightly. Clenched his fists. Stood still for a second. My face frozen in the same come-hither look I had been practicing for another man. Oh, I said, are you waiting for me? He lunged forward suddenly and grabbed me by both shoulders, pushed me back into the apartment, slammed the door behind him, slammed me back against the wall, hard, twice.

I'd never been thrown like that before. Held my elbows tucked in and my eyes closed and felt the wall on my back. It was not a feeling I knew existed. I thought Khloé's death had showed me the fragility of life. That was nothing compared to being slammed against a wall. The look in Q's eyes, not willing to believe he would kill me but afraid of it, a black pit opening rapidly under my feet. What it is to be helpless.

He realized what he had done and stepped back. Looked at me, angry. You need to go to the hospital, he said. I stood, staring at him, paralyzed. He was panicked, mumbling to himself. Fumbled his keys out of his pocket. Dropped his phone, kicked it in frustration. Dropped his keys. Picked them up, fumbled for the kitchen key. Lurched toward the door like a man possessed. I had a moment of déjà vu watching him fumble with the padlock. You need to go to the hospital, he was saying. Finally he ripped the door open. Disappeared into the kitchen. I was shaking all over, like a wet dog. I grabbed his phone from the floor and his keys from the padlock hanging on the kitchen door. Ran out of the apartment and down the hall.

Made it to the elevator and stood shaking. Got in. The doors closing sluggishly. I watched, frozen. Q came out the apartment door. Gigantic. Barely fit in the hallway. Ducked his head so it wouldn't touch the ceiling. Trying to run, his broad shoulders squeezing against the sides of the hallway. The butcher knife in his hand looked the size of a spoon. You need to go to the hospital, he was roaring, swiping the knife in the air as the doors closed between us, you need to go to the hospital.

Panicked in the parking garage, running between the cars, looking for his. Listening for the next elevator coming down. Or the door to the stairwell slamming open. Pushed the button on the key fob frantically. Finally his car went beep, beep. I got in and started the engine. Pulled out of the tight parking spot and turned the corner, gunning for the ramp to the street. Saw him in the rearview. A dark figure framed in the doorway of the stairwell, the knife glinting in his hand. I slammed on the gas, got away.

The shakes started near the south end of New Jersey. I had to pull over and let my body go loose. Got out of the car and jumped up and down a couple of times. Shook all over. Ran in circles around the car until some concerned passerby pulled over. A man in a baseball cap. I nearly screamed. Was back in the car and speeding away before he had shifted into park.

I had no money. Wearing a pair of shower sandals, stolen from Q and therefore much too big, over the socks I'd been wearing for three days. Stopped at a big-box store, tried on a pair of light tennis shoes, left Q's sandals in their place in the shoebox. And walked right out. Have you ever shoplifted before? I never had, not even a stick of gum when I was five. It feels fucking fantastic. Stole, begged, and borrowed several more things on my way here to Bethany Beach. All good stories I'll tell you later: The woman with a van full of kids who bought me a tank of gas. The electronic toll lanes that I breezed right through—this fantastic alarm goes off with an indignant buzzing roar, sounds just like I feel. Q will get the bills in the mail in thirty days or so. The last time he'll ever hear from me.

And now I'm here. At your mother's condo in South Bethany, writing emails on a phone on airplane mode. Emails that I'll never send you.

Because I know what you would say: Alice, why do you always hide behind genre stuff? Why make Q a literal monster, when what he did was so monstrous already? When will you just tell the truth?

Sitting here on this balcony, at sunrise, I'm feeling surprisingly optimistic. And how appropriate that I wrote this on a phone! It's how my love for Q started. He was a text message before he was much of anything else. Now he's just a string of missed calls, and our story is a string of emails, hidden away forever in my drafts folder.

I will tell you what happened. Someday soon. In person, probably; I'll tell you as much as I can (and then you'll fill in the gaps—in your own way, you'll make Q a monster, too). But no matter how much I tell you, you'll want me to talk more. You'll want me to write about Q; you'll want to interview me for another documentary film. You'll want me to be a quote-unquote survivor. But all I want to be is safe. I want my life back.

Or maybe this time will be different. After all, next time I see you I'll live in a new city, I'll have a new job. Maybe I'll be a new person. Maybe, from here on out, it's just you and me.

To us,
Alice

FIFTEEN PIECES

BASED ON THE HORRIFYING TRUE STORY

WHITE DRAFT: 10/15/96

BLUE DRAFT: 11/3/96

PINK DRAFT: 11/13/96

YELLOW DRAFT: 12/20/96

Written by Alice Lovett

Story by Alice Lovett & Haley Moreland

FADE IN:

INT. THE LEDBETTERS' LIVING ROOM — NIGHT

A normal house in a normal neighborhood. So normal, in
fact, that it is IDENTICAL to every other house in the
neighborhood.

The camera tracks around the room to take in the
decorations. The living room is tastefully decorated.
A SLIDING GLASS DOOR overlooks a grassy yard. Family
photos of MR. and MRS. LEDBETTER are on the mantel.

There's only one decorating detail out of place . . .

. . . the camera slowly pans down . . .

. . . to reveal . . .

. . . A DEAD BODY! ! ! !

                                           SMASH CUT TO:

                            TITLE CARD: FIFTEEN PIECES

INT. THE LEDBETTERS' LIVING ROOM — THE NEXT MORNING

The body is covered by a WHITE SHEET, which is dappled
with bright red BLOODSTAINS.

A DETECTIVE crouches next to the body. This is
DETECTIVE MORGAN, thirty, long brown hair and a look
of vigilant intelligence on her face, a look that
says, I WILL NOT ABIDE BULLSHIT.

Detective Morgan LIFTS the white sheet and LOOKS at
the body underneath it. She grimaces.

She lowers the sheet and stands. Contemplates the
room.

She turns and examines the SLIDING GLASS DOOR.

A ROOKIE runs into the room.

                    THE ROOKIE
          Detective Morgan! This is the third
          body in the neighborhood this month!
          All of them have been cut up like
          that!

                    DETECTIVE MORGAN
                 (mostly to herself)
          Fifteen pieces. Who cuts a body into
          fifteen pieces?

                    THE ROOKIE
          It's a serial killer!

Detective Morgan ignores the Rookie. She looks at
the MANTELPIECE, takes out a tissue and dusts for
a FINGERPRINT.

                    THE ROOKIE
          You've got to stop him. You're the
          best man we've got!

                    DETECTIVE MORGAN
          I'm not your man.

The camera ZOOMS IN on the SERIOUS, DETERMINED look on
Detective Morgan's face.

                    DETECTIVE MORGAN
          But I am your only hope.

FADE TO BLACK.

INT. MR. LEDBETTER'S OFFICE — AFTERNOON

A psychologist's office, with DIPLOMAS on the WALL, a
BIG DESK, and a BIG MAN sitting behind it.

MR. LEDBETTER is middle-aged, balding, wears GLASSES.
He's dressed in a SUIT and TIE.

He is CRYING INCONSOLABLY.

We watch him WEEP for a minute.

The camera PANS to the other side of the desk:
Detective Morgan is sitting in a chair.

She watches Mr. Ledbetter with a skeptical look on her
face.

>   DETECTIVE MORGAN
>   (dryly)
>   Mr. Ledbetter, I'm so sorry for your
>   loss.

Mr. Ledbetter SNIFFLES, trying to get a hold of
himself.

>   DETECTIVE MORGAN
>   I know you're upset. I'm very sorry
>   that your wife was murdered.

Mr. Ledbetter WAILS at the word "murdered." Detective
Morgan subtly rolls her eyes.

>   DETECTIVE MORGAN
>   But you have to answer some questions.

>   MR. LEDBETTER
>   Can't this
>   (sobs)
>   wait until
>   (wails)
>   after the
>   (blubbers)
>   funeral!!!

Detective Morgan suddenly stands and BANGS her FIST on
his desk.

                    DETECTIVE MORGAN
          We're dealing with a serial killer
          here! If we wait for the funeral, who
          knows how many more women will die!

The camera ZOOMS IN on Mr. Ledbetter's face, which
looks SHOCKED.

Then for a minute: His face TWISTS into UNCONTROLLABLE
RAGE.

Then it's GONE in a FLASH.

Mr. Ledbetter composes himself.

                    MR. LEDBETTER
           You're right. I'm sorry.

He wipes a handkerchief across his face. As he does,
Detective Morgan subtly leans forward and STEALS a PEN
from his desk.

She holds the pen with a TISSUE. She slips it in her
POCKET.

Mr. Ledbetter folds his hands, ready to answer
questions.

                    DETECTIVE MORGAN
          I only have one question for you.

The camera focuses on Mr. Ledbetter's face. He looks
NERVOUS.

                    DETECTIVE MORGAN
          Your first wife. She was killed in the
          same way. Ten years ago. Police never
          found her killer.

The look of RAGE briefly crosses Mr. Ledbetter's face
again.

                    DETECTIVE MORGAN
          Do you think it's the same person?

A beat.

Mr. Ledbetter BREAKS DOWN into SOBBING again. He's not
answering ANY questions today.

Detective Morgan rolls her eyes.

FADE TO BLACK.

INT. DETECTIVE MORGAN'S HOME — EVENING

Detective Morgan's house looks a lot like the
Ledbetters' house. No dead body, but same sliding
glass door, same mantel, etc.

She lives ALONE. She is standing in the KITCHEN,
making POPCORN.

Suddenly . . .

JUMP SCARE: There is a MAN STANDING OUTSIDE OF HER
SLIDING GLASS DOOR! ! ! !

     . . . IT'S THE KILLER! ! ! !

He's a BIG MAN. He's wearing ALL BLACK and a BLACK SKI
MASK.

Detective Morgan DOESN'T SEE HIM. He is BEHIND HER.

The camera ZOOMS IN on the HANDLE of the SLIDING GLASS
DOOR.

The Killer crouches slightly and LIFTS the HANDLE of
the SLIDING GLASS DOOR from the outside. (Anyone who
owns this kind of sliding glass door knows this
WEAKNESS.)

The lock FLIPS OPEN.

Detective Morgan HEARS and spins around just in time
to see the KILLER THROW OPEN the door and ENTER THE
ROOM.

She SCREAMS.

The Killer LUNGES, knocks her down.

She SCRAMBLES backward.

The Killer is holding a KNIFE.

He LUNGES at Detective Morgan. She KICKS his hand, the knife goes FLYING.

The Detective and the Killer FIGHT.

The Killer THROWS the Detective across the room.

She SCRAMBLES over to the desk, where her GUN is waiting.

She FUMBLES the gun.

> DETECTIVE MORGAN
> God damn it . . .

She GRABS the GUN.

She SPINS around and stands, holding the gun with two hands.

Her living room is EMPTY.

The Killer has FLED.

FADE TO BLACK.

INT. MR. LEDBETTER'S OFFICE — THE NEXT MORNING

The Rookie is standing next to Mr. Ledbetter's desk.

> DETECTIVE MORGAN
> You're not going anywhere, Mr.
> Ledbetter.

> MR. LEDBETTER
> What are you doing here? My wife died!
> You should be finding her killer!

                    DETECTIVE MORGAN
          I found her killer.

The camera ZOOMS IN on the LOOK OF SURPRISE on
Mr. Ledbetter's face.

                    MR. LEDBETTER
          What are you suggesting?

                    DETECTIVE MORGAN
                    (to the Rookie)
          Cuff him. He might try to run.

The Rookie HANDCUFFS Mr. Ledbetter.

                    MR. LEDBETTER
          What is this?!!

                    DETECTIVE MORGAN
          My first clue was the sliding glass
          door. Everyone in the neighborhood
          knows those locks are a joke, so I
          know the killer lives local.

                    MR. LEDBETTER
          That doesn't prove anything!

                    DETECTIVE MORGAN
          I also found the killer's fingerprints
          at the crime scene. And last night,
          someone attacked me in my home. He left
          a knife behind. The fingerprints
          matched the killer's. They also matched
          the fingerprints from this pen, which
          I took from your desk yesterday.

The camera ZOOMS IN on Mr. Ledbetter's face, TWISTED
WITH RAGE. Now he makes NO EFFORT TO HIDE IT.

He TRANSFORMS into the KILLER we KNOW he IS.

                    DETECTIVE MORGAN
          Checkmate, mister.

                      MR. LEDBETTER
          You'll never take me alive!

Mr. Ledbetter TWISTS and HITS the Rookie with his
handcuffed fists.

The Rookie stumbles back.

Mr. Ledbetter tries to run —

Detective Morgan SHOOTS HIM.

Blood EXPLODES OUT OF HIS CHEST.

He falls back against the wall.

He DIES.

Silence.

Detective Morgan shakes her head. The Rookie stumbles
up to his feet.

The two cops stand over Mr. Ledbetter's DEAD BODY.

                      THE ROOKIE
          He killed his own wife. I can't
          believe it.

                    DETECTIVE MORGAN
          I can. I've always known . . .

The camera ZOOMS IN on Detective Morgan's face, which
looks determined.

                    DETECTIVE MORGAN
          You can never trust a man.

FADE TO BLACK.

PART V

OLD FRIENDS

2014

1. Idiot Nick

The first thing Lindsey says when she opens the door is "Jesus Christ!" Then she squints at you and says, "Are you doing the steps?"

Her apartment is in a sprawling brick complex in Brooklyn. She's number H5 (which makes no sense; she's on the second floor). You stood outside, pretending to look at your flip phone, until a guy with keys came up and you slipped in behind him; you didn't want to explain yourself to Lindsey over a loudspeaker. Standing in the hallway now—too late—you realize it's weird to show up already inside her building.

You give her a big, stupid smile. She's right. You're doing the steps. (Lindsey has always been one step ahead of you.)

You say, "Would you rather I were here to borrow money?"

She rolls her eyes but gives you half a smile, and you feel a tick of satisfaction. You're surprised how much you still want to impress her.

"Well," she says, then steps aside and widens the door. "I guess it's been a long time coming."

You keep your hands in your pockets as you follow her inside. Her apartment is unmistakably the domain of a child. In the narrow kitchen, a few pieces of letter-shaped cereal are scattered across the floor; the refrigerator is covered in finger paintings.

"You have a kid," you say.

Lindsey just nods. "Why are you here?" she says. She's got her arms crossed and you have the feeling she's trying to restrain herself, but from what—hugging you or hitting you—you can't tell. You mirror her, unconsciously folding your own arms.

"Look, I know it's been—"

"Nick!" Lindsey exclaims.

You shove your left hand back in your pocket, but it's too late. Lindsey claps her hands over her face like she's hiding from the gory part of a movie. "What happened to your hand?" she says.

"I had an accident," you say. "Just a couple of fingers."

Lindsey doesn't say anything, her face still tucked in her hands.

"Really, it's no big deal. I'm totally fine."

She exhales and looks up at the ceiling, tears pooling in her eyes. "I just always knew you were going to hurt yourself, and, oh God, *of course* you did."

There's so much you need to explain. Things have changed. You know she'll understand. You just don't know how to start. And then there's a flurry of feet on the floor, a child enjoying the sound of her own stomping, and in comes Lindsey's kid.

Short blond curls pulled up into uneven pigtails and her mouth open, her tongue sticking out, as she focuses on a My Little Pony she's trying to balance on her head.

You recognize her right away. She looks like all the baby pictures of you hanging in your mother's front hallway.

"Look, Mama!" the child says, her eyes crossed up toward her own forehead as she holds the plastic horse in place with one hand, fooling nobody.

Lindsey transforms, some bright maternal magic; you can barely tell she'd been upset. "Wow, Katydid," she says warmly, rubbing one eye with one fingertip as if to dislodge a stray lash. Of course Lindsey is an excellent mother. You asshole.

You look from Lindsey to the girl and back. You say, "When were you going to tell me?"

"Not right now!" Lindsey says, firmly bright. "Katie, this is Nick. He's an old friend of mine."

"Katie," you say, slowly.

Katie doesn't say anything. The pony drops off her head and falls to the floor, but she rolls her eyes and twists her small torso backward, posed. She's got her eyebrows raised, like she's doing another impressive trick. She doesn't make eye contact, but she glances your way once, then twice. She's checking to make sure you're watching.

She wants you to be impressed.

The pain is like falling, accelerating into despair.

"I'm an idiot," you say.

And now your daughter, delighted with her own sense of humor, won't call you anything but Idiot Nick.

Lindsey spends two days thinking about it. You're in a hardware store, buying a strip of flypaper for your motel room, when she calls with her answer.

"You owe back child support," she says, "but if you make it square, you can be in her life. And if you really are sober."

You promise you really are sober.

Lindsey has done some calculations. Taking into account your earnings over the course of Katie's life so far, and your future earning potential—which, let's be honest, is almost nothing, after all the jobs you've lost—she decides you owe her ten thousand. "Actually, it's twenty thousand," Lindsey says. "But I don't have to hire a lawyer, and you'll pay me under the table, so we'll do ten." She wants a monthly payment plan, and she wants it in cash. As you hang up the phone, you realize she wants you to prove you'll stick around.

Goddamned right you're sticking around.

You go straight to the nearest ATM. You overdraw your account as much as it lets you—four hundred dollars. You take it directly to Lindsey's apartment. To put an anchor on her. Once she takes your cash, she can't change her mind.

She meets you at the door, says, "Thank you." She even kind of smiles. She doesn't invite you in, but you can tell she's impressed. You walk away feeling like a new man. This is your chance to do things right.

You move to New York in May. You miss that month's payment, but only because your landlord in Virginia rips off your security deposit. Lindsey doesn't mind. You figure she's impressed that you're moving to be closer to Katie. She's impressed that you're following through. She adds another five hundred dollars' interest to the total you owe, but that's fair; you're just glad she never asks where your money is coming from.

By the fall, the three of you have a routine. On the first Saturday of the month, you meet them at a coffee shop near Fort Greene Park. Katie gets an apple, because Lindsey doesn't want her to associate you with treats. Lindsey gets a giant latte and you get a black coffee, and then the three of you walk together to the playground when the weather's nice, and to the library when it's bad.

"Idiot!" Katie says as soon as she sees you, and runs up to give you a big hug. You love it, although you suspect she only does it to annoy her mom.

One Saturday, on your way to the coffee shop, you pass a man selling knickknacks on a table on Joralemon Street. You notice a packet of stickers for sale, twenty-five cents. They're dog stickers. Katie is crazy about dogs. Whenever she sees a dog on the street, she runs straight up to it with her arms spread and gives it a huge kiss. You dig in your pocket for a quarter.

Lindsey doesn't let you bring Katie gifts. You like to buy things anyway. Like you're going to somehow sneak them to her. *Say you got this at kindergarten.* You know that telling your daughter to keep secrets is not a great way to make progress on joint custody. But you can't help buying her things. You've got a whole stack of toy ponies and snap bracelets on your kitchen counter. It accumulates in pieces, like an hourglass, as you try to earn your way into Lindsey's good graces before Katie gets too old for toy ponies. Or too old to get attached to her biological dad.

In line at the coffee shop, you feel the stickers in your jacket pocket. For twenty-five cents, it's basically like you found them for free.

So you wait until Katie is distracted—carefully inspecting her apple for worms—then you say, "Lindsey. Do you mind if I give Katie these dog stickers I found?" You pull the stickers out of your pocket to show Lindsey how small of a gift it really is.

But Katie spots them. She stops, midbite, and removes her teeth from the apple. "Doggies?" she says. She reaches up and holds your good hand, pulling the stickers down toward her face.

It would be weird to hide them from her at this point. "Yeah," you say. "Do you know anyone who might want them?"

Lindsey folds her arms and sighs. But you're watching Katie—her eyes wide, her chin tilted down in exaggerated modesty. You're impressed with her savvy. She understands that you're breaking the rules, and she's being extremely careful to play along. Trying her best not to ruin her chances.

"Well . . ." she says, dragging out the last consonant. "Maybe I could have them?"

Lindsey lets it go, and Katie skips in delight all the way to the park, tapping her fingers on the packet of stickers and singing, "Doggie doggie doggie doggie dogs!" At the park she sits between you and Lindsey on a bench, peeling off the stickers one at a time and flattening them onto Lindsey's purse, your coat, her own cheeks, naming each one as she does. "This is Licker," she says, sticking a golden retriever on her own jacket.

You lean back and try to soak up this moment. It's nearly perfect. You look around the park, trying to appreciate the sunshine and the smell of fall and these precious hours with your daughter.

That's when you notice a pale man sitting on a bench, maybe twenty yards away. Right when you look at him, he looks away.

"This one is Wicker," Katie says, sticking a Labrador on the bench.

Was the man watching you?

You glance away, then back, studying him. He's tall and thin, pale and pasty, with gray hair; he's reading a magazine, wearing a trench coat. He glances over at you again, and then again away. You frown.

"Idiot!" Katie says, patting your shoulder urgently. You look down, and your daughter's sweet face reminds you that you are probably being paranoid. Imagining strange men following you is a thing of your alcoholic past. You're sober now. You're trying to stop seeing things.

"I *said*, this is Kicker," Katie says, and pats the small terrier she has stuck onto your coat.

THE DOG IS COVERED in glitter and wearing a red plaid beret. You keep it on the coat for the rest of the day. It gives you a real feeling of optimism. You're nearly at the halfway mark—you've paid Lindsey four thousand dollars. And maybe letting Katie keep the dog stickers is a sign she's easing up on you. Maybe you did something right for once.

That night you go to a mindless action movie. It's your standard treatment for the depression that sinks in after your monthly visits with Katie, when the lonely month stretches out ahead of you like a sore throat. Today, the movie actually helps. As the credits roll you feel a little lighter than usual, you can see the future more clearly, when you'll be looking back on this hard time instead of living it.

Then you're walking home and you pass a bar with its door open. There's a jukebox in the back outlined in neon red, and a woman with the low-cut back of her blue dress turned to you. The urge to go inside and buy her (and you) a drink is so strong you stop and put your hand on the outside wall to steady yourself.

You look through the door at the jukebox and the woman. It's a perfectly composed scene. Like a noir film still. You shift your body weight, willing yourself to walk away.

You hear the sound of metal and look down. You're standing on one of those basement hatches that dot the sidewalks of New York. There's just a few millimeters of steel between the duct-taped soles of your shoes and a break-your-neck fall down a steep flight of stairs. What a metaphor.

"You are not going inside," you say, out loud.

Then you zip up your coat and notice that Kicker has fallen off and is gone. Whatever was left of the day's good feeling vacuums out of your chest. You gasp twice. Two loud sobs without tears.

You stumble home and spend the night lying on your back on your hand-me-down mattress on the floor, listening through the old plaster to your upstairs neighbors having a fight and wondering whether asking yourself *Am I thinking of killing myself?* counts as thinking of killing yourself.

The jury is still out, and you're still awake, at six o'clock in the morning when your phone dings with a text message from an old friend: *Urgent job. Come ovr.*

2. Fear Safety

00:00:00 So I'm just going to spitball here for a second, with this, with how I think the opening should go. I have the whole thing all worked out. If I just had the time, I could write the book myself.

. . .

It is what it is. You ready?

. . .

It starts out like: I used to be afraid of everything. I'm the youngest of three boys. Also the shortest and skinniest. So I learned fear from a young age.

00:00:30 One of my earliest memories, like six years old, and I'm locked in the basement, with my brothers on the other side of the door telling me that the black fungus in the basement was about to release its spores, that those spores would seep through your nose and into your brain and make you go psychotic. That's what I'm talking about when I talk about fear.

Flash forward twenty years, I was twenty-six. CEO of my own company. Been in business two years and we're already in the black, I had fifteen people working for me, taking home two hundred K, fielding offers from investors left and right. Order of magnitude offers. Do you need me to slow down?

. . .

00:01:00 Right, of course it's recorded. Anyway, I'm fielding offers, running my business, you'd think I'm on top of the world, right? But here's the crazy thing: I was still ruled by that same fear.

Italicize that, Alice. It's a really important point.

Then say—because we want to really hook the guy reading here—say, maybe you picked up this book thinking that you need a new morning routine to kick-start your life. Maybe you're hoping I'll give you some tips about a firmer handshake, or, I don't know, how to stand with your feet spread wide apart, some crap like that to make you more confident. Solve all your problems.

00:01:30 I'm here to tell you all those tricks are bullshit.

Nothing will work—and italicize this next part—*until you overcome your fear!*

And once you overcome your fear?

Nothing—that's in all capital letters—NOTHING will stand in your way. And italicize that, too.

. . .

This is what I was typing—transcribing tapes from a client interview—when Haley called.

I was sitting in a corporate coffee shop in the suburbs. It was my first visit home from Barcelona in three years; my mom was disappointed that I had to work, but I was on deadline. I was auditioning to ghostwrite a book for an entrepreneur, a self-help book about overcoming fear with a method he called "Fear Safety." I'd promised Fox a draft of the introduction by the end of that day; if he liked it and hired me to write the whole book, I'd make enough money to take six months off work. It was almost time for lunch when Haley called, and I hadn't even written the first sentence.

I turned off the ringer and let the call go to voice mail. I told myself it was because of the deadline. It was a question of discipline, I decided, and not my feelings about Haley.

The truth was that I had no discipline. I'd originally become a ghostwriter—composing self-help manuals, memoirs, and other vanity projects—because I was running away from Q, and the job offered privacy. I also envisioned a part-time commitment; I thought the work would fit neatly into four-hour parcels of the day, leaving me plenty of energy to write a horror novel, something I'd been dreaming of doing for years. But in reality I did very little writing at all. I procrastinated on my client projects, wasting a lot of time either reading on the internet or installing new blockers to stop myself from reading on the internet. I'd start working only when it was definitely too late. Then I'd write frantically, ten hours a day, and finish three days after the deadline. Through the subsequent drafts I would alternate between the same procrastination and panic; by the time the book was finally sent to the vanity printer, I'd be too mentally exhausted to do anything but take long walks and browse used book stores until the next client project arrived, and the cycle started again.

Which is all to say: I could have taken a five-minute break and answered Haley's call. The real reason I didn't pick up is that we hadn't spoken in nearly a year, and I was still angry.

I left my phone facedown on the table and went back to the tapes.

> **00:02:00** So this book is the story of how I overcame my fear. Basically the point is that I went from a high school nerd to a Fifty Most Eligible Bachelor in New York.

> . . .

> Right. I went from the skinny kid with hand-me-down glasses, who used to get his mouth stuffed with toilet paper at school—

> . . .

> Yeah, it was pretty bad. But I went from that nerd to the entrepreneur who sold his first company for seven-point-five million dollars, so yeah—the joke's on everybody else.

> . . .

Typing the tapes is one of my favorite procrastination methods. The agency has all of my interviews transcribed for me, but I always end up typing them again. It's a cheap trick to get my fingers moving in the shape of the client's voice. It helps me forget my own voice, too; the agency's software only records the far end of the phone call, to cut down on the cost of transcription. My half of the interview is silence.

But the trick wasn't working that day. I was having trouble getting into Fox's voice.

> **00:13:30** Trust me: I was the kind of guy who used to regularly walk out of my apartment with toothpaste on my

face because I was too embarrassed to look in the mirror. I
couldn't look myself in the eye.

. . .

Swear to God!

. . .

So if I could overcome my fear? Anyone can.

. . .

He sounded like such a jerk on the tapes. During our interview,
though, I'd liked him a lot. He was friendly, one of those business-
people who pride themselves on flouting the stiff etiquette of business. He treated me with casual affection, like a barista at his favorite
coffee shop. True, he was condescending, but all of my clients were
condescending; people are ashamed of hiring a ghostwriter. So when
he acted like it was my job to take dictation, I understood that it was
because he was embarrassed.

00:17:00 Overcoming my fear wasn't easy. But it wasn't
rocket science.

It was a question of a new mind-set, shifted with a daily
practice, and mostly a belief that my life was worth it. That
I was worth it. And I want you to know that you are
worth it, too.

Italicize that, Alice. *You are worth it.*

. . .

There was also the fact that Fox was going to pay me really, really well. He'd asked for me specifically; he offered triple my rate. After our first conversation I hung up and thought, *This will be the easiest twelve thousand dollars I ever make,* giggling to myself because I had never actually made twelve thousand dollars. Of course I liked him.

But his voice! I wondered how I was ever going to turn his ramblings into anything readable. It was like he'd spent years watching nothing but *Glengarry Glen Ross* and motivational speeches by Tony Robbins. He talked precisely, but too fast. I heard desperation pressing out from under his manicured confidence.

> **00:34:00** I'm going to show you how you can overcome your fear. Because once you overcome your fear, you can do anything. You can reach your dreams.

> . . .

I stopped typing and leaned back, letting the tape prattle on. I glanced at my phone, saw that Haley hadn't left a message, and was glad I hadn't picked up; I assumed she'd hit my number by accident. I looked out the window of the coffee shop, trying not to feel sad about our lost friendship, trying not to absorb Fox's desperation. It was a sunny, quiet Tuesday in the suburbs. I watched a woman pulling two children out of the back of her car and nestling them into a double stroller.

I wondered what Richard Fox was so afraid of.

> **00:52:30** It starts with identifying your fear. Fear is constantly rationalizing itself. Fear doesn't want to leave. It tries to convince us that we need it. It tries to convince us that, if we let down our

guard, something horrible will happen. Yes, giving up fear is actually another thing we are afraid of! Stupid, right?

. . .

As the woman from the parking lot maneuvered her double stroller over the curb, I stopped the tape, took out my headphones, and leaped up to hold the door.

"Your children are so sweet!" I said. "How old are they?"

"Almost two," she said.

"Twins?" I asked.

"Yes," she said. "Fraternal." I walked with her to the counter, cooing over the toddlers and asking polite questions. All three of them looked at me skeptically, but I barreled ahead, chattering as we stood in line. I wanted to get more hot water for my tea. Also, I wanted the woman to remember me.

It was a defense mechanism I couldn't shake, even though I wasn't sure I needed it anymore. I had no evidence Q was still interested in me, or still dangerous. But I was still nervous. When I traveled, I checked his social media accounts to make sure he wasn't nearby. I wore my hair cut short and dyed blond; I carried pepper spray. I knew Q had probably moved on—years had passed—but I still felt my vulnerability at unexpected moments, like a dress that rides up too high when you sit down.

So I made a point of being everyone's casual friend; I wanted people to listen if I ever called *Help*. In the coffee shop that day I had already chatted with the pierced-beyond-her-years barista and with the woman in her late forties who had wanted to take the *USA Today* someone else had left next to my seat. And here I was, chattering my way into friendship with this skeptical young mother: "It must be hard with twins! If you need anything, I'm sitting right over there."

I thanked the barista by name and waved goodbye to the twins. As I walked back to my seat, I smiled at the middle-aged woman, who looked up from *USA Today* and smiled back. I reminded myself that everything was going to be okay.

And then I realized that this, maybe, was the real reason I liked Richard Fox. I'd never thought much of self-help books. Life is hard; anyone offering a shortcut is probably lying about the shortcuts they took themselves. But the more I listened to him, the more I believed Fox's confidence was manufactured. If I heard desperation in his voice, maybe it meant that he had really overcome something horrible. Maybe, if I wrote his book, I would learn to do it, too. I opened a new document to start writing the introduction at last.

Then my phone interrupted with an insistent chime. It was a text message from Haley.

> Hey Alice, thought you'd want to know—my mom passed away. It was a couple weeks ago. Would love to talk sometime when you're around. LYLAS.

It took me a few minutes to calm down, but finally I packed up my things and went outside.

"Alice!" Haley answered, saying my name with real warmth. "I wasn't sure you'd call."

"I'm so sorry," I said. "I had no idea about your mom."

There was a pause; I imagined Haley on the other end of the line, blinking back tears. I felt horrible for not talking to her all these months. "Thanks," she said. "She was sick for a long time."

"Last time we talked she was in an experimental treatment, I remember."

"Yeah, she did a few of those." Haley sighed heavily. "Anyway."

"Was there a funeral?" I asked.

"We had a ceremony, just family."

I sat quietly for a minute. "Thanks for letting me know," I said. "I'm just so sorry."

I searched for some warm memory of her mother I might share: The time she taught me to French braid Haley's hair. Or the smell of the cinnamon she mixed in with coffee grounds. Most importantly, the way she never treated me like damaged goods; after what happened in high school, Haley's mom was the only adult who spoke to me with neither pity nor self-conscious terror in her voice. But I wouldn't talk to Haley about that time in my life ever again.

Finally I just said, "I'm so sorry."

"Thanks. But how are you? Are you still in Spain?"

I made a humming noise of assent.

"And are you still ghostwriting?" Haley said.

And like that, my sympathy was gone. Her voice was falsely bright and curious; in her tone I heard all the years of lectures she had given me, about how I should *tell my story*, I should *claim my voice*. I knew she saw ghostwriting as an act of cowardice. "Actually," I said, guilt and irritation wrestling in my throat, "I'm on deadline. I should go."

Haley said, "Oh." She laughed, sarcastically. "I see you're still punishing me."

"No, work is just crazy. It's a crazy day."

She didn't say anything. I wanted her to feel better, but I didn't want to relent. I reminded myself our estrangement was her fault this time (she'd published an op-ed that included a description of what had happened in high school). "I'll call you again soon," I said finally.

She still didn't say anything.

I found myself trapped, waiting for her to speak. The urge to apologize cycled up again, and again I reminded myself not to relent. I closed my eyes. I had nothing to apologize for. I held the phone away from my ear and took a deep breath.

And then I realized what she was doing. Silence is the oldest trick in the interview book.

"Haley, stop it," I said.

"What?" she said.

"You're being quiet so that I'll keep talking, aren't you," I said. "I know that trick. I'm not falling for it."

"Oh, I meant to tell you!" she said. "I found a couple of our old home movies. On VHS."

It was just like Haley to switch from one trick to another; the abrupt change of subject was just another way to keep me talking.

"They were in the attic when I cleaned out Mom's house," she went on. "And they are *wild*!"

I remembered the movies we'd made in middle school—back when we were brand-new friends. Ghostly white-paint handprints on the wall of Haley's little brother's tree house; watery oatmeal, dyed with green food coloring, for a vomit special effect; two girls collapsed in a rec room, laughing so hard we couldn't breathe.

"I totally forgot about those," I said.

"Me too! They're amazing. I've watched them like eight times already. They're such a weird mix of childishness and sophistication, like you can tell we were taking ourselves really seriously, but also we were, what, thirteen?"

"Eighth grade," I said. "Yeah."

"I found the scripts, too. I really want to do something with them. I'm thinking of using them in a film. Right? Like, *A Portrait of the Documentarian as a Young Girl*."

It was yet another tactic, trying to get me to brainstorm. Haley would never stop trying to suck me into her work. Ever since the Teen Scene column she had wanted to write about me when we were eighteen; or her senior thesis film, a documentary short about rape culture in high school.

"Or maybe something about how horror movies shaped our feminism?" she was saying.

"I'm sure you'll figure something out," I said. "I gotta go."

She was silent again.

"I'll call you soon," I said.

I was about to hang up when Haley said, "Alice. We were friends for *twenty years*. Are you really going to just . . ."

I sighed. "Your math is a little off," I said. "We lost those years in high school, and to Q."

"Well, I like to round up."

"I do have to go," I said.

"Hey. Alice."

"Yeah?"

"I really miss you. I wish we talked more often. I know it's hard with you being abroad, and I'm so busy, but—let's try to keep in touch? Can we try to keep in better touch?"

I stood for a minute in the suburban sunshine. She was right: I was punishing her. And why? I didn't trust her anymore. I understood why she had written the op-ed, and I knew that she had not actually stolen my story—she had written only about her experience—and I knew also that my anger was grounded not in that betrayal but in years of exhaustion; I was tired of her constant encouragement to tell my story; being cold to her wasn't going to change any of that. I wondered what I could say that would be both gentle and true. "I miss you, too," I said, finally, and then I hung up before she could say anything else.

I went back inside, turned my phone off, and started writing Fox's introduction:

> I used to be afraid of everything. As the youngest (and
> skinniest) of three boys, I learned fear from a young age.

At last, the writing was going well. I didn't stop for two hours; when I finally stood up, and stretched, and opened my email, I had a note from Haley.

> I'm sorry I always say the wrong thing somehow, I hope you
> know I'm always here for you.
>
> Anyway—I thought you might want to see the actual scripts.
> From our old horror movies, I scanned them for you, and the
> PDF is attached.
> xo

The attached file, labeled "Sister Wife Productions," was a scanned document containing scripts for the movies, typed on my dad's electric typewriter years ago. I glanced through the document, marveling that we had gotten the formatting right. I remembered that we'd asked the school librarian to order the script for *Reservoir Dogs* for us, telling her it was about the SPCA. I chuckled at the bravery of the girls we used to be (and Haley still was), then felt a stab of pain and quickly closed the document. I left it on my desktop to read later. I was on deadline, I told myself; it was a question of discipline, not my feelings about Haley.

I muscled my way through the writing as the hours passed and the coffee shop crowd changed—the young mothers and middle-aged women ceding space to groups of teenagers looking for a place to flirt in the evening. I was still writing when the teenagers went home and were replaced by other people like me, working on our laptops; eventually the baristas turned the chairs upside down and swept us all out. I finished in the guest room at my parents' house and sent the introduction to Fox five minutes before midnight, then went to bed in my clothes, too drained to even brush my teeth.

I woke up the next morning to an email from Fox. *I love it, you're hired*, he said. *When can we start on the whole book?*

3. Final Draft

A few weeks later, back in Spain, we did our last interview. By that point we'd talked for hours, and I'd written nearly forty thousand words in his voice. Any warmth I'd felt toward him after our first interview was totally gone; I was more than tired of him, and we still had another ten thousand words to go.

We did most of our interviews in the evening, to accommodate the time difference with New York. That night I took my laptop out to the patio to look at the stars while we talked.

> **10:00:00** . . . work is nutso these days, it's really insane. I don't know how I'm going to get through the next two weeks, honestly. But. Yeah. But that's why I'm glad to have you! Writing this for me. It's been great to work with you.
>
> . . .
>
> You're blowing smoke. Which, I guess, is what I pay you for!
>
> . . .

Isn't it half of the reason to hire a ghostwriter, getting an ego massage?

. . .

10:00:30 Why?

. . .

For me it's the opposite. I'm not a good writer, I don't care. It's flattering to have someone listen to you talk for—what, we've been working together three weeks now, we've done how many hours of interviews?

. . .

10:01:00 Like ten hours! Jesus. Anyway, yes, let's wrap this up, I don't want to take up a bunch of your time today. I feel like I've given you a lot of great stuff to work with.

. . .

10:01:30 Yeah? Did we say that?

. . .

Oh. No, I don't know, I feel really confident. Seriously, don't worry too much about it. I believe whatever you send me will be great, the book is going to be great.

. . .

10:02:00 You're a really good writer. I almost can't believe it, what you sent me yesterday was incredible. I can tell they're

my words, but you make them sound so—I don't know, they
sound actually good!

. . .

So I was thinking we could just cut the last two chapters.
Cut them out.

. . .

10:02:30 Yeah. I'll be honest, I thought this book was going
to be faster.

. . .

I just feel like, let's not stuff a bunch of extra stuff in just for
the sake of it. Don't worry about your fee—I'll still pay for
the whole word count.

. . .

10:03:00 Yeah. Short and sweet. Get right to the
point. . . . My readers are busy, too. Plus that's easier for
you, then.

. . .

10:03:30 Yes!

. . .

Right. We can do that. Like, what do you need?

. . .

Right, right, so yeah, that's easy, I can give you that right now: So the anthropology of fear is, modern life makes fear build up in our bodies, right?

10:04:00 I think of it like smokers and black lung. Modern man so rarely experiences real danger—and I mean real like italicized *real*—so we have no idea how to handle our fear. Hundreds of years ago our ancestors had real things to be afraid of. Italicize that. Saber-tooth tigers and shit like that.

. . .

10:04:30 Okay, thousands of years ago. Ha, you're probably right. I'll get an intern to fact-check this.

The point is our ancestors were afraid of real things, they knew what to do with the fear. Avoid the tiger, get away, and then you don't have to be afraid anymore.

Today, we live pretty safe lives. So when something sparks fear—like someone shoots up a movie theater in a suburb somewhere—we don't know what to do with it! So we just hold on to it. And it changes our brain chemistry. We never experience the release of fear.

10:05:00 Fear has to be released. Just like you have to sweat when you exercise, you have to let go of your fear after you've been afraid. By the end of this book, the reader is going to learn to physically release fear.

. . .

10:05:30 Physically releasing fear, so anyway, right, I'm not saying you have to put yourself in real danger, you don't have to go get eaten by a saber-tooth tiger.

Nothing? Okay, I thought that was funny. Anyway, I'm not saying that, I'm saying that you have to experience your fears. Then you can let them go.

. . .

10:06:00 Well, it's simple. "Fear safety" is both the concept that there is safety in fear—that we cling onto fear as a kind of security blanket—and the mandate to avoid fear at all costs, to actually fear fear instead of to fear letting go of fear. Right? It's a double meaning.

Is that clear now?

. . .

10:06:30 No, it makes sense. What I mean is that you have to train yourself to fear safety, you have to rewire your brain chemistry to run screaming away from anything that feels too safe or comfortable, because then you'll be motivated to always do the thing you're scared of, then you'll be able to really change and grow. So yeah.

. . .

I don't think so. People will get it.

. . .

10:07:00 I've gotten a lot of good feedback on it.

. . .

Cool, I'm glad you like it.

. . .

I'm gonna be happy no matter what you do. Please don't kill yourself over this. I mean—I don't mean that. That was a bad joke. I just mean, you know what I mean, right?

. . .

Thank you. Yes.

. . .

10:07:30 So what else do you need from me?

. . .

More stories? Like from my life?

. . .

I feel like I've been talking about myself for—well, for ten hours now! What a blowhard.

. . .

10:08:00 I'd have to think about that.

. . .

Yeah, the basement fungus story! I love that one.

. . .

A different one?

. . .

There was this thing in my hometown that's pretty crazy. We had a serial killer.

. . .

Me, too! I'm so fascinated by serial killers. That's a fucked-up thing to say, isn't it? It's gross to be interested in murder.

. . .

10:09:00 Yeah, I see your point. Like looking at what you're afraid of can help make it less scary. Still, I don't know if it's right for the book. Maybe you can tell me, though. I think it just shows . . . I don't know what it shows. But it affected me.

. . .

Maybe that's it: it's about how modern life builds up fear—because I grew up in a middle-class suburb, you know, your basic suburbia. Super safe! But a woman was murdered.

10:09:30 A burglar broke into the house and knocked out her husband. And her body turned up in a dumpster behind

a church, cut into fifteen pieces, which I remember
specifically because I was like—where are those cuts? Even
if you cut at every joint . . .

. . .

Anyway, the point is that it turned out her husband was the
murderer. He'd done the exact same thing with his first
wife, like ten years earlier. The cops there believed his story,
the cops in my hometown would have believed it, too,
except—

. . .

10:10:00 What did you say?

. . .

No. No, it was something else. I actually can't even
remember. But I know the story I'm telling you is different
than what you're saying.

. . .

No. Where?

. . .

10:10:30 That's weird. No, I grew up in Florida. In Florida.
What are the chances? Hey, shoot, can you hold on? I've got
another call.

. . .

I hung up.

I stared at Richard Fox's avatar on my screen—a circle-shaped picture of his face that showed up whenever he called. It was too small to make out his features; I saw only dark eyes and a wide smile. There was a tight feeling in my chest getting tighter. I slammed my laptop closed as my body tightened up around a buried thing I didn't want to know. I went inside and put on my running clothes.

Running is the only thing that has ever worked for me. Thirty miles a week the only reliable cure for despair. Looping long courses through parks and city streets, I amaze myself—the indoor kid who always got a stitch in her side, who was always skipping gym class. I never knew you could learn to endure. Until Haley taught me to run. She came to see me the summer after senior year, found me puddled in depression and a sweatshirt, and took me to the track.

That night I made it out of my apartment and down to the street and started to run. The city was crowded with people making their way to dinner, families still out playing soccer in the parks. I sprinted as fast as I could, but the tight feeling was still there, and Richard's voice was still in my head.

> I know the story I'm telling you is different than what
> you're saying. . . . I grew up in Florida.

. . .

I ran all the way to an overlook near the top of Montjuïc and stood looking out at the Mediterranean. I'd run too fast. My heart was going to explode. I did the leg stretches Haley taught me; I did the breathing exercise Haley taught me to slow my heart. I wondered if she'd been right all along. *If you don't control your story, your story will control you.* I always thought she had no idea what she was talking about. The salutatorian and track star, the golden child who'd never really suffered. How did she know what would help me? But here I was, panting above the city, still running from a story I thought I'd escaped long ago.

I couldn't run anymore. I walked back down the mountain, through the shadows of the park. I passed passionate young couples wrapped up in each other on benches. I passed a gaunt man sleeping on cardboard. I came to the end of a long, curving sidewalk path and reached the street. I walked home, picking up a pack of cigarettes on the way. When I got to my apartment, I finally opened my computer to search for a picture of Richard Roth, a boy who drove me home from a party in high school one time.

I found him in the archives of my hometown newspaper. He was "Teen of the Week." I'd never seen his picture before; I'd always avoided yearbooks and local news articles like this one; I'd never wanted to see him. Now here he was, a wide smile in a school portrait with a marbled gray background. I opened a new window and searched for Richard Fox, the entrepreneur. I saw the same wide smile. I closed my laptop and went out onto my patio and smoked all of the cigarettes.

ALL NIGHT, and all the next day, I dreamed about revenge.

I would meet him in a city park. He would plunge a long knife into his own belly to show me that he was sorry. He would die with apologies still gurgling out of his throat, his body bowed down at my feet.

We would meet at a museum, and I would be the one who plunged the knife in his belly. He would fall to his knees bleeding, asking why I couldn't just let it go.

Or we'd meet in the lobby of an old hotel. As we talked, a ghost would slip out of a painting on the wall. "You're blowing this out of proportion," Richard would say, as the ghost crept up behind him. "You're being crazy," he would say, as the ghost wrapped its fingers around his throat. He would die before the EMTs arrived. The heart attack would be so severe a vessel would burst in his throat.

In some of my fantasies, he would apologize. In others he wouldn't say anything, but in his eyes I would see the moment he realized I was going to kill him, the moment he realized he had brought it on himself. And when the cops came to pick me up, I would tell them what had happened, and they would understand, too.

But that's where my stories broke down. Telling the cops; telling anyone; because who would believe me? What Richard had done was too insane, too horrific, to imagine. If it were a movie you wouldn't believe it. It would have to be a documentary.

The idea arrived like that. Simple, and fully formed. I had the evidence—the interview tapes—I would make a documentary about Richard. Haley would help me.

I bought a plane ticket that same afternoon, using money Richard had paid me. I was so frantic and skittish I accidentally checked the box saying that I would carry explosives and hazardous liquids and guns.

Haley shouted when I told her the news. "You're coming to New York? Really?"

"I'm hoping we can see each other," I said. "I need to talk to you about something." Already I was feeling hopeful. Maybe the movie would start a new chapter in our friendship. A creative project that would bring us back together, like the horror movies we made in eighth grade.

"Shut up," she was saying. "See each other, no, come on. You have to stay with me! Alice!"

Visions of Q loomed—hearing that I was in town, banging on Haley's door. "You moved last year, right?" I asked.

"Yeah, I can't wait for you to see it. I can't believe it," Haley said. "I'm so excited. Stay with me forever!"

She was laughing, joyful, and I smiled despite myself. I had forgotten how good Haley could make a person feel; her confidence was infectious. Plus, Q wouldn't know her address. It would be okay.

"Does this mean you're done being mad at me?" she asked.

"We'll talk," I said.

4. Odd Job

The text message said: *Urgent job. Come ovr.*

But it's your old friend Richard, and "urgent" is relative in Richard terms. Richard lives on Mott Street, which, from your basement in Brooklyn Heights, is either a short subway ride or a long walk. After the rough night you had, you decide on the walk. You like to cross the Brooklyn Bridge by foot once in a while, get a new perspective on things.

You get to Richard's building, a historic-building-cum-luxury-co-op, all carved stone and heavy iron bars on the door. You push the button for Richard's apartment and wait, rolling out the cricks in your neck—the stubborn bastards—and then you notice movement across the street.

You look over and see a bearded man standing near the alley. He's a big guy, and he strikes you as suspicious—hanging out in an alley at seven o'clock in the morning. You decide to ignore him. You remind yourself you're not paranoid anymore.

And anyway just then the speaker crackles, delivering Richard's voice in a blur of fuzz and pops. It's impossible to know what he said.

"It's the pope," you respond, knowing Richard can't hear you, either. That's just how it's always been between you two. The buzzer, at least, groans at your joke.

Inside you find Richard's apartment door cracked open. You knock as you push your way inside. "Richard?" you say.

From the foyer you hear the sound of running water on dishes and NPR. The early morning sun is bright through the large windows, stretching and yawning into the hallway. There's a faint floral smell, maybe hand lotion; you get the feeling there's a woman in the apartment somewhere.

"In here," Richard says, and you come around the corner and see him standing barefoot in a pair of jeans and an undershirt in front of the sink, rubbing a frying pan under the running water. Even this early on a Sunday morning he looks powerful, with his teeth buffed near radioactive white and his dark hair slicked back, like Al Pacino playing the devil.

You pick a coffee mug up from the table; there's a half moon of red on the lip.

"She break your heart?" you say, putting it together: the open door, the smell of hand lotion, and Richard in his bare feet, cleaning up a breakfast that nobody ate. You assume she's gone already.

"Nah," Richard says. He turns and takes the coffee mug out of your hand and puts it in the sink, then pours two fresh cups. "You know my heart is made of pure steel," he says. You both sit down at the table.

"Sure," you say. "Like my dick."

"And your anal beads," Richard says, grinning.

"But you didn't call me over here at dawn for girl talk," you say.

"No, I did not," he says. He leans back in his chair, holding his coffee mug on his stomach with both hands and staring down into it. He does not move or look at you as he says, "Do you remember that girl in high school?"

You immediately think of Haley Moreland.

"I've always meant to look her up," he's saying. "I've always felt bad."

"Wait. The private school girl?"

Richard nods, sighs, and rubs his face.

You haven't thought about that in years. You can barely remember it now; you were frequently drunk in those days; but what you do remember is not pleasant. You remember a leather couch, a room hung with diplomas, lying on your back until you were sober enough to drive. You remember the scandal, the accusations against Richard. But that was so long ago.

Richard stands up to pour himself more coffee. He puts the coffee-pot back on the stove and then puts both of his hands against the counter, as if bracing himself. "Nick, I'm very freaked out," he says. Then he turns and looks at you seriously. "It's Haley Moreland."

And Haley, already hovering at the back of your mind, rushes in like a gutshot bullet, her long, thin runner's legs forever just out of your reach. "What about her," you say. You worry about what your face is doing, a teenage wave of embarrassment surging red over your cheeks. That stupid fear of a crush revealed.

Luckily Richard isn't paying attention. He's looking at something several inches above your head. You hear a beautiful alto voice: "Good morning." You turn and see a woman leaning against the frame of the door to the kitchen. Zaftig and blonde, wearing a shirt that is obviously Richard's.

"I'm Nick," you say. She frowns at you, then frowns at Richard; clearly she wasn't expecting company.

"Nick is a colleague. He's my consigliere," Richard says.

"What's that?" she says, suspicious.

"You've never seen *The Godfather*?" Richard looks at you with his eyes wide in mock scandal. "Nick, she's never seen *The Godfather*!"

He turns away from you, back toward the woman. You look at her and realize how young she is, with a pang that is both jealousy and disgust. "Emma, you need to see *The Godfather*!"

Richard crosses the room, walking toward Emma; as he passes the table, he pauses, reaches over, and grabs a stapled pile of papers. He shoves the pile into your hands like he's throwing it in front of a bus. "Read that, Nick. I'll be right back," he says. Then he's across the room with both of his hands on the woman's hip bones, half-following, half-steering her out of the room. "I'm so sorry, Emma, but I have to work this morning . . ."

His voice fades into a murmur in the hallway. You get a crackle of pangs for bright sunny mornings and women and not having to worry about money. You look down at the paper and see the name *Haley Moreland* listed on the top, on the letterhead of a company called Sister Wife Productions, and the anachronism of high school memories in your New York life is so weird you can barely read. *Women's Fiction* says the title at the top of the page. *A film by Haley Moreland.*

You stare at the first page. It's a letter to someone named Cheryl, asking for money. You read the words *family foundation* and *commitment to gender equality* and *project in development,* wondering what this has to do with anything, until you read that *a group of boys assaulted Moreland's best friend, Francesca.**

You follow the asterisk to the bottom of the page and learn that **The survivor's name has been changed to protect her identity.*

You start again at the beginning, and gradually understand what this is:

> Francesca has never known what actually happened that
> night. Charges against the perpetrators were dropped,
> denying her not only justice, but truth. Now, fifteen years
> later, an uncovered trove of childhood movie projects brings
> Francesca and Haley back together. Collaborating, they begin

to assemble the evidence—home movies, news reports, and found footage—and piece together a collage of what happened in high school.

But just as Francesca is catching a glimpse of some kind of closure, through a strange "coincidence" she gains access to hours of audio recordings—interviews with one of the perpetrators himself. Now a grown man, haunted by guilt but unwilling to confess, the perpetrator's testimony reignites Francesca's anger and makes her question whether closure is possible. The sum of these parts, WOMEN'S FICTION will be a complex film that challenges our conceptions of high school rape culture, justice, and what it means to make amends.

"Emma was an intern at the company." Your head snaps up as Richard comes back into the room. He's got a smile on his face like he's just peed in the pool. "That's not totally gross, is it? I mean, she's not an intern *anymore*. I know it's a little bit gross, but it's only a little bit gross, right?"

You hold up the sheet of paper with Haley's name all over it. Richard's face falls. "What the fuck is this?" you say.

"A grant proposal," Richard says, sitting down with his face in his hands. "Moreland is fundraising to make a movie about me."

"I didn't know the private school girl was Haley's best friend," you say.

Richard shrugs. "Haley always was an ambulance chaser. But anyway, I don't even think it's the actual girl."

Some old piece of heartache dislodges from somewhere deep in your body. It floats around your bloodstream. You feel sad and old. You made this choice years ago; you chose Richard over Haley. Why is he bringing her back to you now?

"I need to stop this film, Nick," Richard is saying.

You flip through the rest of the stapled pages—more writing, spreadsheet budgets, printed pictures, nothing you understand. "How did you get this?"

"My old buddy Ed is on the board at the foundation."

"This says she has 'damning recorded interviews.' 'Hours' of them. Who'd she interview?"

Richard shakes his head. "Might have been Max."

"Shit," you say. You'd long forgotten about Max. You drink your coffee and try to imagine him at thirty-three—eyes still weed-shot, the same sarcastic smile on his face. "I figured he'd be dead or in jail by now," you say. You watch Richard's face tighten and fall and you realize that you're right.

"When?"

"Two years ago. Drunk driving."

"Shit," you say again. "But why would Max talk to Haley?" You're stalling—you don't want to give Richard an opportunity to ask for your help on this. You know that's why he invited you over. You don't want to help Richard on this. "And—Richard, what would Max even say? You never actually touched that girl."

Richard looks away. "I don't think she talked to Max. Like I said, I think she's making this all up."

You look at the paper again. *The film will protect Francesca's anonymity, while giving her a platform to finally share her truth.*

You cringe. *Platform* is the kind of thing Richard says. And here Haley is asking for money from a buddy of Richard's who runs some kind of foundation for women. You push the papers across the table. You don't want anything to do with this.

"So what are you going to do?" you ask.

"I called you," Richard says, pushing the papers back at you.

. . .

You met Richard when you were thirteen. Back then Richard was a real sad sack: the Jewish kid who kept kosher in an otherwise Episcopalian suburb, the last to claim he had lost his virginity, the winner of an award from the English department for his sensitive interpretation of *A Farewell to Arms*. You and he were both on the lacrosse team, but you all used to say that Richard was only *on* the lacrosse team, not *of* the lacrosse team. Now you realize that you were all just jealous. You could always tell Richard was on his way to somewhere better.

It turned out to be Princeton. Then a year backpacking through South America. Then the tech start-up, which he sold five years later for an influx of cash so big you can't bring yourself to remember the exact number.

That's not true. You remember the number: seventy-five million dollars. Richard's company is worth seventy-five million dollars because it cleans embarrassing stories off the internet for a yearly subscription fee. Richard calls it "reputation management." In public, he is a valiant champion of privacy rights in the digital age. In private, he shares his own deeply personal story, how he changed his name from "Roth" to "Fox" to escape the internet results of a false accusation that has dogged him since high school.

Richard was the first person you called two years ago, when you were getting sober and doing the steps, making amends with everyone you'd ever hurt. You guessed that Richard would be the easiest, and you were right. He jumped at the chance to meet you for a beer (and a seltzer for you). You had to insist that he let you do the whole apology thing. "No need!" he kept saying. "No need!" Before that, the last time you and Richard had seen each other, you punched him in the face because of a spilled beer. In other words, you'd been what you used to call a *real pussy dick*. You felt lucky that Richard forgave you at all, let alone so easily. The two of you spent the rest of the night drinking beer (and seltzer) and catching up, and if it wasn't exactly like old times, you still felt relieved talking to someone who so genuinely believed in water under the bridge.

Later, when you moved to New York, your old friend smoothed your way. You moved into the basement of a house Richard owns in Brooklyn Heights, for which you pay just nine hundred dollars a month in rent. It's not a legal rental—the basement has no windows, and it flooded once after a heavy snowmelt—but the upstairs apartments each go for four thousand dollars a month. You feel like you've got a deal. Plus you could never afford the security deposit or pass a background check anywhere else.

He offered you a job at his company, too. But you turned it down after you went in for lunch one day and found the office filled with alert young men with great-looking haircuts. Compared with them, you felt like an elderly drunk coming in to ask for change. You got a job at a temp agency instead. Now you do a lot of paper shredding and data entry; now you work mostly in closets. The pay is not great, and the work is inconsistent, but it's the only job you can get except bartending, and you can't trust yourself to bartend. You're resigned to your fate. Until you pay back Lindsey. Afterward you'll go back to school and dream bigger.

Once in a while, though, you do an odd job for Richard.

The jobs are definitely "odd." You get why Richard wants an old friend for them. Like, sometimes you book a private room at a strip club and arrange with the manager for Richard and some other men to arrive and leave through the back door of a neighboring restaurant. One time you posed as a programmer and went to a job interview at a competing company to gather information. Once, dressed as a food delivery guy, you hid a recording device in a conference room.

These jobs are why Richard introduces you as his *consigliere*. It always makes you squirm. You're more like Richard's hit man, except a lot less cool. But you never complain. Shame is a part of your penance. Plus, Richard fucking pays. While the rate varies, as a whole Richard's odd jobs are responsible for most of the four thousand dollars you've given Lindsey so far.

But this time you shake your head. "I can't do it."

"I know you can do it," Richard says. "Nick, this is what I'm always saying: you have to *believe* in yourself!"

"Thanks," you say. "That's not what I meant."

"So what, you're too busy?"

You roll out your neck, annoyed. "Can't you kill this? You founded a company that basically does this exact thing for people."

"That's what makes this story so perfect. Any guy gets accused, whatever. But a guy who founded a reputation-management company? This would go viral. More than viral. This would go nuclear viral."

He's overreacting, as usual. "You're overreacting," you say.

"Name your price," Richard says. "Literally anything. I'll pay you anything."

"I'm not going to blackmail anyone."

"Stop saying it's blackmail. It's not blackmail."

"You're asking me to dig up dirt on Haley and then give it to a journalist to write a damaging story about her so the movie won't get made."

"That's just what journalists do! Don't be so melodramatic." Richard gets up and pours more coffee.

"You didn't do anything," you say. "I don't understand how this can be such a big deal when you never even touched that girl."

Richard wails. "You don't know how optics work."

YOU DON'T AGREE to do anything except think it over.

You take the subway home, stopping for a dollar slice at the pizza shop on your corner. You eat standing up, looking out the window. You can see Richard's logic—there is no way to prove that nothing happened. The only thing you can do is prove that the premise of Haley's film is questionable. Which it is, since nothing happened.

It's not like you think Haley is a bad person. She's just angry. And Richard made one very good point: This isn't Haley's story to tell. It seems like Haley is just doing it to further her own career.

And you're worried about Haley's *feelings here?* says Richard's voice in your head. *Are we friends, or what?*

You think about taking a walk to the promenade, but it's a beautiful, sunny day and there are too many happy families pushing strollers and chasing toddlers down the sidewalk. You miss Katie.

You go back to your basement and take off your left shoe. There's a hole in your sock. You wiggle your big toe through it. You're a goddamned bum.

Then you take off your right shoe and catch a little flash of white on the bottom. You look closer. It's Kicker, stuck to the heel. Most of the glitter has rubbed off, but you can still see the little red beret and the stupid smile on that dumb dog face.

When you thought you'd lost the sticker outside of that bar last night, you'd taken it as a bad omen. The sight of it now, stuck on the bottom of your shoe, breaks your heart.

You call Richard.

Richard doesn't even say hello. "Tell me your price."

You take the amount you still owe Lindsey and double it. You've seen Richard negotiate and you know he always cuts the opening bid in half.

"Twelve thousand dollars," you say. "If you give me twelve thousand dollars, I'll do it."

"Done," Richard says, and hangs up.

5. Private Eye

There's a new chime over the door at the Happy Pancake Diner. It sounds like you just got the answer right on *Jeopardy!*, and you smile. You've decided you feel good about this job.

That's why you're at the Happy Pancake, after all. It's your favorite place in the city. You rarely eat meals out; mostly you're on a regimen of peanut butter sandwiches, dollar slices, and Nip Chee. Sometimes Richard treats you to barbecue or oysters. But about once a week— when you're either very happy or very sad—you go to the Happy Pancake Diner in the Village and have a milkshake.

Today you sit in your usual booth in the corner, with your back to the wall. One of the waiters comes over and looks at you levelly. You order, and he starts to walk away.

"Wait," you say. He stops and looks at you. The check in your pocket— your half up-front—makes you feel extravagant. "Make it a malt."

You lean back and spread your arms out like you own the place. The Happy Pancake Diner always makes you feel like a man.

As you wait, Haley's films keep swimming up in your mind. She made a short documentary in college, and then a feature called *Truth Booth* in 2010, but you couldn't find them anywhere—they weren't

streaming and the DVDs weren't at the library. So instead you read
what you could. You found articles about her work; press releases
about grants she'd been awarded. You'd read the press kit for *Truth
Booth*, which described how the film was made: Haley retrofitted a
camper van into a soundproof video studio, then drove it around
picking up men on the street—imitating *Girls Gone Wild*—and bully-
ing them into reading memoirs of rape survivors, in the first person,
directly into the camera. Apparently it made most of the men weep.

In all of the articles about Haley, you recognized pieces of the girl
you knew in high school; you saw her confidence, her self-assurance.
But you weren't prepared to hear about her genius. A month before
Truth Booth came out, a short preview piece in *The New Yorker* called
Haley a "rising star" on the "fringes of Hollywood" working to create
"radical experiments into the very meaning of empathy." You got a
sharp kick of jealousy reading that.

But then you started reading the actual reviews.

People *hated* Haley's movie. Words like INFURIATING and DYSFUNC-
TIONAL and DEEPLY MISGUIDED appeared in more than one headline.
The reviews were positively gleeful. One called it "a piece of trash."
You shook your head, amazed at the journalist's viciousness. "It's a
case study in modern feminism gone awry," he'd written. You'd noted
his byline—Willem Connor—then got in touch with him.

And here he is. Willem Connor walks into the diner just as your
malted milkshake arrives. He's tall and trim, with floppy brown hair
and a pair of red glasses that make him look smart. He looks like an
actor playing a journalist. He smiles when he sees you, walks over and
shakes your hand. "Nick Brothers. Good to meet you."

He doesn't want anything to eat. "I'm fasting," he says, putting a
hand over his belly.

"Fasting?" you say. "That's interesting, I've never heard of that."

Then you spend a while listening to him talk about the details of this baffling diet.

You are very patient; you ask thoughtful questions. "But you don't care," Willem says, suddenly realizing.

"No, it's fascinating," you say, but you've overshot. You laid it on too thick, and he's embarrassed now, uncomfortable; it's going to take some finesse to get him on your side. "But, let's get to business."

"Okay: Ed Brand said you have a lead about a filmmaker?" he says. "It was all very mysterious."

You nod. Ed Brand is Richard's old buddy, a powerful guy. You asked Ed to connect you to Willem; Richard is staying out of the details.

"I don't feel great about this whole thing," you say. "So I'm sorry, but I'm not going to tell you everything today," you say.

Willem is taking out a notebook. "Whatever you're comfortable with."

"This is off the record, right?"

Willem writes OFF THE RECORD in big letters across the top of a blank page, then turns it around to show it to you.

"Thanks," you say.

Willem bows his head, pretends to doff a hat. He's not really taking this seriously.

That's fine. He will.

"So," you say, "the first thing you need to know is that Haley Moreland and I were high school sweethearts. She was the first girl I ever loved."

This is true. Sticking to the emotional truth is one of your secrets to lying well. Willem nods despite himself—sympathetic to first love, charmed by your "openness."

"Haley reached out to me a couple weeks ago and asked if she could interview me for a documentary film she's making," you say. "Do you know her work?"

"Yes," Willem says. (Of course he does—you picked him because he does. You're just getting him to voice agreement with basic facts. It's another of your secrets to lying.)

Willem clears his throat. "I wrote a piece for *New York* about her first film, actually." You wonder if throat-clearing is Willem's poker tell. He's being so cautious about that bad review.

"So you know Haley can be pretty strident," you say. "Which is why I didn't want to be in her movie."

Willem picks up his pen. "Are you thinking Haley is going to accuse you of something?"

"No, no. She wouldn't do that to me. Plus, if you know Haley's movies, you know—she doesn't tell her own stories. She uses other people's."

Willem makes a quick note.

"What I'm worried about is, a friend of mine from high school, Max Platt, died two years ago. I think Haley's new film is going to center on a false accusation against him."

You explain the whole story. It's a story that makes sense: How Haley always hated Max. How she spread an accusation against him in high school—using some other girl. A typical sports-star witch-hunt. Charges were dropped. It was fifteen years ago. But now Max is dead and Haley is trying to revive the old charges. You still care about Haley, but you also care about the truth.

Suddenly Willem is writing a lot, in a tight and expert handwriting you can't read. You sit and wait. Patience is part of being a good liar. It's a bit painful—lying is a craft you honed through years of hiding your drinking from people you love—but it is nice to exercise competence.

Willem, still writing, says, "Who's the woman she's working with?"

"What?"

He looks up. "You said she's making a movie with a girl she knew from high school. Is it the girl who made the original accusation against Max?"

"Oh," you say. "The private school girl." Wait. Nick. Don't you know her name? "Right," you say, stalling.

It's true. You don't know her name. And you're shocked you haven't thought about this before. But you play it cool. You shake your head and spread your hands, a gesture like—*who fucking knows?* You say, "I don't know. Apparently Haley isn't going to use her real name. So how can anybody know for sure?"

Willem puts his pen down and folds his hands. "This is a big story, Nick. Can you prove it?"

You pretend to hesitate. Finally you say, "I have proof. But I'm not sure . . . not sure I can give it to you." You look Willem in the eye; he's nearly standing up out of his seat in anticipation. "I want to be sure I can trust you."

This is your last and best secret to lying well: make the other person feel they have to prove themselves to you.

Willem clears his throat, and you know you've got him. "I understand," he says.

"I can tell you're a good guy. I just want to think it over for a day or two. Haley still means a lot to me. I want to make sure—you'll treat her fairly?"

Willem holds up three fingers. "Scout's honor," he says.

AFTER WILLEM LEAVES, you text Richard, asking for the private school girl's name. Then you stay in the diner to finish your milkshake.

Of course Willem is going to try to talk to Haley. He'll probably call her today. You wonder whether she'll agree to an interview. Haley must hate Willem, of course, but also, she isn't afraid of anyone. You admire that about her. She might be brave enough to take him on, actually give him an interview. You're curious to see what she does.

But it doesn't matter whether she talks to Willem or not. It's the fact of his interest that matters—the threat of bad publicity. It should only take a couple of days of digging to find something embarrassing about Haley; as you've learned from Richard and his company, most people are not well protected from this kind of thing. Whether you get it by pulling her police records, hacking her computer, or talking to ex-boyfriends, you'll find something. Then you'll show it to Haley, and she'll do whatever it takes to make sure you don't show it to Willem. It's blackmail, you know, but you've decided that's better than Richard's version—where you give the damaging information to Richard, and he uses it to destroy her career.

You leave a portrait of Hamilton on the table and stand up and straighten your jacket. Things are going exactly as you planned.

But walking out of the diner, your phone chimes with a text from Richard. *I don't know her name*, it says. You're surprised; during the investigation she was kept anonymous, but still, everyone knew her. You assume Richard put it out of his mind long ago, wanting to move on. And for you, it's the alcohol, so many names drowned. You walk out the door, under the same door chime, but now it sounds too bright, falsely cheerful, like an airline steward explaining a two-drink limit.

ON THE SIDEWALK you turn right, on your way to the bank. After that you'll go to the library. You're not meeting your connection at the police department until tomorrow. In the meantime maybe you can find the private school girl's name on LexisNexis, in some article from your hometown paper, or an old school record. If you find her name, you can ask your police connection to pull her police records, too.

As you get to the corner you notice a short guy waiting for the walk sign going west. You slow down and watch him. He's looking both ways, like he's about to cross the street. But he doesn't cross. The walk sign clicks on and he just stands there.

You clock his black jacket and baseball cap, dark sunglasses. He's shorter than you, maybe five-nine, and so stocky he barely has a neck—his head just swivels on those broad shoulders as he looks up the street and then back. Your heart races. He's up to something.

"Sorry," a woman in a leather jacket says, sharp and sarcastic, as she bumps your shoulder on purpose, and you realize that you're standing in the middle of the sidewalk, not moving—doing the exact same thing as the guy you're suspicious about.

You remind yourself not to be such a freak. You're not hallucinating dangerous men anymore. You walk past him and move on.

The bank is in one of those old buildings with two-story columns and a set of wide stone steps leading up to the entrance. You feel a little like Rocky Balboa, jogging up those steps. You haven't had a financial situation that called for a visit to an actual bank since you opened your checking account with two hundred dollars last fall.

The teller doesn't blink at the size of the check. She seems almost bored; you get the feeling she's comfortable around a lot more than six thousand dollars. But she can't deposit anything directly into Lindsey's bank account. She has to deposit it into yours, and then make a transfer.

You drum your fingers. "So it'll arrive by Friday?" you say. You're dreaming of Lindsey calling you, weeping tears of joy. Or better yet: coming directly to your apartment, with Katie in her arms, both of them hugging you. *We always knew you could do it!*

"By Friday at the very latest, Mr. Brothers," the teller says, with a sweet smile. You feel better. It's been a long time since someone called you mister. Walking out through the golden doors of the old bank, there's a spring in your step. You have a feeling you're on the right track.

Then you freeze.

The same guy is standing on the sidewalk. He's facing away from you, calmly smoking a cigarette. Same black baseball cap. Same black bomber jacket. Same squat body. No neck.

You step to the side, tucking yourself half-hidden beside one of the big stone columns. Your mind races through your choices. You could turn around and go back into the bank and hide. You could try to sneak away.

But you know what? Fuck it. Why don't you just be a man?

You walk down the steps. You head directly toward this guy with no neck. *Let's do this, No Neck*, you think, gathering your nerve.

When you're halfway there, he turns, slightly. It's an aimless movement, he's just kind of pacing as he smokes. He glances in your direction. He doesn't seem to notice you in particular. But then he turns away and starts moving very casually out of your path. *Too casually.*

You try to feel angry instead of scared. You check your surroundings. There's a hot-nuts cart a few feet away that smells delicious. At the blocked intersection someone lays on their horn, then other drivers respond, like cicadas, a call-and-response that stretches three blocks north. It's just a regular day in New York. Everything is fine. You walk right up and stand beside No Neck.

He raises his eyebrows at you over his sunglasses. You say, "Hey— can I bum one?"

No Neck shrugs and digs a pack out of his pocket, hands it to you along with a lighter. You light a cigarette and hand both back. "Thanks," you say.

"No problem," he says.

You smoke next to him for a second, looking around. "Cigarettes are expensive," you say. "And I know people who bum cigarettes are jerks. So I really appreciate it."

No Neck shrugs again. The horns have calmed down; the cars are moving again. A fire engine wails from somewhere east.

"You work around here?"

"Yeah. Over there," he says, pointing vaguely, not looking at you. He tosses his cigarette to the curb. "Have a good one," he says, and walks away.

You watch him walk all the way into the bank.

You trash your cigarette and start walking north. You try not to walk too quickly. You try to prove you're not afraid. But ten blocks up you can't help it: you stop in the doorway of a shuttered nail salon and open your flip phone, like there's something interesting on the screen you need to check. You glance around the block, looking for No Neck.

You wait a full fifteen minutes. There's nobody on the sidewalk with you except for eight million people, going about their business. No sign of No Neck.

You shake your head and put away your phone. Then you walk the rest of the way to the library and start looking for the private school girl's name.

6. A Witness

Two days later, you arrive at Quinn Mitchell's building. You have to double-check the address, because it's fancier than you expected—there are sleek, dark potted plants in the lobby, and the elevator is polished the same shining black as the walls. You catch your reflection in the polished black doors. A heavyset guy with bloodshot eyes looks back. You look away.

On the seventh floor, a woman answers the door. She gives you a big smile; she has a charmingly wide gap between her two front teeth and her hair is bright red. "I'm Nick," you say. "I spoke to Quinn on the phone?"

She says her name is Kyra and invites you in. "I won't shake your hand, I'm fighting a stomach bug," she says, over her shoulder, as you follow her into a living room lined floor to ceiling with books. When she disappears into the kitchen to get you a cup of coffee, you wander over to a big bay window. You look down at a gorgeous view of Prospect Park.

This isn't what you were expecting. You were expecting something dingy, dark, because you found this address in the private school girl's police records. "Records for Alice Lovett," your old buddy in the police department said, handing you a razor-thin manila envelope. "There was nothing on Moreland."

Your stomach sank. "This is it?" you asked. You'd spent three hours at the library, combing through school archives and interviews and articles in the local paper; in the end you'd found her name in a list of "special thanks" for Haley's first film—*To my sister wife, Alice Lovett,* Haley had written, and you'd remembered the name of the production company for *Women's Fiction.* You were extremely proud of this detective work, and you'd been expecting more of a payoff than a thin manila envelope from your cop friend.

But when you got home and looked at what was inside the envelope, you understood that it was plenty.

You turn away from the window as Kyra comes back into the room. She hands you a warm mug. "Quinn is just meditating, he'll be out in a second." You take her invitation to sit down on the couch, but she stays standing, as if ready to bring you another cup of coffee at any moment.

"So, you're a journalist," she says, her hands clasped together in front of her heart.

"To my mother's great disappointment," you say.

She laughs skeptically. "What are you investigating?"

"I don't know if I should—" you start.

You're interrupted by a voice from the doorway to the bedroom. "He's investigating Alice."

You look up and see a tall, heavyset man about your age standing in the doorway. Quinn Mitchell. He's got straight blond hair tightened up into a bun on top of his head; he looks kind of like Lee Marvin—big features, rough skin.

"You don't have to hide anything," Quinn says to you. "Kyra knows all about my ex."

"And I don't want to know anything more," she says primly, walking toward the back room. "I'm going to leave you two to it and lie down for a bit."

As she passes Quinn he stops her, putting a hand on her hip and peering into her eyes. "Are you feeling okay?" he says. You feel a flash of envy at the familiarity of the gesture, the obvious intimacy of a secure couple.

Kyra nods. "Just a little queasy." She kisses Quinn on the cheek, gives you a friendly wave, and disappears into the bedroom.

Quinn crosses the room in three long steps and shakes your hand. His grip is huge; it's like shaking a clutch of bananas. "Thanks for agreeing to talk," you say.

"Of course," he says. "Alice is important to me. If you're writing about her, I want to make sure you have the truth."

Quinn sits down across from you. You pull out your notebook and flip to a blank page, doing the whole journalist routine. You clear your throat, look up at Quinn. Then you stop: the man has a look on his face like you're a doctor with bad news.

"Are you okay?" you ask.

Quinn catches himself and laughs. "Yeah, I'm fine. I just—I can't stand the suspense. I haven't heard from her in years." He stretches his arms out, flexing his fingers, then sighs and says, "So, how did you get my name again?"

Yesterday in your basement apartment you slid open the manila envelope and spread out three pages of police records on your floor. They were photocopies, one of an Incident Report (one page) and one a Restraining Order (two pages). Both were dated 2011. Both were fairly brief and not that interesting. Like, the Incident Report didn't seem like much of an incident:

> On DATE listed above OFFENDER-1 was observed
> by WITNESS-1 trespassing in a residential lobby
> building.
>
> Offender-1 was mashing the buttons on the building
> elevator, attempting to override the keypad system.

Alice Lovett was OFFENDER-1, and her offense was PUBLIC INTOXICATION. The notes were brief, and there was no arrest.

The second document was a restraining order taken out by Alice Lovett. You can barely look Quinn in the eye as you say, "It was a restraining order against you."

"That was retracted immediately," Quinn says, immediately.

"Right," you say. You realize you've folded your hands together between your knees; you lean back and tuck your left hand back into your pocket (it's just easier if people don't see it). "I'm not here to accuse you of anything."

Quinn nods. You wait.

"Go on," he says finally.

"I was hoping you could tell me a little bit about your time with Alice. You lived together, right?"

"Is this about drugs?" Quinn says.

You try not to look surprised. You remember the Incident Report. You clear your throat and nod in a noncommittal but inviting way. "What can you tell me about that?"

Quinn sighs and leans back. "Alice has a problem," he says. "I love her, and I tried to save her. That's my problem, my shrink says. I always think I can save people." He shakes his head at his own folly.

"What kind of drugs?" you say.

Quinn has his face in his hands. You wait for a minute. Finally he says, "Pharmaceuticals." Then he sits back up and looks at you, sighing heavily. "This is just so painful," he says.

You close your notebook and wait. It's like Quinn's first AA meeting; he's going limp with the relief of confession.

"I protected her. As best I could. She got the restraining order to punish me. She was vindictive like that. Self-destructive. She was so self-destructive." His story is long and rambling. You don't need to take notes. It's an old story, and the gist is familiar: Quinn would find a new way to save Alice, but it would only work for so long before she would slide back into her addiction. "To be honest, I'm waiting for the day when someone comes to tell me that she's dead," he says.

You marvel at how thoroughly this man's heart has been broken.

"She's still alive," you say gently.

He brightens. "You know where she is?"

"I don't."

"But you're looking for her?"

You make a noise that passes for assent. Quinn nods eagerly. "I can help." He stands and walks over to the bookshelf, pulling down a wooden file box. "I have her medical records."

You say, "You have her medical records?"

"Just copies," Quinn says, coming back with a faux-leather folder clutched against his chest. "I thought I should save them for something like this."

Quinn thrusts the folder at you; the name ALICE is embossed in gold on the cover.

He leans over your shoulder as you flip through the folder. "She was a hypochondriac. Hysterical. Drug seeking. We'd go to the doctors and they would pull me aside and warn me, say that she needed real help."

There are about four dozen pages, loose lines of confident doctors' handwriting, printed on sheets of white and blue and pink paper.

"You made copies of her medical records?" you say.

"This is the most important piece, I think," Quinn says, pulling out a pink sheet dated 2011. He holds it up for you to read. "This doctor—he's explicitly recommending counseling. Says that there's no physical explanation of Alice's symptoms, suggests she has Munchausen syndrome. It's a mental illness where people harm themselves to get attention."

You remember an old rumor. "Was she bipolar?" you ask.

"She's something," Quinn says, shaking his head.

You stare at the sheet. It's hard to believe this is the girl Haley has decided to make a movie about. You've read about Haley's career. You know she's turned radical. But you can't believe she's this brazen.

There's a loud *thump* in the back bedroom. You jump.

Quinn smiles at you for being startled. "It's just Kyra," he says. "She's had a flu."

"Oh," you say.

"At least she's not an addict!" Quinn says and gives a big laugh to cue you to laugh, too.

You laugh to be agreeable. "But is she okay?"

"I'm sure she's fine. I'll just go check on her . . ." Quinn stands.

"Right." You hold up the folder. "I can take this?"

"On one condition," he says. He walks you to the door with one meaty hand on your shoulder. "When you find her, you'll tell me where she is?"

IN THE POLISHED ELEVATOR you look down at the faux-leather folder, the word ALICE printed expensively across the top. You think about poor Kyra, competing with this madwoman in Quinn's attic. You're glad to be out of that apartment; something about it gave you the creeps.

You walk slowly through the lobby and then outside. You want to think for a minute. You head down the hill and then along Eighth Avenue. You pass joggers, nannies and mothers pushing strollers, people sitting on their stoops talking on the phone. You pass a small, expensive-looking restaurant with its windows open, people talking over glasses of white wine, and for the first time in a long time you feel no jealousy. Relationships are wounds, and alcohol is a Band-Aid. Today you're ready to scab.

You get to Grand Army Plaza. You find a bench, grit your teeth. And then you call the number listed on the letterhead of Haley's grant proposal.

As the phone rings you look around at the arch, the fountain. There's a woman attached by six leashes to a fan of dogs. There's a handful of people on the other benches, each of them bowed over their phone screens like deep heroin nods.

Your calls goes to voice mail. *You've reached Haley Moreland,* the recording says. Haley's voice doesn't sound familiar, but what were you expecting after fifteen years? *I never check this mailbox, just text me . . .* she's saying, and then you see a man in a black baseball cap strolling slowly toward the fountain. You stand up quickly. The voice mail machine goes *BEEP!* and you jump two inches straight up in the air. You hang up the phone. You take two steps backward. You duck behind a bench.

Between the slats of the bench you can see the fountain and one of the six dogs, straining to jump into the water. You take two panting breaths, and then the man strolls into your field of view. You recognize him with a firm certainty.

It's No Neck. He walks through the park slowly, his head swiveling around on those broad shoulders. Like he's looking for someone.

Like he's looking for you.

YOU'RE RUSHING BETWEEN the rows of cubicles in Richard's office, panting and panicked, when you run directly into a woman rushing in the opposite direction.

"Sorry!" You double take on the woman's face, riveleted with makeup. "Are you okay?" She closes her eyes, dodges around you, and hurries down the hall. Three steps later you realize: it's the woman from Richard's apartment Sunday morning. "Emma?" you say, turning around, but she's already gone.

You feel sorry for her and whatever you assume Richard has done to break her heart, but as you walk toward Richard's office—a glass prism in the corner, sleek and polished like a spaceship—you can't help thinking she should have known what she was getting into.

Richard doesn't look at you when you open his door. He's got his feet up on his desk and he's looking through a binder, flicking sheets of paper like cigarettes into a gutter.

"Fucking legal," he says, baring his teeth.

"Someone's following me," you say.

Richard slams the binder closed and throws it onto his desk. "Fucking legal department is always up my ass." For the first time he looks at you. He immediately points at the leather folder under your arm. "What's that?"

"Listen: A guy is following me. I've seen him three times now. The same man. Wherever I go, he's waiting for me."

"Why would someone be following you?"

"I have no idea. It's freaking me out. Does someone else know about the job I'm doing?"

Richard nods, slowly, and takes his feet off his desk. "Okay," he says.

"I don't know who would know, nobody else knows, right?"

"Sit down," Richard says, leaning forward, his hands folded like he's praying.

You sit in the black leather chair facing his desk, at the edge of your seat. "I can't imagine what anyone would want from me, unless it's about this—"

Richard interrupts. "You know you've done this before."

"No." You stand up and start pacing. "I'm sober now."

"I'm not saying you're hallucinating . . . again . . ." He lets the last word hang.

You realize you're pacing and make yourself stop. You roll out your neck, sit back down. Your entire body has been tense for the past forty-five minutes—sprinting out of the plaza, spending your last sub-way fare getting here, looking over your shoulder the whole way. You know you look crazy. But the urgency you feel in your body is so thick right now you want to punch something. You clench your teeth and say, "It's never been like this before."

Richard walks over to a bookshelf on the far wall. All of his books are fake; he pulls a panel of red leather classics forward and down and track lighting clicks on automatically. It's a minifridge filled with clear and brown liquids. He cracks open two slim cans of seltzer and hands one to you. "I believe you, Nick," he says, sitting on the front of his desk like a sympathetic middle school teacher. "But it's gotta be just a weird coincidence."

"This guy following me is super sketchy," you say.

"This is New York!" Richard says.

You inhale and exhale. You chug some of the seltzer, then burp.

"Give it another day." Richard is shrugging. "If you see this guy again, call the cops."

"They won't believe me." You suppress a second burp.

"Then call me, and I'll hire you a bodyguard."

You look at Richard. He smiles and spreads his hands wide, backlit heroically by a view of lower Manhattan. Here in his glass office and his easy confidence, burping like an idiot, you can see your panic from a little distance. "Okay," you say. "Okay."

Richard claps you on the shoulder and walks back around behind his desk. He puts his feet back up and his hands behind his head and says, "Now tell me about that other thing."

You give him the high level. The police records, the medical file. How Haley has gone too far; how she's exploiting a drug addict. How you believe she's just gotten carried away, that she'll be embarrassed, that she'll correct course as soon as a rational observer explains it to her.

As you talk, Richard starts vibrating in a carefully controlled way, like a panther. "Now I just need to get in touch with Haley," you finish.

Richard points at the leather folder. "So that's it?"

You nod.

His eyes widen in excitement. Then he throws his head back and howls, kicking his heels on his desk like a happy baby. "Fuck, you got her medical file! You animal! You did it, Nick!"

"Don't look so gleeful," you say. "This whole thing is icky."

"I know. It's very icky." Richard grins. "Can I see the file?"

"Absolutely not."

Richard begs, but you're not budging. You remind him that he's paying you to take care of everything. "I'll let you know when Haley agrees to cease and desist."

But Richard is shaking his head. "You cannot show that to her."

"How else do I blackmail her?"

"If she sees that file, she'll figure out a way to kill it. No, Nick, you have to take it to Willem right away. Get him to run a killer story on her. Make sure no one ever believes her work again."

"No. That's not what we agreed. I won't do that to Haley."

"You're being sentimental."

"I'm handling this. Didn't you want to stay out of the details?"

Then something occurs to you.

Richard says, "You're enjoying fucking with me like this, aren't you."

You say, "How did you know his name is Willem?"

Richard freezes for just a hair of a second. "What?"

"The journalist. You said, 'Take it to Willem.' But I never told you his name."

"Did I say Willem?"

"You said you wanted to stay out of this."

Richard grins slowly. "You got me." He spreads his hands wide, like he's showing all his cards. "I asked Ed Brand. I had to know. I've been dying of anxiety over here."

You look at him steadily. He looks back at you with the same steadiness, still smiling. He folds his hands in prayer. "Please, Nick, just give me that file. I'll give it to Ed to give to Willem. You can be done here, take the rest of your fee and go home."

"I'm doing this my way." You stand up.

Richard stands up, too. "No," he says.

You pause, frowning. "You really are freaked out, aren't you."

"You have to let me take that folder."

You walk over and put your hand on the doorknob. "Don't worry," you say. "Just give me one more day."

You look at each other. Richard looks like he's thinking hard. You figure he's just worried. "You can trust me," you say.

Richard nods, frowning. "Okay," he says. "Fine." He turns away and picks up the phone. Already on to the next piece of business.

"I promise it'll be done tonight," you say.

"I know," Richard says, just before you close the door.

IN THE BUILDING LOBBY you run up against a tide of young professionals, all sweeping back to their offices with cell phones and cups of coffee. You grapevine four steps to the left, getting out of the way, then lean against the wall and pull out your phone. No new messages.

You write a text to Lindsey: *Notice anything special in your bank account?* You think about it for a second, then delete it. It's better if Lindsey finds it on her own. And anyway, you're just stalling.

You call Haley, and get her voice mail again. "Hi, Haley," you say. "This is Nick Brothers. From high school? Out of the blue, I know. I know you said you don't check these messages but it's worth a shot.

I'm in New York, and I just had the weirdest coincidence—anyway, I need to talk to you. Call me back."

You hang up the phone. She's not going to call you back. You'll have to do this the old-fashioned way.

You check your watch—it's a little after four, so you'll have to walk fast. You're going to go to her building, the address on her film company's letterhead, and catch her when she leaves for the day.

You pass through the revolving door and head west, imagining what it will be like to see her again. Will she still be angry at you after all these years? She's mad at Richard, but maybe she's forgiven you; maybe she'll feel nostalgic for old times. You think about asking if she remembers smoking a joint with you in the backyard of somebody's house. You imagine her laughing. *We were just kids!* You look up and realize you're approaching Broadway; you went the wrong way. You stop abruptly and turn around—and there on the sidewalk behind you is No Neck.

You make eye contact. His eyes widen in surprise; clearly, he wasn't expecting you to turn around. He blinks and turns quickly away, cutting right. He strides through a sliding glass door and disappears into a Duane Reade.

You turn and run.

You pass the Brooklyn-bound subway entrance and cross the street, heading for the northbound side. You dodge a group of teenagers giddy with shopping bags and swing around a row of periodical boxes. You tap dance down the steps of the subway station, swipe your card, and slam into the turnstile.

"Insufficient fare," says an old man behind you.

You look both ways and then swing yourself over the turnstile. The old man hollers righteously, but you ignore him and keep moving, toward the sound of an approaching train. You jog downstairs and across to the opposite platform, Brooklyn-bound. You make it just in time, barely clearing the closing doors.

The train is mostly empty. There's a young couple in matching sweatshirts holding hands. Three men in MTA uniforms. A woman reading a book. An advertisement for a personal-injury lawyer. *If you see something, say something,* says a recorded voice. You take a seat. You're okay for now. You decide to go back to your apartment; you can go see Haley tomorrow; right now you need to think.

You can't call the cops, and after what just happened you're not going to ask Richard. You have to figure this out if you're going to stop it.

No Neck appeared the day you met Willem. Did Willem hire him? Willem seemed like a straight shooter, but that could have been an act. Maybe he was suspicious from the beginning, and hired a tail to get the full scoop.

But journalists don't work that way. You know who does work that way? Richard. Following you is the kind of thing Richard would hire *you* to do. Except Richard trusts you. You've known Richard forever. And if he didn't trust you, why would he hire you in the first place?

The only thing that makes sense is the thing that scares you most. No one sent No Neck. No Neck sent himself, to reap some cosmic debt.

After an eternity, the train doors open at High Street. You get out and hurry up the long escalator. You're panting by the time you reach the top, but you don't stop to catch your breath. You push yourself forward, straight out of the station and across the concrete park toward Cranberry Street, on your way to your basement apartment.

Then a voice from behind yells, "Hey!"

You turn.

It's No Neck. He's running at you, full speed. Panic sweeps you up like a big wave. You spin around to run, and at the same moment No

Neck dives, tackling you with a shoulder to your kidney, a sick stab-
bing pain, and you fly forward and down and your head hits the

YOUR PHONE IS RINGING.

Your face is cold.

Your phone is ringing again.

You blink your eyes open. The light is dusky, gray. A bus roars past.
You're in a park. You're on a bench. You sit up slowly and fish your
phone out of your pocket.

"Nick?"

It's Haley—you recognize her voice this time. Your stomach flips
over itself.

"Hello?"

You should say something. "Hullo, Hah-lee." You sound like you've
got a mouth full of peanut butter.

"I got your message! Seriously out of the blue, Nick!"

"I thought you didna check tha," you say.

"What's that?"

A coughing fit overtakes you. You hold the phone away from your
ear and cough into your hand.

Haley is talking when you bring the phone back to your ear. "—to
hear from you, but this is an absolutely insane time for me. I'm in the
early stages of a new film, it's a really important one to me, and I really
don't have time right now."

There's a splatter of pink in your palm; are you coughing up blood,
or did you lose a tooth?

"Maybe this summer?" Haley says. "Can you call me in a couple
months, and we'll find a time for coffee?"

"Waith," you say. "You won' talk da me?"

"No, no, it's just, this month and next are super insane, with this project, I barely have time to sleep. I'm sorry. But this summer will be better, we'll talk this summer."

You can't believe it. Haley is blowing you off.

"Shoot, Nick, I have another call, I have to take this—I gotta go. But it's great to hear from you! We'll catch up this summer," she says.

"But—" you say.

But she's already hung up.

You stare at your phone. "You bith," you say.

You try to stand up. Your right kidney disagrees. You sit back down. Your kidney thinks you should go to the hospital. Lindsey would tell you to call the cops. But what would you say? And you don't have insurance for the hospital.

You check your pockets: keys, wallet. You run your tongue around your teeth: nothing loose, just a big gash inside your bottom lip. You touch your head: there's a bump on your forehead, about the size of a golf ball. Except for that, and your kidney, everything seems to be in order.

"Okay," you say out loud, and with both hands and teeth clenched you stand up again, and then you realize that Alice's medical file is gone.

7. The Truth

Your neighbors are fighting again.

You've never seen these people. You've only heard them through the walls, you know them only by the loudest words they hurl at each other: *childish* and *goddamn you* and *bitch*. Your neighbors have money, their apartment has windows, but they, too, are alone.

You spend an hour trying to write a text message to Lindsey. You describe what happened a hundred different ways, hoping for her sympathy—mugged in the park! attacked in the park!—you delete a hundred versions. Finally you hit SEND: *Just wanted you to know I'm thinking about you and Katie.*

At midnight the walls of your apartment shake when one of the neighbors slams out the door. You get up and piss, and thank God there's no blood. You check your phone; no response from Lindsey. You wonder why Haley called you back so fast. She said she didn't check those messages. As the night thins into early morning you snap the pieces into place.

If No Neck were out for vengeance he would have killed you. If he were working for Willem he wouldn't have known to take the file; if he were working for Richard he wouldn't have attacked you.

The only thing that makes sense is that he was working for Haley. Taking the file benefits Haley the most.

Why else would Haley call? An hour after you get attacked? And she's calling just to blow you off? No fucking way. If she really wanted to blow you off she would have sent a text message. Nice try, Haley. She called an hour after No Neck attacked because she was obviously checking to make sure you weren't dead. It's the only evidence you've seen that she has any conscience left. You pace around until you realize that you're pacing, then you make yourself sit.

You get up and drink water straight out of the tap, your head underneath the faucet. You check your phone, again and again. You dream of bourbon, thick syrupy sleep, oblivion.

Finally you shower and shave, and at seven o'clock you're outside of Haley's office building, a cup of black coffee and three double doses of ibuprofen doing their job. For an hour you watch people pass, thousands of them, lucky bastards on their way to gainful employment. You can't wait to yell at Haley. You can't wait to tell her you don't need the file; you'll bluff, you don't care, you want to scare her; you'll tell her you have plenty to ruin her with. Even without the file, you now know the truth. You were going to let her off easy—but she upped the ante, and now you're going to ruin her.

Then she walks down the block and your knees go weak.

She looks just like she did at seventeen. Her hair is darker blond, but pulled back in that same high ponytail. She's wearing faded jeans and bright-red lipstick, and she's tucked into a cream-colored jacket as neatly as a thank-you card in an envelope.

You dodge through traffic across the street. You call out "Haley!" sounding like Bobcat Goldthwait. You clear your throat and jog, you catch up, you touch her shoulder. "Haley?"

She turns and frowns.

"It's Nick," you say. "You know: Go Spartans?"

Her eyes turn into dinner plates. You laugh. "Have I really changed so much?" You're fifty pounds heavier and a decade pickled in hard liquor, and you've got a black eye from where the lump on your forehead drained. You knew all of that five minutes ago—but now you see it starkly, reflected in the mirror of Haley's face, and she hasn't even seen your bad hand. "I know," you say. "I've changed."

Her mouth opens for a few seconds before she says anything. "Hi, Nick," she finally says, and then she smiles, bright and fake. "What are you doing here?" she says.

You laugh, a bitter bark. "You wanted to meet me for coffee!"

She blanches, confused. "What?"

"Oh, wait, my mistake. That's right, you said you *didn't* want to meet me. I must have been confused! Sorry, I've been having a hard time keeping things straight, ever since your goon gave me a concussion."

She takes a step backward. The frowning, confused fear on her face looks genuine. You're amazed at her acting skills.

"Don't play dumb," you say. "I *know*."

She takes another step backward. "I'm sorry . . . I have a meeting, I need to go meet a funder . . ."

"No, you have to talk to me. I read Alice's file before you stole it. I know *all about your movie*. I know the truth. The file doesn't matter. This isn't over. Your movie is dead in the water, Haley, okay?"

The fear on her face disappears, and she frowns deeply.

You've got her.

She says, carefully, "What do you mean, you know about my movie?"

"I mean I know everything," you say.

She studies you for a second. "Are you doing this for Richard? Did he send you?"

"Your conscience sent me," you say.

She looks around the street.

You say, "This time you've gone too far, Haley."

She seems to make a decision, nodding to herself. "Let's go somewhere and talk."

You follow her into a bodega on the corner. It's one of the nice ones, with a couple of metal tables in the back. There's a line of people getting coffee and breakfast, but all the seats are available. Haley chooses a table and you sit down across from her.

"So," Haley says, folding her hands. "Are you here to threaten me, or to offer me money, or what? What does Richard want?"

"It's not Richard's plan," you say. "It's my plan. I found out about Alice, and I think what you're doing is despicable. Making the movie is despicable enough—but then hiring some goon to follow me, to attack me, that was really beyond the pale."

She leans forward and slaps both of her hands flat on the table, interrupting you. "Nick! Listen to me. I have no idea what you're talking about."

"You don't know about your movie?" you say, narrowing your eyes sarcastically.

"I don't know about someone attacking you." Her face looks worried—worried for you—and suddenly you're a little worried, too.

"Just stop lying for once in your life," you say, petulantly.

She spreads her hands and shakes her head. "I don't know what to tell you. Who attacked you? Did you talk to the cops?"

You look at each other for a second. Your anger is draining away and embarrassment is creeping in. You'd expected her to cave by now; instead you're the one who sounds crazy.

"No," you say. "I didn't think the cops would believe me."

"Are you okay, Nick? It seems like . . . like maybe you need some help?"

There's a euphemism. You feel tears swelling up, clogging your sinuses. "I'm fine," you say. You sit up straight and clench your teeth. "Fine. Forget the goon. What matters is that you have to stop this movie."

She looks away and down, waiting for you to get yourself together.

You cross your arms and fight off the crying feeling. "You're hurting people. This is such a mess."

Very gently, Haley says, "How did you get involved in this?"

"Why couldn't you just let it be? The old rumors. The stupid accusations. You had to go drag them up, trotting out that poor girl for a movie."

"But Richard is the one who dragged her into this."

"Oh, so Richard's the one making a movie now?"

"Didn't he tell you?" she says.

You watch her, the tears hot and threatening right behind your eyes. You want to get up and run away. You wipe roughly at your eyes, and wipe your nose. Haley's eyes are spotlights.

She says, "Richard tracked Alice down, he reached out to her."

"What?" you say. In a flash you think of the fundraising document: ten hours of damning interviews. Richard said it was Max; Richard said he didn't remember Alice's name; but Richard didn't look you in the eye when he talked about it.

Haley folds her hands in her lap, looking down. "Alice is a ghost-writer. A few months ago she got an offer to work on a book project for a lot of money. She interviewed this guy for weeks, over the phone. She wrote a whole book for him. She had no idea who he was." She looks up and searches your face.

"It was Richard?" you sputter. "But that's crazy."

Haley's eyes widen and she spreads her hands. "It's *maniacal*."

"So the interviews in your movie . . ."

"Alice tapes her client calls."

"Oh," you say.

Haley frowns and leans forward. "You know about those interviews?"

You put your forehead down on the table.

"Did you see my grant?" she says, her voice a register higher.

You keep your forehead on the table as you nod. "You should be careful about where you fundraise," you say.

And then you hear Haley's phone chime.

You sit up and watch as she pulls her phone out and reads what's on the screen. Her face falls. She blurts out, "Oh, Alice!"

"What happened?" you say.

"I have to go," she says. "I have to make a call." She's gathering her things up to go, frantic, typing on her phone with one hand while pulling her purse onto her shoulder with the other.

You look around the bodega. "But I don't understand," you say. "Why would Richard hire Alice to write a book?"

Still typing, she says, "He was trying to pay her off without having to apologize. He wasn't going to tell her who he was, but then he slipped up. She came to New York and asked me to help her make a film about it."

"So you're not exploiting her," you say.

Haley looks up at you sharply and suddenly. Then she looks away. "I'm not so sure about that," she says. She shakes her head and goes back to typing some frantic message on her phone.

"I don't believe you," you say.

This time, Haley raises her head very slowly. She gives you a stony stare.

"Richard would have told me," you say.

"Can you imagine, Nick?" She stares at you, eyes wide, like she's waiting for you to react in some way. "Can you imagine what it's like to realize you've been talking to your rapist without knowing it?"

She just keeps staring. You don't know how to answer. You feel numb and confused. "But Richard never actually touched her," you say. "It was just a rumor."

"Fuck you, Nick," she spits, and stands up roughly, her chair scraping against the floor.

But you don't understand yet. You need her to explain things. You reach out and grab her wrist. "Wait."

She rips her hand away from yours. "Don't touch me!" she yells.

The sound drops out of the bodega. Everyone in line looks at you. You feel them hovering, ready to help, and they're not going to help you.

In the silence your phone starts to ring. Haley spins around and walks away. "Wait!" you say, as you fumble your phone out of your pocket. "I just want to—" The caller ID reads LINDSEY.

You answer, "Hey, Lindsey, hold on—" standing up at the same time, reaching for Haley, but then you run up against what seems like a dozen burly construction workers stepping into the line. They're crowding the bodega, blocking your exit.

"Nick," Lindsey says in your ear, and her voice is a warning.

"Just a second," you say. You duck your head and try to break through the crowd. "Could I just get through, excuse me—" you say, but the men ignore you. You watch, in the space between their elbows, as Haley bangs out through the bodega door.

"Nick, why is there six thousand dollars in my bank account?" Lindsey says. Your attention snaps back to the phone, your heart leaps. You sit back down in the chair.

"Yeah," you say. "I did it."

"Nick, you're not listening. You ruined my mortgage application!" Lindsey is screaming now. You hear Katie wailing in the background. "You ruin everything!"

"Wait, it's not like that," you say, and stand up too quickly. You bump into one of the construction workers from behind. He turns around and frowns at you, but you're focused on the phone. "I'm sorry, Lindsey, I can explain—"

"What is *wrong* with you, Nick? I *knew* I couldn't trust you," she says, and hangs up.

You stare at your silent phone.

"Asshole," the frowning construction worker says, and turns his back on you.

RICHARD ISN'T ANSWERING HIS PHONE. He's in the Brooklyn office on Fridays, his receptionist says. But then the receptionist at the Brooklyn office says he's in Manhattan.

You find him at his apartment in the early afternoon. "I know you're in there," you shout, banging on the door.

"Jesus, Nick," Richard says as he opens the door. "What happened to your face?" He's dressed in spandex and drenched in sweat, a towel around his neck.

"We need to talk."

Richard breaks into a big grin. "So—you heard the news?"

You push past him into the apartment. All you can think about is the liquor cabinet he keeps in the living room. You walk over and look at it longingly. Then you breathe and turn and sit on the couch. "I fucked up."

Richard is pulling on an old gray sweatshirt. It takes you a beat to recognize it, the heat-press number 36 cracked and peeling—his old lacrosse team sweatshirt. "What are you talking about? Haley's movie is dead, right? Ed told me it was dead."

"No," you say. "I fucked things up with Lindsey. Maybe forever."

Richard laughs in relief. "Oh! I thought you meant you'd fucked up the job!"

"She's not answering my calls. All I did was transfer her the money I owe her, I thought she would be impressed."

"I'm sure it's no big deal. Come on, Nick, this is a good day: You did it. You got Haley's movie pulled."

"I'm worried she'll take Katie away."

"I'm sure she'll calm down. Listen to me, Nick: Maybe you haven't heard? I just got off the phone with Ed Brand. You did it. Haley is calling funders with some crazy story about how Alice left New York suddenly this morning. It's a lame excuse; Alice left because Willem is on to her *mental health issues*. The movie is obviously fucked. I was so excited I had to bike twelve miles."

"She won't calm down."

Richard looks at you blankly for a second. "Oh, you're still talking about Lindsey." He sighs and pats his knees and stands up. "Okay, we'll talk about your problems first, as usual." He walks over to his liquor cabinet. "You don't mind, do you? I'm about to explode." He takes a shot of bourbon, then looks at you. "Do you wanna join me? Make an exception?"

You clench your fists and shake your head. He pours himself a second drink and walks back over to sit across from you. "Okay. What happened."

"I transferred six thousand dollars to her. I was excited about it. Paying off the rest of my support. I was thinking I'd get to start seeing Katie every week."

"And why is she mad?"

"Apparently she's trying to buy an apartment. An unexplained cash influx in her bank account sunk the deal, or something? *I* didn't know that."

"Oh yeah, shit, man. The mortgage companies are sticklers about bank statements. Unexplained cash is a doozy." Richard puts a hand on your shoulder; the smell of bourbon hits you like a blown kiss. "It'll be fine. If she's buying a place, she's stressed. She'll figure things out. Lindsey is smart. And she'll come around when she calms down."

"I don't think she will."

He shrugs. "Then you can sue her for custody."

You get a vision of Lindsey, weeping in court. You get a vision of her screaming at you. "I can't do that."

"This is your problem!" Richard says. "You wait for other people to do things for you. You've always been kind of a victim that way. You don't take what's yours."

You look at him steadily. "Also: you lied to me."

Richard blinks but keeps smiling. "What about?"

"The tapes in Haley's movie. It's you on those ten hours of tapes."

He blinks and laughs. "That's crazy!"

"Fuck off, Richard. I can tell when you're lying."

He keeps smiling, finishing his drink. He carefully sets the glass down, then folds his hands and looks you in the eye. "So Haley told you."

You nod. "And that's why you didn't want me to talk to her."

"No, I didn't really care if you talked to her. Like I said: she would have buried the file. It had to go right to Willem."

You lie back and put your hands on your face. You hear Richard standing back up; you listen to him walk back to the liquor cabinet.

You say, "Actually, I will take a drink."

"I figured," he says. After a minute, you hear the solid clack of the glass on the coffee table in front of you.

"I think you're overreacting," Richard says. "You're missing the big picture here: You solved this case. You pulled off an incredibly elegant job in, what, four days? This is a huge accomplishment, my friend. I think this is the start of a new chapter in your life."

You pull your hands off your face and look at the glass of bourbon. If you sit up, you can reach it. "You lied to me about those interviews."

"If I'd told you all that, you wouldn't have helped," he says.

You see Lindsey again, screaming at you in court. But now she's not yelling about child support. *You discredited a girl who tried to kill herself in high school?* she yells. *What is wrong with you, Nick?*

"I'll be honest. I wasn't sure you'd be able to find something," Richard says. "But you did it!"

"Why did you hire me, then?"

Richard smiles. "Because you're my oldest friend."

"But you didn't even trust me," you say. "You had me followed."

You watch Richard's face and know that you're right. You lean back and cover your face with your hands again.

"He was just an insurance policy. Listen, I'm sorry he gave you that black eye—he wasn't supposed to do that. I just had to get the medical file to Willem! You were going to take it to Haley, Nick—how naive can you be? If Haley had seen that file she'd have gotten a team of PR people to kill it in thirty minutes. No, we had to get it right to the press. And I tried to tell you that! You did half the job but you were too sentimental to finish. Think of it like teamwork." Richard starts pacing as he adds, "I really am sorry about the black eye."

You sit up and reach for the glass of bourbon. You hold it, looking at it, as Richard says, "I don't think you understand how important this was to me, Nick. You don't know how I've suffered this week."

"You didn't have to go find her in the first place." You hold the bourbon under your nose and inhale. The familiar smell floods you with queasy guilt.

"I felt bad, okay?" he says. You set the glass of bourbon back down on the table. You let it go. You stand up.

"Then you could have just apologized."

He spreads his arms as if for a firing squad. "I don't have anything to apologize for!"

Richard walks over to you. He puts both hands on your shoulders and looks you square in the face. "You were part of this, Nick," he says. You feel yourself tensing. Your fists clench. "I'm sorry, I know you feel bad now, but you'll get used to it."

You say to yourself, *Don't do it.*

"But think about it: In the long run, hasn't your loyalty always paid off?" Richard says.

You do it.

You catch him with a square hit in the center of his face. He yells in surprise and stumbles back, knocking into the coffee table; your glass of bourbon topples over, a brown stain blooming on the carpet.

Richard bends over, holding his nose with both hands. "Fuck!" he yells. He works his nose, then drops his hands by his sides and straightens. You stand looking at each other for a minute, stunned. Then Richard's eyes go dark. "You are such a deadbeat," he says, "even when you do something right you fuck it up." Then he lunges forward.

You both tumble over the couch and onto the floor in front of the liquor cabinet. You scramble on the floor, straining for a leg lock; you get a punch on Richard's rib, and he kicks a heel into your bad kidney. Finally you separate, scooting away from each other on your asses. You sit a few feet apart, panting.

Richard touches the blood on his upper lip. He laughs, a quick, bitter *ha.*

You don't say anything. You scoot farther back so you can rest your head on the wall.

"That was out of line," he says.

You close your eyes. You hear your phone beep in your pocket.

Richard says, "We can both apologize, right?"

You fish out your phone. It's a text from Lindsey.

> I have to cancel your visit this month. I'm sorry,
> Nick, but I have no idea where you got that
> money, and honestly I don't need your sketchy

shit right now. Please stop calling and texting.
I'll call you in a couple of weeks.

"This is a lot for me to say, because I'm really the one being hurt here," Richard is saying. "This is my life that was being ruined, okay? You're walking away with twelve thousand dollars."

You roll forward onto your knees, then get up to your feet. You waver slightly and hold the edge of the liquor cabinet. You look at your phone screen again. *Cancel your visit this month.*

"I know how to apologize. So: I was out of line," Richard is saying. You look over at him. He extends his hand, asking for you to help him stand up. You fold your phone into your pocket and close your eyes.

"Old buddy," Richard says, "seriously?"

You turn away and head for the door. "You're an asshole," you say—to Richard, to yourself—and shuffle out.

8. Black Eye

It's dark, Irish, and empty. Your favorite kind of bar.

The bready, soapy musk of spilled beer is almost primitively relaxing; you have to pee as soon as you walk in. The scattered graffiti in the bathroom brings on another wave of nostalgia—meaningless life advice, annotated in pencil over the urinal, hits you so hard you lean on the sink like you're already drunk. You look at yourself in the mirror. The blood drained out of the lump on your forehead is now brilliant black-purple under your left eye. There's dried blood crusted on your lip, split from the fight. You look like a monster. You turn away.

You head back out to the empty bar, happy hour stretching out ahead of you. The bartender is at the top of a ladder, pulling a box of wine down from overhead storage; he nods nonchalantly in your general direction, *Be with you in a minute.* You set your belly right up against the bar and lean forward like it's the railing of a ship. *Bon voyage*, you think.

It's your first drink in four years. It doesn't taste as good as you remember. It's not the glorious homecoming you were expecting. It's a little metallic. It's fine. But it's not home.

You take the second sip to dull the disappointment and to stave off the thick wave of guilt you feel rising inside. The second sip tastes a little better. Everything is better with lower expectations. You finish the rest of the glass of white wine in one gulp.

And so you're drunk later that night when you leave a long message on Lindsey's voice mail about impossibly high expectations designed to make you fail.

You're still drunk when you leave a short message immediately afterward: "Sorry sorry sorry, Lindsey. I'm so sorry."

You're still drunk the next morning when you stumble home to find an envelope slid under your front door with *No hard feelings old friend!* handwritten on it. Inside is six thousand dollars cash and a printed-out article from the *Times* with Willem Connor's byline. You crumple it up without reading it. You set aside three of the hundred-dollar bills—beer money—then dump the rest into your kitchen sink and light them with a match. They burn orange, smoke, and collapse. You leave the pile smoldering, glad your apartment has no smoke alarms. You carry your brand-new bottle of bourbon over to lie with you on the mattress.

You're still drunk when you wake up, late that afternoon, but you bring the bottle into the shower with you for good measure.

You're still drunk later, when you dial Haley's number. *I never check this mailbox,* she says, and the machine goes *BEEP,* and you don't know what to say. You hang up. You're still drunk when you call again, and again, but even on the fourth try you can't speak. You make yourself stop. You grab your jacket and the three rescued hundred-dollar bills and take the subway back to Manhattan. You want a milkshake. You make it a malt. When you're done you head for another bar. You're not sure where you're going. You're in the mood for something dark and desperate. You're just going to walk until you find it.

You're still drunk, so after a few blocks of stumbling, when you get the feeling someone is following you, you don't care. "Yeah, yeah," you grumble. "Come and get me, No Neck."

You amble east. People pass in both directions. The footsteps keep following you. "Fuck it," you say, finally, and you turn around.

You see a gigantic man. At first you don't recognize him. He waves, then crosses the distance to you in four quick steps, and his face clicks in your mind.

"Quinn?" you say.

"Where's Alice?" he says. He grabs both of your shoulders and kind of shakes you. His eyes are wide and wild.

"I don't know," you say, and step backward out of his grip.

"I read the article in the *Times*. She's in New York," Quinn says, taking a step toward you. "You have to tell me where she is."

You take another step backward before you realize you're emasculating yourself. You set your jaw and take a step forward. You put a hand on Quinn's chest and push him backward. "I don't know where she is," you say. "That job is done."

Quinn pushes you back. "I gave you her medical file. You were supposed to find her."

You see a couple people cross the street to avoid you. A stupid bar fight. You're not drunk enough for this. "I don't know what to tell you," you say, and start to turn. "I'm off the job."

But he grabs your shoulders and pulls you back around. You're amazed again at the size of his grip. "You were supposed to find her," he growls.

"I quit," you say.

The two of you look at each other for a second, searching each other's eyes. The street around you is empty. It's like the start of fight in a movie. But you're not getting into a fight with him—with his size, it would be suicide. You just want to be ready to dodge his punch.

He grits his teeth and you brace yourself. "It's not that hard to find a woman," he says.

"Then find her yourself," you say.

"I don't want her to know I'm looking for her," he says. "It's a surprise."

You take a step, turning away. "I said I can't help you. We're done here."

"I found *your* woman, no problem," he says.

You pause. "I don't have a woman," you say.

"Apartment H5," he says.

The world around you expands into an infinite, silent black space.

He says, "And the little girl, too."

The world zooms back, contracting to a very small, hot point.

"Don't you fucking touch them!" you scream, and you run at him. You're flailing wildly. Quinn catches your wrist and squeezes painfully. You scream and kick at his shins, but he easily holds you at arm's length. If you weren't flooded with adrenaline you would be horrified by his size and strength. Instead you just keep kicking at him. "Don't you touch them," you spit.

Quinn pulls you forward roughly, knocking you off your feet; he holds you up, puts his face right into yours. "You find Alice for me by tomorrow, or you won't ever be able to find Lindsey or the little girl," he says.

He drops you. You massage your sore wrists, for a second you close your eyes in pain; you open them just in time to see Quinn's punch flying toward your face.

It's a solid hit. You fall back against a parked car, the car alarm starts hollering. "Find her," he says, as your vision goes dark and sparkly, your inner ear swims.

You stumble in three directions and then fall back against the still-hollering car. You can just barely see him in the darkness. He's walking away, halfway down the block.

You want to kill him.

You push yourself off the car and catch your balance. You steady yourself. You touch the blood on your upper lip. You take a deep breath, and your vision sharpens.

You see Quinn at the street corner. He starts to cross without looking. He's almost hit by a passing truck. The truck roars past, blaring its horn; Quinn barely flinches, lifting his middle finger and continuing on. Like he wouldn't even care if he got hit by a truck. But maybe you'll push him in front of the next truck and then we'll see how he feels about it.

You keep seeing him holding Lindsey by the wrists. You can't even bring yourself to imagine him hurting Katie. And what about Alice? Or Kyra, falling down in his apartment. You shudder at all the thoughts of the harm this man could do. You push yourself forward. You keep a hand on your head for the dizziness. You walk as fast as you can.

Five blocks away, you're about ten feet behind him. You fall into step. He doesn't turn around, doesn't seem to notice you. You make your plans: You'll follow him to the subway entrance and push him down the stairs. Or you'll push him onto the tracks.

And then you see a metal hatch on the sidewalk, propped open. It's in front of one of those massage places with a waving cat in the window. It's on a dark, quiet block.

The moment takes on the intensity of focused attention; it happens the way you jump off a diving board. You don't think about it. You start to run. At the last minute you lean down and hit him with your shoulder. He grunts, surprised, and stumbles forward two steps and steps directly through the open hatch and keeps going.

You ricochet off of him, stumbling to the side. You see his head hit the edge as he falls. His neck snaps the other direction, his tall body collapsing like an umbrella through the open space and then gone.

For a minute you can't hear anything but the sound of your own breath.

You look around, staring at the night city. There's a couple half a block away on the other side of the street, holding each other so tightly they're like one big creature with four legs. There's an old drunk on the other end of the block, stumbling with his coat turned up. Otherwise the street is empty.

You take a step forward and finally look into the cellar. You see Quinn at the bottom of the steep metal stairs, his head resting on the bottom step and the rest of his body at strange angles. The floor under him is spattered with blood.

You turn and go. Like there's a rope attached to your chest. It takes you about three blocks to really understand what you just did. Then you walk a lot faster.

Time passes. You walk until your legs ache.

You didn't touch him, so you're pretty sure there won't be fingerprints. Quinn wouldn't have told anyone he was following you. Kyra might pick you out of a lineup, but there's no reason she would connect you to him tonight, no reason you'd be chosen for a lineup in the first place. And nobody saw.

You're going to get away with it.

The thought almost makes you feel worse.

You find yourself on the Brooklyn Bridge. That's good, you think. It's good to cross the bridge by foot once in a while. You have to step back from the streets and look at the city. It's all about perspective.

You try to remind yourself that you did the right thing. You think of Katie. You were just keeping Katie safe. Maybe Kyra, too. And whatever Quinn had planned for Alice—whatever his reason for wanting to find her—you're glad you stopped it.

The bridge is quiet at this time of night. You stop right at the peak. You look out over the city. You think of calling Lindsey. You want to let her know that you will always, always keep Katie safe.

And then you feel a surge of hope. You'll call Lindsey!

Not now. You'll wait until the morning, of course. You'll wait until you're sober. But for the first time in your life you understand what it means to atone for what you've done. You can't just expect Lindsey to forgive you. You're going to apologize to her. You're going to earn her trust. You're going to become the kind of guy who deserves to see his daughter once a week. You will always keep Katie safe.

And not just Katie. Quinn was dangerous, full stop.

With Quinn gone, how many more women will be able to get back to their lives?

EPILOGUE

BARCELONA

2015

Oh, Haley. I'm so sorry for the way I left New York. We had such a good week together, and then I left without saying good-bye. When you came to Barcelona six months later, I stood you up. Now a year has passed, and you still haven't given up on me. You're still sending me emails every so often, checking in. Few people get a friend as dedicated as you.

I'm grateful to have you, old friend. Even now that I know about the guilt braided into your loyalty, and the long-running apology you've never been able to say.

WHEN I ARRIVED IN NEW YORK, I felt sure I was doing the right thing. I walked into your apartment—the familiar poster of *Grey Gardens* on the wall, the familiar smell of cinnamon in coffee—and relief washed over me. I sat at your kitchen table and told you what had happened, how Richard hired me. When I finished, I stood up to stretch and my back cracked, so loud it made us both laugh. I knew I'd been right to come to you for help.

Of course you agreed to make a film with me. You were thrilled.

We started right away, taking long brainstorming walks, sketching out a plan for production. We planned to use found footage from the movies we'd made in eighth grade, old VHS tapes labeled with masking tape and Magic Marker (you'd bought a VHS player just so we could watch them). The movies were mostly unintelligible; our thirteen-year-old voices were too quiet to hear on the crappy camcorder microphone, and because we'd done all the edits in camera, our characters jumped around on the screen, defying time and space.

But they were a joy to watch. I saw, in those movies, the girl I used to be. A girl who thought she could act. Who thought she could be a witch, a police detective, or whatever she wanted. Who wasn't afraid of anything.

I fell asleep on your couch dreaming that, by making this movie with you, I could become that girl again.

We agreed that I would start by writing a narrative outline, a script-like document to guide the collage of a film we had planned. Meanwhile, you were going to fundraise.

You kept up your side of our plan. You shifted the schedules of your other projects and made time to write an excellent grant proposal almost instantly. You lost no time in sending the proposals to funders and started setting up coffee dates and pitch meetings. You were confident, competent, as always; you were sure of the story we were going to tell.

But I couldn't keep up my end of the bargain. It was too hard to write about Richard.

All week I sat at your kitchen table, unable to write. I plucked dead leaves off of your houseplants, and went for long runs, and bought myself nice pens and new notebooks, but nothing worked. I stared at a blank Word document, so overwhelmed with revulsion I thought I might throw up. I wanted revenge, I wanted justice, but I didn't want to write about what had happened.

Or maybe it was just that I couldn't figure out how.

. . .

EVERY NIGHT, OVER DINNER, I lied to you. I told you that writing was going well. I just needed more time, I said. If I told you the truth, I worried you would want to interview me, to *get the juices flowing*. I worried you'd offer to write a rough outline for me, *to get rid of that first blank page*. I worried you'd push me into one of the hundreds of ways you'd tried to get me to tell my story over the years. I worried I'd end up telling your version of the truth, not mine.

"Yeah, it's going great," I'd say. "I just need a little more time."

ONE DAY, WHILE NOT WRITING, I opened the document where I'd transcribed Richard's interviews. The text was so familiar it was almost comforting. How many hours had I spent among those words? I almost started typing them again. I slammed the laptop closed.

What if I never got Richard's voice out of my head?

MAYBE I COULD have done it with more time. Maybe I could have written the movie we imagined. Maybe I would have eventually broken through.

Instead, on Thursday afternoon, Richard sent me an email. The email was breezy, all lowercase.

just checking on you!

i hope you're not working too hard on this last chapter.

no matter what you do it will be great!

It had been ten days since our last interview. I'd assumed Richard had been silent because he was ashamed of what he'd done. I'd assumed he was avoiding me.

Actually, he just thought I was a fool.

That night you found me under a blanket on the couch. "It's a migraine," I said. "I need to just lie here and not move and not talk."

THE NEXT MORNING we left the apartment together. You were on your way to coffee with a funder. I told you I was going to a doctor you had recommended, who specialized in migraines. Afterward, you and I were going to meet up for lunch.

Instead I left New York. I haven't seen you since.

Because the truth is that when I left your apartment, I went to meet Richard.

He'd suggested a Mexican restaurant near the Meatpacking District, a tourist trap in an old building swathed in wrought iron.

He had chosen a quiet spot; it was ten o'clock on a Friday, and the place, just opened, was still empty. Two servers in black polo shirts leaned against their station in the back, joking with each other in Spanish. They gestured to indicate we should choose our own table. I walked to one near the door and sat with my back to the wall, my baggage resting at my feet.

"Thank you for coming," Richard said. "When I got your email yesterday, I can't tell you how I felt. I'm glad we have this chance to talk."

I looked around the restaurant—cheap swag from beer companies, neon signs and multicolored flags and a cardboard cutout of a pirate with a palm tree. "It's so empty," I said.

"That's why I picked it," he said.

"Afraid I'll make a scene?"

"I thought you'd want privacy," he said.

A waiter came by and dropped a basket of tortilla chips and a bowl of salsa between us. Richard looked up and said, "Thanks," but the waiter ignored him, walking away without saying a word.

I watched Richard. He was not the Richard you've been reading about in this book. Shorter, for one thing; shorter than his voice suggested. He wore a suit with no tie, the collar of his light-blue shirt open below his Adam's apple. He had broad shoulders and a baby face; he looked polished, like he had spent a lot of money on his health. But his hair was not slicked back, his teeth were not pointed. He did not know we'd been working on the movie, had not sent any journalists to stop it by blackmailing us. He was not the monster I'd been imagining all these years.

"I've thought about this for a long time," he told me. "I'm so impressed, again, that you're willing to talk, to give me this chance." He talked fast, and too much, just as he had during our interviews, filling up all of the space. "It hasn't been easy for me, either. I've been wanting to do this for a long time."

"Do what?" I asked.

"Well, apologize."

"Why didn't you?"

He gave a pleading laugh. "I guess I was too scared," he said.

"Fear safety," I said.

"I know," he said. "I know it was hypocritical."

He leaned forward and picked up a tortilla chip, unconsciously. Then realized what he was doing and put it back. He smiled, gestured vaguely at the chip. "Stupid," he said.

"So, are you going to apologize now?"

He started talking. It had happened in his late twenties. Over dinner, a dear friend confided in him that she had been assaulted in college.

Richard was plunged into a torturous guilt over what had happened to him in high school. It was awful, he said. He still believed he was a good person, despite the mistakes that were made. But it was awful. He had wanted to find me, and somehow make amends, but he didn't see how it was possible, until he got the idea to hire me. "I didn't want to bother you, dredge up old feelings, you know? But I wanted to see if you were doing okay. And I had the money, I thought maybe I could help you out, career-wise. I thought it would be like a secret gift," he said. "Like a guardian angel, you know?"

He almost smiled as he talked, as if forgetting himself, then, seeming to remember, he would look at me with an exaggerated frown, pleading for my approval. But even when he looked at me, I got the feeling that I was not really there. He was talking for himself. I could have asked anyone from the street to come take my place and it would have made no difference to him. I could have been a mannequin sitting in the chair.

"Can you excuse me a second?" I said. He stood up at the same time I did, like a gentleman. From the back of the restaurant I saw him checking his phone, distracted and frowning. Our meeting was one thing among many for him. I hadn't eaten anything all day, but still I vomited in the bathroom.

When I came back to the table he put his phone away and stood up politely. But I didn't sit down.

He looked down at his chair, wanting to sit again. "Are you okay?" he asked.

"No," I said. "Not at all."

"What can I do?" he asked.

"I can't stay," I said. "I'm sorry, but I can't." I wished I hadn't said *sorry*.

"What can I do," he said again.

I almost left. Instead I closed my eyes. I thought about you, Haley. You're always asking me, *When will you tell the truth?*

When I know the truth.

I opened my eyes.

"I want you to tell me the story," I said. "Just the facts of what happened. From the beginning. And then I'm leaving."

"Okay. Okay. But let's sit," he said.

I sat on the edge of my chair.

Richard cleared his throat, reached for a chip. I watched him dip it in the salsa and put the whole thing in his mouth, frowning and chewing. "I don't know what to say," he said when he had swallowed.

"Why was I in your car that night?" I asked.

"I was giving you a ride home." He shifted backward in his seat.

"I didn't know you," I said.

"You were with a friend of mine," he said. "You were dancing with him. At the party."

"No," I said, so sharply that Richard glanced over to see if the waiters were listening. I raised my voice even louder. "I want you to tell me the whole story from the start."

"I don't really remember much," he said.

"More than me."

He spread his hands and smiled, desperate. "It's so hard to talk about," he said.

"You could start with why you went to the party," I said. "Say, I went to the party because I wanted to find a girl to have sex with."

He frowned, not understanding.

"I went to the party because I wanted to get drunk."

Richard sighed heavily. "I wasn't that kind of kid."

"I went to the party because . . ."

"Kids go to parties," he said. "There's no reason."

"Tell me the story," I said.

He ate another chip.

I said, "I went to the party because all my friends were going. I went to the party because I had nothing else to do. I went to the party because I was . . ."

"Because when you were on the team, that's what you did," he said.

INT. MEXICAN RESTAURANT — PRESENT DAY

RICHARD eats a chip, composing himself.

He puts his hand over his eyes, shakes his head. Then he sighs, gathering his nerve, and starts.

                    RICHARD
          They called it "the party where we all
          get laid, even Richard." They gave me
          so much shit for not hooking up with
          enough girls.

INT. THE PARTY — 1999

A bunch of teenagers hanging around a living room. "Juicy" blaring on a stereo, kids laughing and taking shots.

TEENAGE RICHARD is standing against a wall, sipping from a red Solo cup. He is skinny, sensitive. Alone. He's wearing jeans, a black T-shirt, and his VARSITY LACROSSE JACKET.

RICHARD'S POV: A huddle of giggling girls are looking over at him, gossiping with their hands over their mouths.

They see him looking and then turn away, bursting into laughter.

Richard looks down, then at the ceiling, awkward.

                    RICHARD (V.O.)
          Actually, I wasn't hooking up with any
          girls. But I would never tell the team
          that.

INT. THE PARTY — A LITTLE LATER

Richard pours the rest of his beer down the sink. Just
as he turns, a DRUNK KID pushes Richard out of the way
to VOMIT into the sink.

Richard grimaces and walks out of the kitchen.

He's leaving.

                    RICHARD (V.O.)
          I was an awkward kid. It never seemed
          fair. Why girls should be the ones
          with the power to decide.

EXT. THE PARTY HOUSE, FRONT YARD — CONTINUOUS

Richard slams the front door behind him and heads down
the sidewalk.

                    RICHARD (V.O.)
          Guys have to keep trying; only girls
          get to say yes or no.

Richard stops as the volume of the party behind him
gets suddenly louder — someone opening the front door.
The door slams and the party music gets muffled again,
and there's the sound of a guy laughing, drunk.

Richard stops walking, rolls his eyes, and gives a
heavy sigh. He already knows who's behind him:

                    MAX
          Tricky Dick!

Richard turns. MAX is a big guy with small eyes. He's
got his arm around a GIRL, half-carrying her. They're
totally smashed.

                    RICHARD
                   (annoyed)
        I'm going home, Max.

                      MAX
        Give us a ride, man!

RICHARD's POV: Max stumbles off the front porch and
falls into the grass, pulling the girl down with him.

Richard watches her face as she tries to get back on her
feet. She pushes her long brown hair behind her ears.

                  RICHARD (V.O.)
        I just kept thinking . . .

INT. MEXICAN RESTAURANT — PRESENT DAY

Adult Richard is explaining the story to ADULT ALICE.

                  RICHARD (CONT)
        . . . she's way too pretty for Max. I
        thought, He doesn't deserve a girl so
        pretty.

Alice STARES at him, shock and anger on her face.

                    RICHARD
        If you can believe it, I was thinking
        of asking you out.

Close-up on Alice's face. She stares.

INT. RICHARD'S CAR

Richard holds the door open as the girl climbs into
the back seat.

RICHARD'S POV: The girl searches around for the seat
belt, then manages to buckle herself in.

Richard gives her a thumbs-up. She laughs, drunkenly,
and gives him a big, sarcastic thumbs-up back.

Too late, he realizes: Max is also climbing into the
back seat.

> RICHARD
>> Max, come on.

Max groans, rolls his head back on the back seat, and
PASSES OUT.

> RICHARD
>> Asshole, sit up front. I'm not going
>> to chauffeur you around.

Max lets out a snore.

The girl laughs. Richard sighs, then has an idea.

He leans across the girl, grabs Max's seat belt, and
buckles Max in.

> RICHARD
>> Sleep well, sweetie.

He pats Max's forehead.

Max is truly passed out. He grunts and shuffles.

> MAX
>> (mumbling)
>> Lemme 'lone.

The girl laughs again. Richard smiles at her, gives
her another thumbs-up. She gives him a sleepy
thumbs-up back, leaning her head against the window.

Richard gets into the driver's seat, starts the car.

He drives; from time to time, glances into the back
seat.

> RICHARD
>> (trying to be casual)
>> So, where do you live?

                    GIRL
     Tutwiler's Cove.

                    RICHARD
     Oh, cool. I have a friend who lives
     there.

                    GIRL
     A lot of people live there.

Richard looks out the window, kicking himself. Then:

                    RICHARD
     I'm Richard, by the way.

He glances into the back seat.

The girl is passed out.

INT. RICHARD'S CAR — A LITTLE LATER

Richard turns onto a dark street. He stops the car,
leaves it running. He turns to look into the back seat.

Max and the girl are both passed out, heads rolled back.

Richard gathers his nerve, then reaches out —

RICHARD'S POV: He touches the girl's BARE KNEE,
through the rip in her jeans.

                    RICHARD
     Hey. Hey.

She sits up, blinking and confused.

                    GIRL
     What?

                    RICHARD
     I'm Richard, remember?

She frowns at him.

                    RICHARD (CONT)
          Where's your house?

The girl looks out the window, still confused, very
drunk.

                    RICHARD (CONT)
          We're in Tutwiler's Cove. Which house
          is yours?

                         GIRL
          Three-eighty Poplar.

There's a loud, inarticulate GROAN from Max.

Max has rolled over and is trying to open the door,
pawing at the handle, his eyes still closed.

                    RICHARD
          Max, we're not there yet. Hold up.

                         MAX
                    (mumbling)
          Gotta pee.

Max gets the door open and nearly falls out of the
car.

Richard and the girl look in opposite directions. Out
the window, Max stumbles over to the side of the
street and PISSES LOUDLY.

                         MAX
                (groaning in pleasure)
          Oh, yes! Yeah, baby, yeah!

Richard drums his fingers on the steering wheel,
hating Max.

The back door opens. Max slides into the back seat. His
eyes are open now. He slaps his own face, wakes up.

                         311

MAX

Whoo-yeah!

RICHARD

Welcome back, cowboy.

MAX
(to the girl)
So we're gonna party at your house,
Alice?
(a short pause)
. . . Alice?

Richard turns. The girl — Alice — is unconscious again.
Max is leaned across the back seat, one arm around her
neck, patting her cheek with the back of his other
hand.

RICHARD

Dude!

MAX

What?

RICHARD
Get off her. You just peed on those
hands.

Max doesn't move. He grins at Richard.

Then he turns and slowly, deliberately, LICKS ALICE'S
CHEEK. He turns back to Richard.

MAX
All clean.

Richard, frustrated, reaches for Alice's knee again,
tries to shake her awake.

She just rolls over onto Max's shoulder. Max smiles,
cradles her under his arm.

                        RICHARD
        Fuck you, dude.

Richard puts the car in drive and SPEEDS down the road.

INT. MEXICAN RESTAURANT — PRESENT DAY

Adult Alice has her eyes closed, breathing.

                        ADULT RICHARD (O.S.)
                So yeah, he licked your cheek, but
                that was really the worst of it.

Adult Alice squeezes her eyes closed, trying not to cry.

EXT. 380 POPLAR — ALICE'S FRONT YARD

Richard opens the back door and leans in to pull Alice
out of the back seat. She's still unconscious.

Max gets out of the other side and walks around to help.

They each get one of her arms around their shoulders.
They start carrying her toward the door.

Her head is rolled onto Richard's shoulder.

                        RICHARD
        She smells like Skittles.

                        MAX
                (rolling his eyes)
        Gaywad.

They carry her up the front stoop. The porch light is
on, but the house is dark.

The two boys look at the front door, considering for a
minute.

                        MAX
        Let's just leave her here.

He gestures: There's a wooden BENCH on the stoop.

                         RICHARD
              Dude. It's freezing out here.

                           MAX
              You wanna wake her parents up?

Richard tries to shake the girl awake.

                         RICHARD
              Alice. Alice, wake up. Alice, we need
              your key.

Max rolls his eyes.

                           MAX
              She's *out*, dude. Come on, let's go.
              It's not that cold, she'll be fine.

Richard sighs, looks around.

                         RICHARD
              Okay.

The two boys lean over and set her on the bench.

She slumps over to one side.

                           MAX
              She looks like a bum.

                         RICHARD
              You asshole.

Richard TAKES OFF HIS LACROSSE TEAM JACKET and drapes
it over Alice.

                         RICHARD
                        (to Alice)
              I'll come back and get it later.

They turn and jog down the front lawn back toward
Richard's car.

Behind them, a LIGHT goes on in the house. The front
door starts to open.

ALICE'S MOTHER comes out and SEES the name on the
jacket:

ROTH
#36

Alice's mother SCREAMS.

INT. RICHARD'S CAR — A LITTLE LATER

Richard is still frustrated, gripping the wheel with
both hands.

Max is rolling back and forth in the back seat,
laughing hysterically.

                    MAX
          Did you hear the way her mom screamed?
          Jesus, she was mad! Oh my God, dude,
          that was so nuts!

EXT. 7-ELEVEN — A LITTLE LATER

Richard sits huddled in the front seat of his car,
sipping a Slurpee.

RICHARD'S POV: Through the window, a PUNK GIRL behind
the register, blue lipstick and bright orange hair,
laughs and shakes her head at Max, who's leaning on
the counter, leering and flirting.

INT. DENNY'S — A LITTLE LATER

Max and Richard walk into the all-night diner.

The place is empty except for a table full of lacrosse
guys.

And one girl:

HALEY MORELAND. A beefy guy has his arm around her, and she's goofing around with everyone. She turns and smiles as Richard approaches.

> HALEY
> Hey, Richie Rich!

> RICHARD
> 'sup, Moreland.

They fist-bump as Richard sits down at the table.

> ALICE (O.S.)
> Wait, what?

CUT TO:

INT. MEXICAN RESTAURANT — PRESENT DAY

Alice is staring at Richard.

> RICHARD
> Haley Moreland. God, I haven't thought about her in ages. We used to be good buddies. She was dating a friend of mine. But she was like one of the guys, you know?

Alice closes her eyes.

> RICHARD (CONT.)
> What's wrong?

> ALICE
> Just keep going.

Alice's eyes are still closed.

INT. DENNY'S — A LITTLE LATER

The pitch of the conversation peaks, as Max gets to the climax —

                    And we left her on the fucking bench!

Everyone explodes in laughter, everyone talking over
each other.

"I don't know why I went along with it," Richard said when he finished. "I guess I didn't want to get into it with Max—he could be such a dick. And maybe part of me thought I could get them to stop giving me such shit about being a virgin. I was a dumb teenager! I didn't think about the consequences. I never thought the story would get around the way it did."

He ate another chip. I drank some water. There was nothing to say.

"What made me crazy, what drove me so crazy about the way everyone talked about it, was that I actually *saved her*. You, I mean. Max probably would have—done bad things, if I wasn't there. It's unfair to say I did anything but stop that from happening. But I know it was my fault. I was dumb for going along with the story. I should have told everyone he was lying, that it didn't happen."

He exhaled, as if he'd been crying. "I know it went bad." He said, "It feels good getting that off my chest."

I couldn't look at him.

"How do—are you okay?" he asked.

"You never even touched me," I said to the table. I meant it as a question, although it sounded like an accusation.

"No," he said.

"I thought you did," I said.

"Like I said, I touched your knee. And Max licked your cheek."

"I used to tell people I wasn't a virgin," I said. "I didn't know how else to say it."

Finally I looked up at him. His eyes were wide, and he was shaking his head slowly. "I always thought you knew," he said. For a second I saw the boy he was in high school, who didn't even realize that nobody had ever told him he was wrong.

"Richard," I said. "How could I have known?"

He looked down at his hands in his lap and said, "I always thought a girl could tell." The sound in the room was fuzzy, like static on a VHS. I thought I might throw up again. He was still talking. "You don't know how this has weighed on me, all these years." He laughed a bit at his own hands, astonished.

I grabbed my bags and stood up. I didn't look at Richard as he started to stand, saying he was sorry, asking if I was okay, but my vision was contracting, and I rushed out of the restaurant and onto the busy street and down the block, gasping for air, the strange, empty nothingness of Richard's story opening like a pit under my feet.

I SENT YOU A TEXT MESSAGE to say that I was leaving New York. *I'm sorry,* I wrote. *Something happened this morning and I need some time to think.* You rushed out of your coffee meeting, texting, *Wait Alice, no! stop!* But I was already gone.

A headache started on the plane back to Barcelona. By the time we disembarked, it was squeezing; there were dark clouds gathering at the edges of my field of vision, and I knew it was going to be bad.

I found my apartment just as I'd left it. The sun on my patio was as bright as ever, the succulents still creeping out of their pots. A week of mail had piled up behind the front door, all of it addressed to previous tenants; I kicked it aside, turned the dead bolt, and burrowed my head under my pillow as my vision shrank to a pinpoint.

The migraine lasted a week. I hoped that it was the worst of my grief, but when the pain finally began to ebb, I found actual despair waiting for me, heavy as a sedative. I tried to run, bisecting the city over and over again. I sat on benches and watched people go by. I went days without speaking. I lingered in secondhand bookshops; I couldn't concentrate enough to read, but I found it comforting to pace around in the familiar smell of the mystery aisle.

A month passed before I realized I was buried in rage.

God damn Richard for taking so much of my life. For the hours I'd talked to him on the phone. For the years I didn't speak about what happened—what I *thought* had happened—and the years it ate me up inside. For the dark nights when I felt so damaged I thought I should die, or so damaged I should be grateful to Q as he took me away from the people I loved. For the work it took to keep that damage inside; for the constant crunch of terror that someone would spot it in my voice. God damn Richard for creating a story that shaped my life, even as he tossed it behind him like spilled salt. He didn't have to touch me in the back of that car. The story damaged enough.

This is what I wanted to tell you when you showed up in Barcelona for the film festival. When I heard your voice on the phone, my heart leaped. I rushed out the door. I couldn't wait to see you, because I finally understood how your story was tangled with mine, and why you'd been pressuring me all these years. You were friends with Richard, and Max; you were dating another lacrosse player; you were there the night the rumor began. You've been wanting to atone ever since. That's why you brought me cookies the summer after senior year. That's why you've built your career making space for women to speak.

I wish I could have told you years ago: I forgive you. It wasn't your fault.

I would have told you in Barcelona. I would have explained why I ran away from New York and abandoned our movie. But as I walked in circles around your hotel, I realized you might not believe it. I imagined how the conversation would go—*You're arguing for their side of the story, Alice!*—and I knew I didn't have the strength to fight you on it.

Maybe you still don't believe, even after all this. *Why should we believe Richard?* you'll say.

But Haley, I'm begging you: believe it. It was the level of detail he gave me, and the tone of his voice. I'd already spent ten hours listening to him talk. I know he was telling the truth: the story that fractured my life was a lie.

ON THE PLANE back to Barcelona, before the headache got bad, I glanced over the shoulder of the guy next to me and saw he was watching *Black Christmas* on his laptop. When he noticed me looking, he smiled and took his headphones out. "It's a horror movie called *Black Christmas*," he said. "But don't worry, it's not too gory!"

"I love *Black Christmas*," I said.

"Really?" He sat up a little straighter, excited. "You know it basically created the whole genre of slasher films? You wouldn't get *Halloween* or even *Saw* without this movie." He paused, watching to see if I was amazed yet. "And the craziest thing is that it was made by the same guy who made *A Christmas Story*! You know, the one with the leg lamp?"

"Right, Bob Clark," I said. "He made *Porky's*, too."

The guy looked at me like I'd pulled a quarter out of his ear.

"That's what my thesis is about!" he said, nearly shouting.

I was glad for a distraction from my own thoughts. We ended up chatting for an hour, as our plane accelerated the sunset. He was a know-it-all, but eager to please, with eyes as big as a puppy's. He was on his way to Spain to make a dramatic proclamation of love to a woman who had left him years earlier but had remained a dear friend. He was overwhelmed by romantic anticipation and eager to talk about it.

"She doesn't know I'm coming," he said, widening his eyes as if to convince me he was doing the right thing. "But I think she'll be happy to see me."

I nodded encouragingly and asked questions. I had no advice to offer. I just wanted to know what it was like to be a man like that, so sure of your righteous heart.

When they turned off the overhead lights, he closed his laptop and fell into a heavy sleep. I was jealous; I couldn't remember the last time I'd slept so deeply. He was still rubbing his eyes as we got off the plane. "Good luck, Nick," I said, squinting against my headache, and left him struggling to get his ratty backpack out of the overhead bin.

I thought of that guy again on the night after I stood you up in Barcelona. It was a bad night, desperate and dark. Wrapped in a blanket, sitting on my patio, hating myself, I wished I could talk to you without worrying that you wouldn't believe. I wished I could tell you my story with the same firm certainty the guy on the plane had told me his; the same firm certainty I'd heard from Richard.

And then I heard a voice in my head.

Why can't you? the voice said. *It's not like his story was so great.*

At first I thought it was your voice, Haley. But then I realized it was mine.

I sat up and tossed the blanket aside. I found my laptop and opened a new, blank document. I started writing.

> In the fall of our senior year, my buddy Max Platt was arrested for shining a laser pointer at an airplane. We didn't even know this was illegal. It was one of the least bad things Max ever did, and it was hilarious that it ended up being the thing he got in trouble for. (This was still a few months before the whole thing with the private school girl.)
>
> We were at Denny's when we heard the story . . .

I decided to write about a bystander. It was the best way to show a truth I'll never know firsthand. He was a teenage boy—a jerk and an idiot—but the more I wrote, the more I liked him. He just wanted to fit in; fitting in was invincibility. He was easy to write—so easy I was startled, at first. But I guess it's not really such a big surprise; we've spent our lives listening to men like him.

The freedom I felt in writing from his perspective was exhilarating. No matter how I punished him, he always felt certain he was on his way somewhere better, and always felt certain he deserved it, too. He always felt safe in his body. He was even strong enough to kill Q.

I named him Nick, after the guy I'd met on the plane; I gave him the same confident heart. Then I used him to push Richard's voice out of my head.

AND THAT, HALEY, is the book you've just finished. It's the horror novel I always dreamed I would write. An unconventional horror story, maybe, but the scariest story I know. I hope you'll accept this, at last, as the story you've always wanted me to tell.

I wrote it my own way. I made it a thriller, a horror, a memoir, a noir. I used my college essays, emails, and other found documents to ground the story in the truth—they're the closest thing I have to "evidence," proof that my memories, however few, are real. I let some of Richard's transcripts into the text, but when it came to his confession, I turned his voice into a movie script; I didn't want to give him the last word. I peopled the story with the ghosts and monsters that have haunted me for so long, and then I slayed them; in a way, this book is an exorcism. But it's also the kind of book I'd want to read. Because storytelling doesn't belong only to perpetrators, and neither does having fun.

I admit there were times I used this book to punish the people who have hurt me. But sitting on my patio now, the few visible stars above me and the million lights of the city all around, I'm realizing I've also used it to forgive.

Which is why I've decided to send it to you, Haley.

I'm hoping you'll help me publish it. We'll have to call it fiction, of course (we both know the danger in presenting a woman's story as truth). But I'm trusting you to see this is true. And even if you don't believe—even if nobody believes me again—I will know this is true, because I made it; because it's mine.

THANK YOU

Emily Forland for being the best.

Lindsey Schwoeri for your brilliance.

Ryan Boyle, Meighan Cavanaugh, Allie Merola, and everyone at Viking for taking such good, artful care of this demanding book. Jon Riley and Oliver Gallmeister for bringing it overseas. Rose Tomaszewska for the title.

Bloedel Reserve, the Robert W. Deutsch Foundation, and The Mount for time and space. Robert Knisely for sharing his cabin in the woods.

Paul Dobry, Heather Wells Peterson, JT Petty, and R.F.I. Porto for reading and improving many drafts, along with Elena Burgueño, Dana Cann, Amal Giknis, Sarah Langan, Emily Meredith, Patrick Murray, Tim O'Brien, and Jasmine Oore.

JT Petty, again, for introducing me to *Men, Women, and Chain Saws.* Lina Brunton for always having good advice.

Reed Petty. Susan Bell Knisely.

And Oliver Baranczyk with a bullet.